GOING

GONE!

Other Titles by Award-Winning Author
Anita Dickason

SENTINELS of the NIGHT

Messengers of death, they ride the night wind and hear the cries of the dead. Can they stop a serial killer? FBI Tracker Cat Morgan is about to find out.

"Will have serial killer mystery fans and paranormal urban fantasy junkies alike getting excited over a new series which has something for just about everyone. A compelling debut novel." Readers' Favorite Review

"A riveting high stake read — Sentinels of the Night proves an edgy and notable debut for Dickason with the promise of more to come." Book Viral Review

A u 7 9

What connects the two largest Texas Universities to a missing Laredo ATF agent? A chilling discovery puts Homeland Security on high alert. Pressure mounts as the President demands answers. When a Laredo homicide detective and a truck load of explosives disappear, FBI Tracker Adrian Dillard has one question left. Who dies next?

"A riveting and suspenseful page-turner. The release of A u 7 9 sees Dickason's series go from strength to strength." Book Viral Review

"Dickason's nail biting A u 7 9 is among the best in its genre." Readers' Favorite Review

Available in hardback, paperback, and eBook

Paul
Best
Wishes

GOING

GONE!

Anita Dickason

A Trackers Novel

❧

ANITA DICKASON

This is a work of fiction. Names, characters, places, and incidents either are the product of the author's imagination or are used fictitiously, and any resemblance to actual persons living or dead, events, or locales is entirely coincidental.

Publisher: Mystic Circle Books
Cover Design: Mystic Circle Books & Designs, LLC
Cover image courtesy of Pixabay

ISBN
978-0-9968385-3-5 (paperback)
978-0-9968385-4-2 (hardback)
978-0-9968385-5-9 (eBook)

Library of Congress Control Number: 2017915446

To my daughters
Julie and Christy
Thank you for your support
and helpful comments.

To my grandson
Tyler
who was the inspiration for Tristan
and his infatuation with dinosaurs.

One

Texas

His heart raced, and lungs heaved as he gulped in air. Huddled under low-hanging branches, rocks and pine needles jabbed his bare feet. Tristan's body trembled, but not from the cold, damp air that seeped through the thin material of his pajamas. He was afraid, so very, very afraid. A dirt-encrusted hand swiped at the tears trickling down his face, leaving muddy streaks across his cheeks.

He'd escaped, but, where was he? What happened? He knew he had gone to sleep in his bed. Tristan remembered his momma tucking the blankets around him and kissing him on the forehead. But when he woke, he was in a room he'd never seen and on a bed that stunk. His head and stomach hurt. A strange man with an angry face stood beside the bed and peered down at him.

Hoping this was just a bad dream, Tristan had whispered, "Who are you?" As a deep, harsh voice told him to shut up, he leaned over the edge of the bed and threw up. That's when he knew it wasn't a dream. The stuff hit the floor and splattered the man's pants and shoes.

Shouting, he grabbed Tristan by the arms and shook him, then tossed him back on the bed. No one had ever done that to him. Scared, he had scooted backward until his back was against the wall. Still yelling, and using words Tristan wasn't supposed to know, the man stomped out of the room and slammed the door shut.

Tristan didn't move until the footsteps faded away, then he slid off

1

the bed and crept across the room. Gripping the doorknob with both hands, he slowly turned it to keep it from squeaking, just like he did at home. He peeked out before stepping into the hallway.

Tiptoeing on the wood floor, he passed the living room where two men sat, their backs to the door as they watched TV. Another doorway led to the kitchen. The room was empty though there was a strong smell of coffee. The odor made his stomach rumble, and he had to breathe through his mouth to keep from getting sick again.

When he reached the back door, he eased it open. If he could get outside, he'd find someone to help him. That's what his momma said—find people, then run and scream to get their attention. When he slipped through the doorway, there were no people, no houses, no lights, only trees covered by a gray mist.

The awful voice shouted, "He's gone."

He ran, weaving around the trunks and bushes as he headed deep into the woods. When his feet slipped, he belly-flopped on the ground. Sobbing, he'd picked himself up. The slam of a door had him scurrying under the nearest tree to hide.

Footsteps crunched the pine cones that were everywhere. Tristan pushed back, pressing against the trunk until the bark dug into his back. Arms hugged his chest as he tried to stop shaking. If he made any noise, they'd hear him, and he didn't want to go back into the room with that man.

The footsteps came closer. A beam of light flashed over the ground. Pulling his knees tight to his chest, he wrapped his arms around his legs, tucked his head under his arms, and squished his eyes shut. Tears clogged his throat. *Momma, where are you?*

The harsh voice sounded over his head. "I don't see him over here. I'll circle the other way. The damn brat can't get far."

When the noisy steps faded away, Tristan scrambled from under the tree and ran. Pajama bottoms flapped around his bare ankles. Ahead was a break in the woods, and he raced toward the opening.

A shout echoed not far behind him. "He's running toward the road."

It was the man from the bedroom. Terror pushed him. His legs pumped, but he couldn't go any faster, and it hurt to breathe. He had to find another place to hide, but where? It was getting dark, and the mist made it hard to see. Behind him, footsteps kept getting louder.

Ahead was a fence, a road—then—lights. There was a car. Could he reach the road before it passed? Dropping, he crawled under the barbed wire and felt a hand scrape the sole of his foot.

Her back rigid, Kerry Branson's hands gripped the steering wheel as she peered over the hood, her gaze intently focused on the edge of the narrow road. The thought of ending up in the bar ditch or worse, meeting another car sent a tingle of alarm through her. She was lost. Not just any ole' ordinary lost, but lost in a thick fog with visibility down to a few feet.

This was her reward for waiting until the last minute to leave. She'd spent the weekend in East Texas visiting her best friend and planned to leave by mid-afternoon. Instead, Cindy talked her into staying another couple of hours. If Kerry took a back-road shortcut that weaved through the Piney Woods, it would save at least an hour or more in reaching the interstate.

Her gaze flicked to the navigation system to see if the message had changed, then grunted in irritation. It hadn't. 'You are in an area where no information is available. Follow the route on a map.' Even the damn GPS was lost.

Oh yeah—the map—what a joke. Kerry glanced at the paper, the so-called map, lying on the console next to her phone. When Cindy handed her the directions, she had chuckled as she read them—stay left at the Y, turn right at the burned tree, go a half mile and turn left, take another right after she passed an old metal gate with a flying horse, turn left at the chicken farm sign, then right at the Tucker convenience store.

Well, she wasn't laughing now. Somewhere, in the murky mess, she'd taken a wrong turn, and now it was getting dark. She should call for help, but the thought of being the butt of her friend's jokes kept her hand off the phone. 'Yep, my friend Kerry, the super sleuth, got lost and needed help.' Oh, no, listening to Cindy's hilarity wouldn't happen. She'd get out of this.

Forced to use the edge of the road as a guide, her speed had dropped to a crawl. *What?* A surge of exhilaration shot through her. There's the dang gate again—the one with the flying horse. She'd passed it at least thirty minutes ago. Since she had a reference point, time to regroup and look at the stupid directions again. God, what had she been thinking when she agreed to Cindy's plan.

As she braked, something, barely visible in her headlights crawled under the fence bordering the edge of the road. For a few seconds, she stared at it through the gloomy haze. It appeared to be an animal until it cleared the fence and stood. *My god! It's a small child.* Stunned, she shoved the gearshift into park and jumped out.

A deep, guttural voice bellowed in the gloom. "Goddamn! A truck stopped."

The child scrambled across the ditch and raced toward her. Bare feet slapped the asphalt as he screamed, "Don't let the bad man get me."

Kerry had moved in front of the truck. At the sound of the terrified voice, her cop mode kicked into gear. She stepped toward him, grabbed him around the waist, then spun to reach the driver's door. Tossing the boy on the front seat, she jumped behind the wheel.

A burly man had crawled over the fence. Seeing a gun in his hand, she shoved the boy's head down, and her foot stomped the gas pedal. Tires squealed in protest. A shot rang out. Kerry flicked her eyes at the rearview mirror, but the man had disappeared into the gray mist that filled the roadway.

Racing along the road, she could only spare a quick glance at the boy who cowered on the seat. Wild-eyed, he stared at her. His face was ashen, and the small body trembled as he sucked in deep breaths.

Hoping to reassure him, she said, "You're safe now."

Who is this kid, and what the hell happened back there? Somehow, she had to find her way out of this maze of roads, get him to a hospital, and let the local cops sort it out.

Not wanting to stop and look at the directions, she had to rely on her memory. *Once I pass the gate, it's right at the next road, then the chicken sign, then the store.* When Kerry spotted the crossroad, she realized where she had made her earlier mistake. She had veered left, not right.

Once she reached the main highway that led to the interstate, she pulled to the shoulder. Flipping on the overhead light, her eyes skimmed the thin body that still shook.

Thank god, there's no blood, though dirt smeared his face and pajamas. Twigs stuck in the shaggy red hair that hung over his forehead. Kicking the heater to full blast, she grabbed towels and a bottle of water from the emergency container of supplies on the floor behind her seat.

"I'm Kerry. What's your name?" Her arm slid around his shoulders as she helped him sit up before tucking a large towel around him. Not wanting to increase his fear, she was careful to keep her movements slow and easy.

His voice weak, he said, "Tristan."

"Tristan. What a neat name," Kerry said and handed the bottle to him. "Drink some."

After a few swallows, he handed it back.

Dampening the edge of the other towel, she wiped the dirt from his face and hands. "How old are you?"

His voice still a low murmur, he replied, "Six."

Her palm rested on his forehead. His skin wasn't feverish. Fingertips lightly probed his scalp, searching for bumps or cuts before she picked the small pieces of pine needles and stems from his hair. "That's a lot of dinosaurs on your pajamas. Which one is your favorite?"

"Uh …" he pushed the towel away and pointed to one that covered the front of his pajama top. "That's T-Rex. I like him the best."

Her question certainly perked him up. "He looks like he'd be my favorite too. Do you hurt anywhere?"

"My feet."

The cuts on his ankles and feet were superficial though several still bled. Kerry swabbed the dirt and blood with the wet end of the towel, then wrapped the dry end around his legs.

"Does anything else hurt?" she asked as her gaze flicked over him. The glassy look had disappeared from his dark eyes, and the trembling had stopped. His cheeks had color, and now that the dirt was gone, a faint dusting of freckles across his nose was visible.

"My head did, but it's better now," Tristan said and snuggled under the towel.

She breathed a sigh of relief, and the tension in her shoulders rolled away. He didn't appear to have any severe injuries. Pulling the seatbelt around him, though he was too small for it to fit right, she asked, "Tristan, who was the man who ran out of the woods?"

"He was in the room when I woke up."

"Your bedroom?"

A frightened look crossed his face. "No. It was dirty and smelled bad."

"Do you know his name?"

When he shook his head no, Kerry asked, "Do you know your last name?" A smile crossed her face when he cast a scornful look her way that he wouldn't know.

"Murdock," he emphatically said.

Since her first sight of him, a memory had niggled in the back of her mind. Hearing the name, the connection clicked. Her boss, Mike Bradford who was the head of Bradford Security and Investigations had mentioned a call he'd received from a local FBI agent. Senator Murdock's son had been kidnapped from his Austin home, and the Bureau wasn't releasing the news. The agent wanted Mike to know in case any of his investigators picked up rumors from their sources on the street.

Dumbfounded, she stared at the child nestled in her old towels. Was it possible? "Tristan, is Senator Anthony Murdock ..."

"He's my daddy." His head nodded, and eyes drooped as he fell asleep.

Holy Hell! Well, there went her plan to contact the local cops. An Austin police detective turned private investigator, Kerry was familiar with kidnapping protocols. When the FBI went into lockdown on details, especially in a high-profile abduction, there must be a problem.

Kerry pulled onto the highway, inserted her earpiece, and hit the speed dial for her boss. When Mike answered, she said, "I came across a kid running from an armed man on a deserted county road not far from where Cindy lives. He's in my truck, but the guy took a shot at us before I could get away. Turns out the boy is Tristan Murdock."

His voice incredulous, he said, "Senator Murdock's son! Good, God! Are you okay?"

"Yeah, though my truck may have a hole."

"What about the boy, is he injured?"

"Other than a few scrapes, he appears to be okay. I can't be certain, though, until I get him to a hospital. Call your FBI friend and tell him I'm headed to Mt. Pleasant."

"I'll get back to you," Mike said before disconnecting.

When her phone chimed, a quick glance at Tristan reassured her he was sound asleep. The caller ID showed—unknown. This was probably the agent. "Branson," she answered.

"Special Agent Will Cooper. Mike Bradford said you found Senator Murdock's son. Are you sure he is Tristan Murdock?" Skepticism was evident in the man's sharp tone that bordered on rude.

Kerry never ceased to be amazed at how fast the FBI could tick someone off. Not bothering to hide her irritation, she said, "He told me his name. If that doesn't convince you, how about his clothes? I bet Tristan was wearing pajamas printed with dinosaurs when he was kidnapped."

A deep sigh echoed, followed by a short silence before the agent replied, "Yes, that's right. How'd you find him?"

Kerry quickly detailed the circumstances.

"I wonder how he got away? Well, the questions will have to wait. Where are you now?"

"A few miles south of Mt. Pleasant. I'll be at the hospital in a few minutes."

"Mike said the boy wasn't injured."

"Minor cuts and abrasions are all I could find. Since I don't know what happened to Tristan, a doctor needs to examine him."

"No, you can't do that. Hold on."

His voice muffled, Kerry couldn't hear what was said. Her irritation kicked up another notch.

"Branson, a plane with two agents is leaving Austin. Get him to the Mt. Pleasant airport."

Her tone emphatic, she said, "Unless you have a doctor on board, I'm going to the hospital."

Cooper's voice vibrated with anger. "You don't understand. The hospital will require his name. We can't risk a leak of his identity."

Undeterred, Kerry snapped back. "No! You're the one who doesn't understand. My only concern is this child's welfare, not whatever is pushing your agenda. Your agents can wait at the airport or meet me at the hospital." Jeez, just what she didn't need—a pissing match with a fed.

"Damn it, Branson! This is a matter of national security."

Over the years, she had worked with the FBI on several investigations. They liked to play the 'national security card' to enforce their edicts even when it wasn't applicable. Still, she couldn't take a chance and ignore Cooper's warning. This time, when they cried wolf, there might be one.

"I'm still headed to the hospital, but I'll figure out a way to conceal his identity. How long before your agents arrive?"

Evidently, her answer pacified him. His tone was less agitated as he said, "A couple of hours. I'll have them meet you at the hospital. Mike told me that someone shot at you. Any chance you were followed?"

"I don't see how. Even though the gunman saw my truck, he doesn't know where I went."

"Do whatever is necessary to keep Tristan safe but don't, I repeat, don't let anyone know he's the Senator's son. I'm texting you my number if you need to contact me. Otherwise, I'll call when the plane lands." The line went dead.

Now what? She didn't have a clue how to hide Tristan's identity and only a few minutes to come up with a plan. The highway sign she passed read, 'Mt. Pleasant—5 miles.'

❦

Moore's instructions were specific. Report in at the prearranged times. If something went wrong, he was to call, let the phone ring twice, hang up and wait for a callback.

He had no choice. The call had to be made. Two rings, and he disconnected, then paced. Two men, Sanford and Boyd, leaned against the wall, stoic as they kept their gaze fixed on their boss's face. A third, T.J., waited in a chair.

In the background, the cries of a child exacerbated his anger and pushed his icy control to the limit. "Your instructions were to keep them drugged," he said, scowling at the men against the wall.

Defiant, Boyd replied, "They got sick, so I stopped. I didn't sign on to clean up vomit."

Moore's voice vibrated with rage. "Why the hell didn't you lock the damn door."

Boyd shrugged his shoulders. "Thought the brat was too sick to get away."

Moore glanced at his watch. Only a few minutes had passed. He had no idea how long he would have to wait. When the phone buzzed, he swiped at the sweat on his brow and answered.

A derisive voice on the other end said, "Explain."

"A package is lost." As seconds ticked by, the lack of a response increased his uneasiness. He hastily added, "There was a mistake in handling it."

"Which package?"

"The priority shipment," Moore said.

A sharp intake of breath echoed in his ear before the toneless voice said, "What have you done to locate it?"

"A woman found it before it could be retrieved."

After another extended period of silence, the caller asked, "Do you know who was responsible for the loss?"

"Yes."

"Take care of him. What is the status of the other package?"

"Safe," Moore said.

"Then divert to the alternate plan."

Slipping the phone into his pocket, he glanced at the person responsible for his current predicament. Boyd had a history of screwing up assignments. It wouldn't have happened if one of his team had been here. The operation, though, had his men spread thin, and Moore was forced to add Boyd and Sanford as guards. Another two days and Boyd's demise wouldn't be a loss. His only decision was where and how.

"We're moving. T.J. get the girl ready. Take Boyd and Sanford's car, deliver her to Creel, then hook back up with us. You two," he said, stabbing his finger in their direction, "get your gear. You're coming with me."

T.J. held a rag saturated with chloroform over the girl's face. Within seconds, she was unconscious. Cradled in his arms, he carried her outside, laid her on the backseat, and tossed a blanket over her to hide her from anyone who looked inside the car.

Moore positioned several explosive devices throughout the house.

He couldn't take a chance the cops would find it. Since it was in a remote section of the county, the explosion shouldn't attract any attention. Still, he set the timers to allow ample time to get out of the area.

As he followed T.J. to the main highway, his phone rang.

"Mt. Pleasant hospital," the voice said, a click, and the line went dead.

Two

Turning off the engine, Kerry scanned the hospital parking lot, then checked her watch. In all her law enforcement experience, she didn't believe she had ever eagerly anticipated the arrival of the FBI. *This had better work, or I'm up a creek without the proverbial paddle.*

She flipped open the center console, picked up her pistol, and stuck it in the waistband of her pants. As she slid from the truck, she grabbed her jacket to conceal the gun.

Opening the passenger door, her hand gently shook the boy's shoulder. "Tristan, wake up. I need to talk to you. Come on sweetie, wake up."

His eyes slowly opened. "Momma?" he cried before he realized she wasn't there, and panic flashed across his face.

Her hand brushed a strand of hair from his forehead. "It's okay. Your mother is waiting for you at home. Until we get there, let's play a game."

Games caught his attention, and he straightened in the seat. Head tilted, he gazed at her with a hint of suspicion on his face. "What kind of game?"

"A pretend game, and I get to be your mother. Since I don't have a little boy, it would be so much fun for you to call me momma. It'll be like Halloween when you try to fool everyone."

"I was Spiderman and got lots and lots of candy. Do I get candy?"

This has to work, even if I have to promise him candy every day for the next year.

"I bet I can find some. Since we don't have costumes, you can have a new name." The dinosaur Tristan had pointed out gave her an idea, one he might remember. "Let's use Rex, like your dinosaur. If someone asks your name, you say Rex Smith. Can you remember it?"

"Rex Smith," he said.

"Let's try it here in the car. Now, young man, what is your name?" Kerry asked in a clownish voice.

Tristan giggled, and what a welcome sound.

"Rex Smith," he shouted.

"Wow, aren't you smart. I think we'll have everyone fooled," she said and hoped she had not outsmarted herself, and he'd blurt out T-Rex.

Pushing the towels aside, she lifted Tristan, holding him close to her body. "Now, who am I?"

Tristan giggled. "You're my momma."

"Good boy," she said and kissed him on the forehead.

Inside the emergency room, she approached the front desk. A nurse looked up and rushed toward her. "What's the problem?"

"This is my son, Rex. He was playing in the woods behind our house and got lost in the fog. I found him huddled under a bush." Shifting his weight on her hip, she added, "Scared the bee-Jesus out of me. I don't believe he's injured, but he said he tripped over a log. I want to be sure. His feet are scratched and bleeding."

"I'm Nurse Simpson, let's get him into a treatment room. What's your name?"

"Kerry Smith," she replied and followed the woman to a room located along a hallway. Inside, she laid Tristan on the table.

Simpson surveyed his dirty and torn pajamas. "My goodness, you look like you fell into a hole just like Alice in Wonderland. Do you know who Alice is?"

Tristan giggled, then said, "Nope."

"She chases a rabbit down a hole and has all sorts of adventures."

She paused to take his blood pressure, then asked, "And who are these fearsome looking animals?" Her hand motioned toward his pajamas.

"Dinosaurs."

"Oh ... and which one is your favorite?"

"T-Rex," he said, pointing to the large head.

"Just like your name." She unbuttoned his shirt and examined his chest and back.

"Uh-huh," Tristan said and gave Kerry a wide, mischievous grin.

A warm glow spread through her. This kid will be a danger to the female population once he gets older. He'd already tugged at her heartstrings.

"He went through some brush and tore his pajamas. These are his favorite. I told him we'd get a new pair, but he couldn't scare me like that again."

While Kerry rambled on, hoping to keep Tristan from talking, she had stood close to the table, holding his hand. As the nurse examined him, she also scanned his body and choked back a sigh of relief when there were no injuries under his pajamas.

Simpson started on his feet. Once the cuts were clean, she applied a salve. "He looks fine except for his feet. Young man, next time you wander in the woods make sure you remember your shoes." She grabbed a blanket from the warmer and wrapped it around him. "This should get you nice and warm."

She turned to Kerry. "To be on the safe side, Doctor Harper should examine him. It's why I didn't wrap the cuts on his feet. He's with another patient. In the meantime, I'll bring you the insurance forms," she said and left the room.

Kerry's eyes flicked to the wall clock. She might get to the airport after all and glanced at Tristan. He had fallen asleep on the table. Poor kid, he's exhausted. What kind of hell did he go through in the few days he'd been missing?

Simpson walked in with several documents on a clipboard. "It will be at least another twenty or thirty minutes before the doctor can see Tristan. He's stitching up a man who got tangled in barbed wire. I'll be back in a few minutes."

Kerry leaned back in a chair and studied the forms. Okay, now what? She'd have to wait for the agents to arrive, but how long could she stall? Frustrated, she took another look at the clock, then sighed. When the nurse opened the door with a questioning look on her face, Kerry said, "Still working on them."

Several minutes later, Simpson returned. "I need the forms. The intake clerk is waiting for them."

"It'll be another few minutes," Kerry replied as she held the clipboard to her chest. She couldn't risk the nurse seeing they were still blank. "I forgot to bring my insurance information and called my husband. He's on his way home from work. Once he gets there, he'll call and give me the policy number." *Oh, that was a good one. It should buy me time.*

A mulish expression crossed Simpson's face. "Mrs. Smith, let me have the forms. You can add the policy number when you get it." she held out her hand for the clipboard.

A voice sounded in the hall, the door opened, and a man in blue scrubs walked in. He looked at the nurse. "Would you help Mr. Lewis get dressed? He's ready to leave."

Kerry stifled a sigh of relief as the woman left the room.

Turning to Kerry, he said, "I'm Doctor Harper. Let's take a look at this boy of yours. I understand from my nurse he had a bit of an adventure tonight."

Kerry said, "He decided to imitate a character from his favorite video game, only he did it in the woods behind our house."

Harper scanned the nurse's notes, then pulled the blanket back to examine the sleeping boy. Tristan never stirred during the light probe of the doctor's fingers. "Other than his feet, he appears to be fine. With a good night's sleep and an ointment I'll prescribe, he should be back to normal in a few days," he said as he repositioned the blanket around Tristan's shoulders.

A quick glance at her watch—okay, where's the cavalry? The door opened, and a deputy sheriff walked in. Damn, wrong cavalry!

The deputy said, "Evening, Doc. You doing okay?"

"Just fine, Jerry, just fine. I'll be at the nurse's station if you need me."

The officer turned to Kerry. "I'm Deputy Benton. Do you have a driver's license or another form of identification?"

Kerry's mind rapidly considered her options. There weren't many. "Oh, I was in such a rush to get my son into the emergency room I left my purse in the car. What's the problem, Deputy?"

"We got a call from a hospital representative regarding the child's injuries. What's your name?"

Hospital personnel were trained to look for suspicious injuries. Evidently, her cover story didn't pass inspection with the nurse.

"Kerry Smith, this is my son Rex. As I told the nurse, he was playing in the backyard. He didn't have on his shoes, and his feet are scraped and cut. Those are his only injuries."

"I still need your identification. I'll wait here with the boy while you get your purse."

The deputy's forceful tone disturbed Tristan. "Daddy?" he mumbled.

Kerry walked over and lightly ran her hand over his head. "No, it's not daddy. Go back to sleep, sweetie." She pulled the blanket around his shoulders before turning to the deputy.

"I don't want to leave him. He had a bad scare in a hospital, and I need to be here in case he wakes up again. If you talk to the doctor, I'm sure he will reassure you my son's injuries are not suspicious."

"Ma'am … I need your identification. He will be fine for the few minutes it will take for you to get your purse."

Kerry had no choice. The deputy's gaze was unwavering, and his expression grim. She had to leave. She glanced at Tristan. He had gone back to sleep. Hopefully, the deputy wouldn't try to talk to him.

Laying the clipboard upside down on the chair, she turned to the door as screams erupted. They seemed to come from the front entrance.

"What the hell," the deputy said and opened the door.

A voice shouted, "Everyone—on the floor. Where's the kid that just came in?"

The deputy pulled his radio and requested backup for a disturbance at the hospital before moving into the hallway.

Kerry stuck her head out the door and watched him ease along the wall toward the lobby. Shifting her gaze, she looked at the opposite end of the corridor. Overhead signs pointed to labs and the X-ray.

She stepped to the side of the table and picked up Tristan. Wrapping the blanket tight around him, she pulled a corner of the material over his head. With the sleeping child snug against her chest, she peeked out the door. The deputy's attention was focused on whatever was happening in the lobby, and she slipped into the hall. At the end of the corridor was an exit. The door opened onto the parking lot on the side of the hospital. Tristan groaned and twisted in her arms.

In a whisper, Kerry said, "Tristan, this is another part of the game. Can you pretend to be a ghost and not let anyone know you are here?"

At the sound of her voice, he relaxed. "I think so."

Hugging the outside wall as she moved, Kerry scanned the parking lot for any movement. At the corner, she stopped to peep around the edge. A man, wearing a dark ski mask, leaned against the front of her truck.

Damn! The boy's weight was heavy in her arms, and she leaned back against the brick wall. What was she going to do now? She hated to leave her truck, but she had to find a place to hide.

Shouts, then a shot rang out from inside the hospital. Bending forward for another peek, she watched the man straighten, hesitate as he looked around the parking lot, then race to the front door.

With Tristan balanced in one arm, her fingers groped in her pocket for the keys. Hitting the remote, she unlocked the doors, then sprinted to the truck. Opening the back passenger door, Kerry set Tristan on the floor and told him to stay down. As she slid behind the wheel, she shoved the pistol into a holster mounted between her seat and the console instead of inside the compartment where she usually kept it. Before exiting the parking lot, she darted a quick glance at the entrance, but couldn't see what was happening inside.

Turning onto a side street, she weaved through several neighborhoods. For the second time that day, she had no idea where the hell she was.

Once Kerry was sure that no one had followed her, she stopped on a residential street and peered into the backseat. Tristan's large dark eyes stared at her, and his hands gripped the edge of the blanket. "Are you okay?" she asked.

"Uh ... huh," he said, though his voice quivered. Rage bit deep into her gut at the men responsible for the fear in his eyes.

"Let's get you into the front seat," she said and helped him crawl over the console. Tucking the blanket around him, she bunched a section of the material for his head to rest against. "It won't be long until you are home."

Checking her text messages, she found Cooper's number. As she waited for him to answer, she watched Tristan's eyelids droop, then close.

"Cooper."

Anger resonated in her voice, though she kept it low, not wanting to disturb Tristan. "The kidnappers followed me to the hospital!"

"Damn! What about Tristan, is he okay?"

"He's safe, though I'm certain they're searching for me. How soon before your plane gets here?"

"It should land in a few minutes. Can you get Tristan to the airport?"

"Yes, but make sure your people know I have a problem."

"Here's the number for one of the agents, Ryan Barr. Call him."

Kerry programmed it on speed dial.

A deep voice answered, "Barr."

Her tone terse, she said, "This is Branson. I was followed to the hospital. I'll meet you at the airport. How soon will you be on the ground?"

"Fifteen minutes or so. When we stop, pull your vehicle up to the door. Once Tristan is on board, we'll take off again. What is his condition?"

"Before my hasty exit, a doctor examined him. His only injuries are the cuts on his feet. I'm driving a black Ford pickup."

"Any idea how they found you?"

"Since I wasn't followed, I sure as hell don't."

After disconnecting, Kerry pondered his question. How did they know she was at the hospital? Heading to town, she had kept a close eye on her rearview mirror, and no one had followed her. Plus, she could have turned south instead of north. Nerves tingled. Something wasn't right, but she didn't have time to figure out what.

She pulled up a map of the city. The airport was south of town, and she remembered passing the entrance. *Not good.* The kidnappers could be watching the main highway. Studying the streets, she discovered another route, longer as she had to circle around the west side, but it let her approach from another direction. She also didn't like the setup at the airport, only one way in and out. A lumber yard across the road from the entrance might be the answer.

A few minutes later, she pulled into the parking lot and backed into the shadows near the loading dock. From her position, she could scan the hangars and terminal with the binoculars she kept in the glovebox.

Two cars were parked by the terminal's front door. Lights gleamed inside the small building and along the sides of the runway. There was nothing suspicious. Still, she couldn't shake her uneasiness.

Occasionally, a car passed on the main highway. When a black SUV slowed to turn into the airport, hackles on her neck rose. The headlights had been turned off. Instead of parking next to the terminal, the vehicle headed to the end of the hangars. Three men exited. With rifles slung over their shoulders, they moved to positions along the sides of the buildings.

Oh, my, god! They're waiting for me.

She tapped the number for Barr's phone. When he answered, she said, "It's a trap! There are three armed men at the hangars on the south end of the runway."

"Where are you?" he asked.

"In a parking lot across the road from the airport."

"We're on final approach and will land in a few minutes. I'll come to you, stay put."

Not bothering to keep the sarcasm from her voice, she added, "Yeah, and how do you plan on doing that without them seeing you?"

"I haven't figured it out yet. I'll get back to you," he answered and disconnected.

She glanced at Tristan. Sound asleep, he slumped in the seat with his head against the pad of the blanket. Kerry hit the button to slide the window down. The sound of an engine grew louder. Lights twinkled in the sky as a plane dropped lower and lower. Her phone rang.

"Where are you again?" Barr asked.

"In the parking lot of a lumber yard across the road from the entrance."

"I'm dressed in black pants, a black jacket and will be carrying a backpack."

Well, this ought to be some magic stunt, as she had no idea how he could get off the plane and the men not see him.

Ryan examined his backpack to make sure everything was secure before tightening the straps on his shoulders. He didn't want to damage his laptop.

Fellow agent, Nicki Allison sat across from him. "Are you sure this will work?" she asked.

"No, but it's our only option. We can't risk getting Tristan to the plane, not with three gunmen waiting to stop us. I've got to get to the woman. I don't understand how the kidnappers found her. Branson said she wasn't followed, but she must be mistaken. If she is right, though, we've got an even bigger problem ... a leak."

Nicki's anxiety was reflected in her face. "I don't like how any of this has gone down. This was to have been a routine pickup, not one that has turned into a potential firefight. And ... I don't like the fact we don't know anything about this woman. All Cooper knew was that she was a private investigator. How the hell did she find the kid? Too many questions and no answers."

The pilot's voice came over the speaker. "Five minutes out, turning off the cabin lights."

Ryan had worked out a plan. As soon as the plane landed, the pilot would turn and taxi to the terminal. Once the door was out of view of anyone at the hangars, he would jump and hide in the trees along the edge of the runway. If he timed it right, the waiting men wouldn't know someone had exited the plane. The pilot would sit for a few minutes as if waiting for the woman to show up with the boy, then take off again.

His phone rang. It was Cooper.

"What's your status?"

"Getting ready to land at the airport."

"Let me know as soon as you have the boy and are back in the air."

Disconnecting, he glanced at Nicki. "Until we know who we can trust, I don't want Cooper to know there is a change of plans."

At the jolt of the wheels hitting the concrete, Ryan moved to the doorway. The co-pilot waited to open the door. The plane slowed and began to turn. The pilot's voice sounded over the speaker. "Now!"

Wind swirled through the open doorway. Ryan's hands gripped the door frame, then he bent his knees and jumped. When his feet hit the concrete, he twisted, allowing his body to roll. The backpack dug into his back. Ignoring the sharp pain, he picked himself up and raced to the trees.

Kerry watched the plane land, roll toward the end of the runway where it slowly turned, then taxied to the terminal. The gunmen had slipped from hangar to hangar as they worked their way closer to the plane. Heads repeatedly turned to glance over their shoulders at the entrance to the airport.

The cabin lights came on, and a woman exited. *Must be the other agent.* She paced in front of the open door, occasionally looking at her watch, then made a call. A few minutes later, she re-entered the plane. It taxied to the end of the runway and lifted off.

The men walked to their vehicle. One held a phone to his ear. Before leaving, they slowly drove around the hangars, then exited, turning north, back into town.

As soon as the car was out of sight, Kerry grabbed her gun, opened the door and slid out of the truck. Shoving the weapon in her waistband, she scanned the tarmac and entrance with the binoculars. A shadow flitted across one end of the runway.

Well, I'll be damned. I bet that's Barr, and how did he get off the plane?

Three

The phone rang twice, and Moore hung up.

Within seconds, it rang. "Do you have the package?"

"No, the woman never showed. The plane landed, then left after several minutes," Moore said.

"Did anyone get off?"

"A woman, but she got back on before it left."

There was silence for several seconds. "What's the status of the next package?"

"It's being delivered. What are your instructions for the one that's missing?"

"As soon as I learn its location, I will call you."

Kerry watched the man stroll onto the parking lot. Six-foot, with a slim build, he moved with the fluid agility of an athlete. His gaze flicked across the parked vehicles. She recognized the moment he spotted her truck. There was a slight hesitation before he continued his visual search.

As he approached, Kerry hung the binoculars around her neck and pulled her pistol. Until she was sure this was Barr, she wasn't taking any chances. "Stop! Put your identification on the hood."

As he peered into the deep shadows, he asked, "Are you, Kerry Branson? I'm Agent Ryan Barr."

"I still want to see your ID."

Pulling a black case from his pocket, Ryan laid it on the hood.

"Now, step back, away from the truck." With silent footsteps, she eased along the side of the vehicle.

As a slim, lithe figure, dressed all in black, her face shadowed by the brim of her ball cap came into view, his eyes widened in shock. *The damn woman has a gun pointed at me!* Anger rippled through him. "Hey! I sure as hell don't like a gun pointed at me."

"Right now, I don't give a damn what you like or don't like!" Picking up the badge case, she flipped it open. Her gaze flicked between the picture and his face.

Sliding the gun into her waistband, she handed the case to him. "I'm Branson."

His tone terse, he said, "Yeah, I figured that one out. Where's the boy?"

"Asleep in the truck. How'd you get off the plane, and did anyone see you?"

The implied criticism piled irritation on top of his anger. "When the pilot turned, I jumped and hid in the trees on the other side of the runway, and no, I wasn't seen. I waited until the men left. I don't suppose you got a license plate number?" he jabbed back.

"I couldn't. There was no front plate, and the back had something over it. They were prepared. How about telling me what's going on."

"I will, but let's get out of here first," he said, stepping to the car door.

Her voice amused, she said, "You'll have to sit in the back, Tristan's in front," as she slid behind the wheel and tossed her ball cap on the dash.

Glaring at her, he climbed into the backseat, then leaned forward to look at the sleeping child snuggled under a blanket. His anger and irritation vanished. Branson might be a pain in the ass, but she had saved the boy.

"Are you familiar with this area?" he asked.

"Enough to get us on secondary roads to head south to Longview. I want to get away from this town. Those men are likely still searching for us."

"As soon as you reach a place where we can pull over, let's move Tristan to the backseat."

Kerry turned onto the same road she had driven to get to the airport. When she spotted the parking lot of a feed mill, she pulled in.

She studied him as he unbuckled Tristan's seatbelt and picked up the boy. *How far can I trust him?* Ryan didn't even look like a federal agent. The man had a pretty boy look, a classical elegance in the high cheekbones, narrow nose, and blue eyes. Strands of blond hair with a hint of a curl drifted across his forehead, and brushed his collar, long for a fed. She guessed he was in his early thirties.

No, until she knew more, she would err on the side of caution. When he laid Tristan on the back seat, she moved her pistol into the holder beside the console.

The child never stirred as Ryan wrapped the seatbelt around him. With Barr in the front seat, she pointed out her route on the GPS screen. As she pulled onto the roadway, his phone rang.

"I'm checking to make sure your butt wasn't plastered all over the runway," Nicki said.

"Yeah, rough landing, but I'm still in one piece. I'm with Branson and will keep you posted on our progress. Any problems on your end?" Ryan listened, then said, "Okay," before disconnecting.

"That was my partner, Nicki Allison. She's on the plane."

"Time to start talking," Kerry told him.

Ryan stared at her, debating what to say. His few experiences with private investigators had not left a favorable impression of their knowledge or experience. The abduction was already mired in the political currents swirling around Senator Murdock. The inept bungling of an individual, no matter how well-meaning, could have disastrous consequences.

Her appearance didn't inspire confidence. Age-wise, she looked to be in her late twenties. Slim, around five-seven, her face had a pixie look with its heart shape and large dark eyes. The long hair pulled into a ponytail, trailed over her shoulder. Still, she had kept Tristan out of the hands of the kidnappers. Until he knew more, he would tread lightly.

"Before I do, tell me how you found the boy."

Kerry recapped the series of events from the moment she had spotted Tristan on the side of the road.

"Did you get a look at any of the men?"

"Only a glimpse of the one who took a shot at me, big and burly. Dark clothes and a cap. The one at the hospital had on a ski mask, and at the airport—well, too dark and too far away."

"Since the details haven't been released, how did you know about the abduction?"

"I'm a private investigator and work for Mike Bradford, head of Bradford Security and Investigations in Austin. An agent called Mike and told him the Murdock boy had been kidnapped, just in case we picked up any rumors from our informants."

"I've heard of BSI." Ryan's opinion of Kerry shot up. If she worked for Bradford, she had to be good, he only hired the best. This might not be as bad as he first thought. "The kidnapping happened at Murdock's home in Austin. So far, there's been no contact with the kidnappers."

"That's strange. Why would you kidnap a child if you are not asking for a ransom or make some type of demand?" Kerry asked.

"Since we don't know, it's one of the reasons we haven't gone public with the abduction. Senator Murdock is the head of the Senate Appropriations Committee and is one of the most powerful men on Capitol Hill."

His phone rang. Caller ID showed it was Cooper. Ryan let the call roll to his voice mail as he continued. "He is negotiating a series of contracts with the Chinese government. If the Chinese delegation finds out his son has been kidnapped, it could cast doubt on his credibility in the negotiations."

When Kerry's phone chimed, she picked it up from the console. "This is probably Agent Cooper."

"Don't answer. Cooper called me, but I don't want to talk to him yet."

She laid it back down, glancing at him with an inquiring look.

Ryan picked up the phone, turned it off, popped the back and removed the SIM card.

"Okay, now you do have me concerned," she said as he laid the pieces in the cup holder.

"How do you know you weren't followed after you picked up Tristan?"

Since Barr didn't know her, Kerry tried not to let the question irritate her and tempered her sarcasm. "Because I'm damn good at what I do and can spot a tail. I wasn't followed when I found Tristan, and I wasn't followed from the hospital. They knew I was there, and I only told two people. My boss, who I trust, and Agent Cooper." She took a deep breath, then added, "I'd say you've got a leak and a hell of a problem."

"Yeah, I've figured that one out too."

He punched another number on his phone. "Scott, Tristan Murdock is safe. He's with me, but we've got a serious dilemma."

Kerry listened to him explain their predicament and suspicions to whoever Scott was. When Kerry's name came into the conversation, she glanced at him. Their eyes met, and his hard gaze revised her assessment. No, Ryan Barr wasn't just a pretty boy.

Disconnecting the call, he explained, "My boss, Scott Fleming."

A small voice, barely audible, came from the back seat. "I have to go potty, and I'm thirsty."

"Oh, boy," Kerry said. How was she going to handle this? Her only experience with a child was the few hours she'd spent with Cindy's new baby.

Ryan smiled at the note of panic in her voice. He looked at the passing terrain. They were on a deserted stretch of roadway.

"If you'll pull over, I'll take him outside."

Kerry stopped on the shoulder and turned on the overhead lights. Tristan had sat up. The blanket was clutched tight in his hands, and he had a look of fear on his face as he gazed at Ryan.

"Where did you come from?"

"Hi, Tristan. Your daddy sent me," Ryan told him.

"You know my daddy?" Reassured, he wiggled higher on the seat.

"Yes, and he'll be happy to know you are with me."

"I want my daddy." Lips quivered, and fists rubbed his eyes.

Hoping to avert the tears, Kerry quickly said, "Tristan, we'll get you home as soon as we can. I know your daddy and mommy are waiting to see you. Ryan, there are bottles of water in the container on the floor."

Ryan stepped out and opened the back door. He picked Tristan up and within a few minutes had the boy back inside. Grabbing a bottle of water from the box, he removed the cap and handed it to the child.

After several sips, Tristan asked, "Are we still playing a game, are you my pretend momma?"

Ryan sent a questioning look at Kerry as he secured the seatbelt around the boy.

"I'll explain later," she told Ryan, then looked at Tristan. "Not now, sweetie. We might want to play it again later."

Ryan stood by the open door. He hated to question the child, but they needed all the information he could get. "Tristan, what happened after you went to sleep in your bed?"

Tristan took a long drink from the bottle before saying, "I woke up, but it wasn't my room. It smelled and was dirty."

"Do you know how you got to the room?"

"Huh-uh … I got sick. He didn't like it." A smug tone of satisfaction crept into his voice. "It hit his shoes."

"Who was there?" Ryan asked.

"A man. He shouted, said some bad words, and shook me."

Ryan hesitated, then asked, "Is that the only time he touched you?" Relief swept over him when the boy nodded yes. "Did you see anyone else?"

"Yep, another man. He was watching TV with the bad man. They didn't see me," he replied with another smile of self-satisfaction.

"Why didn't they see you?"

"I snuck out of the bedroom and was really quiet when I walked."

"How did you get out of the house?"

"I ran out the back door and hid under a tree, then I ran again. I screamed at Kerry like mommy told me to do. Kerry grabbed me."

"Wow! What a brave boy you are. Your daddy and mommy will be very proud of you. You did good. Is there anything else you remember about the house?" Ryan asked.

"A girl. She was crying."

Four

Kerry had twisted to look over the seat as Ryan questioned Tristan. Her gaze shot upward to stare into Ryan's eyes, their faces mirrored the shock from Tristan's words. Was there another kidnapped child?

After several more questions, it was evident, Tristan had told them all he could remember. When the boy yawned, Ryan grabbed the bottle, then positioned him so he could lie down and tucked the blanket around his body.

As she pulled back onto the highway, her thoughts swirled at the implication of another kidnapped victim. She glanced in the rearview mirror at Tristan. He had fallen back asleep.

"Are you thinking the same thing I am? There's another kidnapped child?" she asked.

"It's exactly what I am thinking," he said.

"Do you work for Cooper?"

"No, I work for a specialized unit, the Trackers. We're based in Washington, D.C. My boss received a call to help on the Murdock kidnapping."

His phone rang. Answering, he activated the speakerphone. A female voice asked, "Where are you? Cooper called again."

He laughed and said, "Careful what you say, you are on the speakerphone. Nicki Allison, say hello to Kerry Branson."

"Hmm, Barr ... not nice to do that to someone. Remind me to return the favor one of these days. Hello, Kerry. Sounds like you landed in the middle of a mess."

Kerry grinned at the bubbly voice on the other end. "Nice to meet you, and yeah, I did."

"Nicki, we may have another victim. Tristan heard a little girl crying."

Her voice turned somber as she said, "If that's the case, why haven't we heard anything?"

"Good question. And, if our suspicions are correct, we have a mole. The kidnappers followed Kerry to the hospital and then to the airport. Her only calls were to her boss and Cooper. If you can, steer clear of the agents in the Austin office until we figure this out."

Disconnecting, he said, "Nicki and I had finished an investigation in Clinton, Mississippi when Scott received the call and sent us to Austin."

"I'm curious how you got to Mt. Pleasant so fast."

"We had just landed and were on our way to Cooper's office. When your boss called him, we were only minutes from the airport."

As she listened to Ryan talk, a new worry wormed its way into her thoughts. "If someone in the FBI is involved, is it safe to take Tristan home?"

Startled, he glanced at her profile as she drove down the highway. He had the same concern and said, "I'm not sure since we don't know the reason he was kidnapped. There is certainly a determined effort to get him back. If I had a place, I'd stash him for a few days. Plus, I need to find the house."

"I know where we can leave him. It's the home of the person I visited this weekend. Cindy is a friend from college and lives in the middle of several thousand acres. No one would even think to connect her to Tristan. Plus, her husband is ex-military and as tough as they come. His brothers live nearby and are also ex-military."

Ryan agreed, saying that would at least solve their problem for the night. He'd wait and make his own assessment before deciding to leave the boy.

Up ahead was a convenience store, and she needed gas. Ryan stepped out to fill the tank.

A quick stop at the restroom, then a pass along the cookie aisle to pick up a snack. Just in case Tristan woke up, she wanted to have something he could nibble on. Uncertain what a six-year-old boy liked, she decided on a package of animal cookies. On her way to the checkout counter, Kerry spotted the display for paid cell phones. Grabbing a half-dozen, she paid for the items and her gas, glad she had acquired an ample supply of cash before she left Austin. She didn't want to use her credit card.

Back in the car, she waited while Ryan made a trip inside. Activating one of the cell phones, she called Mike. "It's Kerry. Get a burner phone and call me back at this number." He always carried one in his truck.

A few minutes later, the phone rang. It took several minutes to explain what had happened and the suspicions someone in the FBI was involved.

"I don't like your situation. Can you trust Barr?"

"Umm ... I didn't at first. But, after talking to him, I believe I can. He's not part of Cooper's team."

Mike knew Kerry's instincts were reliable as he considered her one of the best investigators he had ever worked with. "Who's his boss?"

"Scott Fleming, and it's the Trackers Unit in D.C."

"I've heard of it. It's new, and only the elite of the elite get offered a position. If Barr is a Tracker, I would agree with your assessment he's not involved," Mike said.

"You may get a call from Cooper, so be careful what you say. Right now, Ryan's not talking to any of the local agents."

"I've known Coop for several years and can't believe he's involved, but still, it's better to not take a chance."

"If you need to call, use this number. My phone is disabled."

Her next call was to Cindy. Luke answered. She told him she was on the way back to their house and would explain when she got there.

Ryan opened the door as she disconnected. Kerry motioned to the bag sitting on the console. "There are several burner phones if you need one along with cookies for Tristan."

She pulled back onto the highway and within a few miles turned onto the county road that led to her friend's house.

"Do you think you can find where you picked up Tristan?"

"Yes, even though it was foggy, I remember the damn gate—the one with a flying horse. I went by it twice when I got lost. Is there any way you can check on what happened at the hospital?"

Ryan hit a key on his phone. "Nicki, find out what happened at the Mt. Pleasant hospital. Kerry's worried. Anything on a second victim?"

Nicki said, "I talked to Scott, and he didn't know either. I got the impression if there was another abduction, he wasn't happy over being kept out of the loop. I'll check on the hospital and call you back."

Surprised at his astute observation since she hadn't mentioned her concerns about the hospital, she glanced at him. He looked her way and grinned, sending a shiver down her back. The man was way too good-looking for her peace of mind.

A few minutes later, his phone rang. Ryan activated the speakerphone again for Kerry's benefit.

Nicki said, "Three armed men charged into the waiting room looking for Tristan. They disarmed a deputy sheriff and tied him up. When they found out the boy had disappeared, they hauled ass and left, but not before they shot out the tires of the squad car parked in front. Since they wore ski masks, there's no description, other than three men of varying sizes."

"I bet it's the same three who showed up at the airport. One of them was on the phone before they left the airport," Kerry said. "I called Agent Cooper within minutes of leaving the hospital and told him I would meet the plane. If he isn't the leak, I wonder who he talked too?"

"You can bet they're still looking for you. Can anyone find you?"

Nicki asked.

"I don't think so, even though they know what my truck looks like and probably have the plate number. My phone is deactivated. I'm using a burner phone and staying off my credit cards."

"Sounds like you know what you are doing. Oh, by the way, the sheriff is also looking for you and the boy. Ryan, what's your next step?"

"I may have found a safe house for Tristan. Until we know who is behind this, I don't want to take a chance on someone stopping us on the way to Austin. And, I don't want to leave until I find the house where he was kept."

"We're getting ready to land. I'll contact you once we are on the ground. I'm sure Cooper will be waiting. He's called several times and isn't happy at either of you for not answering his calls."

"See if you can find out who he is talking to on his end," he said and hit the disconnect button.

"Are you sure your phone is safe to use?" Kerry asked.

"It's on an encrypted link which prevents anyone from getting a lock on it."

Ryan glanced at the back to check on Tristan, then reached for his backpack and pulled out his computer. While Kerry drove along the dark and lonely back roads, he mined the internet. Everything he found confirmed what he already knew. Murdock was rich, powerful, and had made his share of enemies over the years.

"Cindy's driveway is up ahead."

Ryan looked out the window. "My god, but it's dark. I can't see a light anywhere."

"She lives in the middle of nowhere and loves it."

She turned onto a narrow lane and followed it for about a half mile before pulling in front of a large two-story farmhouse. A porch extended across the front and down the sides. Yard lights came on as she parked in front.

"Impressive house. What does your friend do for a living?"

"A large part of the land is a tree farm for lumber, the rest is dedicated to cattle. The family also owns quite a few oil and gas wells across the state. Wait here."

As she exited and walked to the front steps, the door opened. A man, wearing an unbuttoned shirt and a pair of jeans, filled the doorway. A pistol was held against one very solid looking thigh.

His deep voice rang out. "Kerry, are you okay?"

"Yes, but I need your help."

"Well, come on in."

"Wait a minute, someone is with me." Kerry turned and motioned toward the vehicle.

Ryan stepped out, then picked up Tristan from the backseat. The movement caused him to wake.

"Daddy?"

The hope in the child's voice was heartbreaking to hear. "No, not yet, but soon," he said as he walked into a large entryway with stairs leading to the second floor.

A woman, in a long robe, appeared on the landing. Cindy was the same height as Kerry, but a few pounds heavier. During Kerry's visit, she had lamented several times on how long it was taking to lose the added pounds from her pregnancy. Short, auburn hair tousled around a face furrowed with concern. "Kerry, what's wrong?"

"Cindy, it's a long story. This is FBI Tracker Ryan Barr, and the child is Tristan Murdock. Ryan ... meet Cindy and Luke Shelton."

The woman rushed down the stairs.

"Before any explanations, I need to get Tristan taken care of," Kerry said.

Cindy took one look at the child in dirty pajamas, clinging to a blanket that dragged the floor and instantly went into her newly acquired mother mode.

"Let me have him. Tristan, are you hungry?" she asked as she took the boy from Ryan's arms.

"Uh huh," he said as hands came up to rub his face.

"Well, let's get you a bath, and once we're done, there will be chocolate chip cookies and a glass of milk waiting."

The mention of cookies lit up his face and instantly cemented his friendship with her.

She looked at Kerry. "You talk to Luke, and I'll take care of Tristan," and headed up the stairs.

Luke slid the pistol into a drawer of a cabinet near the front door. Buttoning his shirt, he led the way to the living room. It was warm and inviting with a large sectional in the center and smaller chairs grouped to face a rock fireplace on the opposite wall.

"Would you like coffee or do you want something stronger?"

Kerry said, "As much as I would like something stronger, I'll settle for the coffee."

Luke looked at Ryan with raised eyebrows.

"Coffee works for me."

Luke nodded and walked out of the room.

Ryan settled on one end of the couch while Kerry eased back in a chair. "Nice place. Are you sure this will work?" he asked.

"I can't think of any place safer for Tristan. It would be hard for someone to spring a surprise attack on this house. Luke will explain."

"What will I explain?" Luke asked as he walked back into the living room. "The coffee will be ready in a few minutes."

Kerry recapped what had happened since she left earlier in the afternoon. As the story unfolded, a look of shock mixed with anger on Luke's face intensified.

"We need a place to leave Tristan until we can sort out why he was kidnapped and by whom. I told Ryan this house was as secure of a location as I could ever find," she added.

"Holy hell, Kerry. When you land in the middle of something, you don't do it by halfway measures. This is as bad as when you were shot."

His words sent Kerry into an instant flashback, the excruciating pain when the bullet struck her head. At that moment, her life changed forever, though she didn't realize it until several weeks later.

Luke's comments caused Ryan to stare at Kerry. *What was he talking about?* It suddenly occurred to him he had been so busy researching Murdock, he hadn't considered he needed to do the same with Kerry.

"Yeah, I know, but this is worse," Kerry said. "There is a possibility another child has been kidnapped. Tristan said he heard a girl crying. Until we can come up with some answers, we can't risk taking him home."

He looked at Ryan. "I have an extensive alarm system to warn me if anyone is approaching the house. When you arrived, I knew a car was coming as soon as it turned into the driveway. I have two brothers whose houses are only a few miles away. All three of us are ex-military. I also have an underground bunker with fully equipped living quarters. No one will get to Tristan as long as he is here."

The ding of the coffee maker sounded. "Let's go into the kitchen."

Ryan's phone rang. "I have to answer this."

He stepped outside as Kerry followed Luke to the kitchen. "Nicki, where are you?"

"Still on the plane in Austin. There have been two more abductions, the daughters of Senator Berkstrom and Wademan. It's possible the girl in the house with Tristan was Wademan's daughter. The Berkstrom abduction was only a few hours ago."

"Unbelievable! Any details?"

"No. The lid is clamped down on both. Cooper is livid and has stonewalled me. As soon as we landed, he stormed into the cabin. When he realized, you had left the plane, he went on a tirade, demanding to know where you had gone. He even threw out accusations you had gone rogue and was off the reservation. Who talks like that? Anyway, when he didn't get any information from me, he called Scott wanting your head on a plate."

"What did Scott do?"

"What I gathered from Cooper's comments is Scott told him to back off and let you handle it. The boy was safe, and it was all anyone needed to know. He stomped off the plane with some not so nice names for you. Cooper must not have the clout to overrule Scott. The boss man has some serious pull in the department, more so than I knew."

"How'd you find out about the kidnappings?"

"I happened to see an email to one of the agents involved in the Murdock investigation."

Ryan didn't bother to ask how she'd seen the email. There wasn't anyone better in the Bureau at research or hacking into computer systems.

"Does Scott know there are two more abductions?" he asked.

"I don't know. I'm getting ready to call him."

"Any idea who leaked the information on Tristan?"

"Not yet. I've identified every agent associated with the Murdock investigation, and so far, nothing is coming up in the initial search. What's next on your end?"

"To locate the house, though I'm sure they are long gone. I'll talk to you in the morning."

"Scott ordered the pilot to refuel and get me to Washington. We will be taking off in a few minutes."

❧

Luke glanced at Kerry as he poured her a cup of coffee. "This could get nasty before you're done."

She nodded and turned her head at the sound of footsteps. Ryan walked into the kitchen, his face grim.

"Nicki called. There have been two more kidnappings."

Stunned, Kerry and Luke stared at him for several seconds, before Kerry asked, "Who?"

"Senators Berkstrom and Wademan's daughters."

Shock held everyone quiet. Cindy walked in with Tristan at her side,

38

clean and in a t-shirt, that hung over his knees, and a pair of socks that were several sizes too big. She glanced at the bleak expressions and knew something was terribly wrong.

"Let's get this young man some cookies and milk, then I'll put him to bed," she said as he hopped onto a kitchen chair.

Kerry shook off the distressing thoughts as she looked at Tristan. His red hair was clean and curled a bit as it hung over his forehead. The aroma of baby powder wafted in the air.

"Tristan, you look so cute, I think we may have to play pretend momma again."

He giggled as he looked up at her. The sound tugged at her heart. "Are his feet okay?" she asked as she watched Cindy set a plate of cookies and a glass of milk in front of him.

"They seem to be, but that's why the socks," Cindy answered.

While Tristan ate, everyone kept the conversation off the topic at the forefront of their thoughts. By the time he started on the second cookie his eyelids had drooped.

Cindy picked him up. "I'll be right back." When she returned, Kerry went over everything for her benefit.

"Well, of course, he can stay here. What about the other child?" Cindy asked.

"I need to find the house where Tristan was held," Ryan said.

"I can help. Let's go to my office," Luke said and led the way down a hallway along the back of the house.

Surprised, Ryan scanned the extensive computer equipment in the room. A large monitor sat on one desk in front of a ceiling to floor window. An impressive security control panel was mounted on a wall along with a flat-screen TV. Filing cabinets and an oversized safe were positioned along another wall.

Luke hit a wall switch, and drapes slid across the window. As he sat in his chair, he asked, "Where were you when you found Tristan?"

"I was lost in that damn fog trying to follow your wife's cockamamie directions. I had gone past the gate with the flying horse which I'd already passed once," Kerry replied as she glared at her friend.

Used to Kerry's verbal jabs, Cindy smiled and ignored her.

"There is only one farm near there, and it's been abandoned for years." Luke tapped a few keys and pulled up an aerial map. He zoomed the map to the roadway to locate the gate, then expanded it looking for a structure. "There it is, the only one for miles."

"This must be the place. Do you know anything about the owner?" Ryan asked.

"No. It belonged to an old man who died several years ago. I don't have any idea what happened to his estate."

Ryan sent a text message to Nicki with the GPS coordinates of the location and a request to locate the owner of the property.

As they studied the screen in detail, Ryan said, "Well, there goes any hope of getting to the place tonight." Trees surrounded the property, and the narrow road leading to the house was overgrown with thick brush.

"No, it would be better if we went in at daybreak," Luke said.

"We!" Ryan responded.

"Yeah, you've got company for this little excursion."

Kerry pointed to a corner of the screen. She had spotted an easement that had been cut through the trees and passed along the backside of the property.

"Luke, if we pick up the trail here," pointing to a road a half mile or so from the house where it intersected the wide swath of cut timber, "we can use the easement, then cut through the woods to reach the back of the house." After what happened at the airport, she had no desire to make a frontal approach.

Luke picked up the phone and called his brothers to set up an early dawn meeting. He suggested they all go to bed since there was nothing they could do until daylight.

Ryan seconded the idea.

Luke asked if he needed any clothes.

"If you have anything that fits," he said before grinning at a man a couple of inches taller and at least thirty pounds heavier.

"Cindy's brother is around your size and usually leaves a few clothes here," Luke said.

"Kerry, you have the same bedroom," Cindy said. "Ryan, I'll show you where you can stay. Leave your clothes in the hallway, and I'll wash them."

In bed, the events of the day circled in Kerry's mind. What could possibly be the motive to kidnap the children of three senators? She had never been one for conspiracy theories, but she had to ask herself—was this a plot against the government?

Since this was a scheduled call, Moore let the phone ring. After three rings, the toneless voice answered. "Yes."

"We have the next package," Moore said.

Five

A faint light had slipped around the edges of the drapes when the tap sounded on Kerry's door. It opened, and Cindy stuck her head in. "I wanted to make sure you were awake."

Seated on the edge of the bed, Kerry laced up her boot. "I didn't get much sleep. How's Tristan?"

"Still asleep. He sure is a cute little guy," she said as she leaned against the side of the door frame.

"Are you okay with all of this? We can tell Luke and his brothers to stay here and not get your family involved any more than I already have."

Cindy laughed before saying, "Oh, yeah, like he's going to listen to you. You know Luke. There won't be any holding him or his brothers back on this one. I'm fine with it. Remember, I went through the years when he was in Iraq and Afghanistan. At least, he is home."

Kerry pulled her belt through the loop on the holster, then slid the gun into place. "Is Ryan up?" she asked.

"He's in the kitchen. Seth and Butler are here. They're huddled over the aerial map Luke printed."

Kerry grabbed her jacket and jammed her ball cap on her head, pulling her ponytail through the back as she followed Cindy downstairs.

She'd never met Luke's brothers, though she knew they were single and lived nearby. When she walked in, the men looked up from the map on the table.

"Kerry, meet Seth and Butler," Luke said.

Both shook her hand. They were a younger version of Luke. Dressed in army fatigue pants and t-shirts, they sported impressive biceps. Muscular thighs stretched the material covering their legs. They looked tough and confident. An aura she had observed in many ex-military men, including her boss.

Somewhere, Cindy had come up with a set of fatigues for Ryan. Even with his elegant good looks, he had the same rugged appearance as the other men.

Kerry poured a cup of coffee, leaned against the counter and gazed at a sea of fog through the window.

Luke said, "We were studying the approach from the road to the farm," as he noticed the direction of her stare. "The fog will provide cover. It'll take around thirty minutes to get into position behind the house," and passed small headsets and portable radios to each. "We use these when we are herding cattle. Makes it a lot easier to talk when we are on horseback. I suggest we take two vehicles. Ryan, you go with Kerry," and grinned at her. "I'll take the lead ... so you don't get lost again."

Crinkling her nose at his smirk, she took the last swallow of coffee, then followed the men out the door. It was the first opportunity to look for a hole which she spotted at the back of the truck. The bullet had entered the right side of the bed and exited on the left.

Ryan walked up as she examined the damage. "Well, he didn't miss."

"I thought I heard a ping but wasn't sure."

Kerry followed Luke's vehicle out the driveway. When he reached the section of the road where the easement had been cut, he pulled into an adjacent pasture.

After a final weapons check, Luke took the lead. On each side were the thick piney woods common to East Texas. The ground was rough, and tree stubs and deep ruts made for a treacherous surface. It would be easy to twist an ankle, and she was thankful she had on high-top hiking boots.

When Luke moved into the trees, they picked their way through the dense underbrush. Stopping, he motioned with his hand toward the faint outline of a building visible through the thick mist. They had already agreed on the position each person would take. Her pistol clasped in her hands, and her body slightly bent, Kerry sprinted to the back corner of the house. The quick peek through the kitchen window revealed an empty room. On the opposite corner, Ryan checked another window. His whisper sounded in her ear when he called the all clear. Luke and his brothers had run to the front corners of the house. Luke's voice was next when he signaled there was no one visible.

Ducking under the window, Kerry crept to the back door and twisted the doorknob. It was unlocked, and she eased the door open. Ryan moved up behind her as she darted through the doorway. Within minutes, they determined the house was vacant, though there were signs it had been recently occupied.

Holstering her gun, she said, "Let's check each room for evidence."

A long hallway ran the width of the house with bedrooms on one end and the kitchen, dining room and living room on the other end. While Luke and his brothers searched one side, Kerry and Ryan started on the bedrooms.

In the first room torn drapes hung from the dirty window. A thick layer of dust covered the bed and dresser, and cobwebs hung from the ceiling. With a quick glance, she moved to the next one.

When she stepped inside, the vision started. A shimmering haze shrouded the room. When it cleared, it was dark. A lamp on the dresser cast shadows across the floor. The sobs of a small girl curled on the bed filled the room. Dressed in a nightgown, her body shivered under the thin material, and long blond hair was twisted and matted around her tear-streaked face. A footstep sounded behind Kerry, and she looked over her shoulder. The harsh voice of a heavyset man, his face covered with stubble, told the child to shut up, then closed the door, followed by the click of the lock.

The images faded, and she was back in the present, standing in a room with an empty bed.

"Bomb! Get out! Get out!"

Luke's warning blasted her eardrums. Spinning, she raced toward the back door with Ryan's footsteps close behind. The brothers were ahead of them. Luke's broad shoulder rammed the door, knocking it off its hinges as he burst outside.

They ran and barely reached the tree line before the house exploded. The heat of the blast swept over her. She fell, her arms covering her head, as dirt and debris rained down.

Coughing, Luke staggered over to her. "Are you okay?" Blood trickled down his forehead.

She pushed up and rocked back on her heels. Her gaze flicked over him. "Yes. How bad are you hurt?" she asked.

He swiped at the blood with his sleeve. "It's nothing."

Kerry looked around to find the others. Seth and Butler were getting to their feet. They didn't appear to be injured. Ryan was near them on his knees. Blood ran down the side of his face.

"Ryan!" Kerry shouted.

"I'm okay. Just got nicked by a flying piece of wood," he said as he stood and wiped his face. "What the hell happened?"

"The house was wired to explode," Luke said. "When I spotted the timer, there was less than a minute."

Stunned, everyone was silent as they absorbed the implication of what Luke had found. If he hadn't it, they would have been inside.

"There was more than one explosion," Butler said, wiping the dust and pieces of debris from his shirt. Seth nodded his head in agreement.

Luke replied, "Yeah, I know. Someone who knows explosives set those devices and did a damn good job of it. The house imploded, going inward, with a minimum of flying debris. It's probably what kept our injuries to a minimum."

Ryan added, "Well, there went our evidence."

Kerry thought to herself. *No, not all.* She had seen the little girl and one of the kidnappers.

Luke's phone rang. "Yes, we're all okay and are headed back," he said, then disconnected. "Cindy heard the explosion."

"Ryan, do you want to contact the sheriff's department? I doubt anyone other than Cindy heard anything," Luke said. "There are no other houses close by. It's your call."

Ryan studied the remains of the building through the dust that overrode the fog. There wasn't any danger of fire to the surrounding woods. "No, I don't. For now, I would rather keep it to ourselves."

"Let's head back. Nothing more we can do here," Luke said.

"You go ahead. I want to look at what's left." Ryan motioned toward the huge pile of rubble. "Kerry, do you want to go with Luke?"

"I'll stay and help."

Luke nodded and turned to catch up with his brothers.

Stepping around a pile of bricks, Kerry said, "I think I found the room where the girl was kept."

Ryan's phone rang. It was Scott.

"Where are you?"

"Still in East Texas with Kerry's friends, Cindy and Luke Shelton," Ryan answered. "It's where she spent the weekend and was on her way back to Austin when she found Tristan. We located the house the kidnappers used. It's several miles from the Shelton ranch. Though, it's not a house anymore. It was rigged to blow."

"Anyone hurt?"

"No, we got out in time," he said and explained what happened.

"Did you find anything?" Scott asked.

"Not much. There were at least two adults and two kids. Kerry believes she found the bedroom where the little girl was kept, and I located the room Tristan was in. He told us that he got sick, and it was still on the floor. We're going to search what we can, though, before we leave."

"Do you plan to move the Murdock boy?"

"No. Tristan's safe, and I believe we need to keep him hidden. After meeting the Sheltons, and seeing their home, I agree with Kerry their ranch is the best location. What have you learned about the kidnappers?"

"Someone knew what they were doing. All three were a smooth operation. They disabled the security system, grabbed the kid from the bedroom, and were gone. It couldn't have been accomplished without inside knowledge of the home."

"Any evidence?" Ryan asked.

"None, and still no contact with the kidnappers. I called Senator Murdock to reassure him Tristan was safe. He wasn't happy I wouldn't provide any details and adamant that he wanted to speak to you."

"I plan to meet with him as soon as I get to Austin."

"Is Branson still with you?"

"Yes."

"Good. From what I discovered, she'll be a valuable asset."

Disconnecting, Ryan remembered he still hadn't researched her. He pocketed the phone and relayed the gist of the conversation to Kerry who poked through the debris.

All they could do was search the perimeter of the mound of brick, concrete, and wood, moving smaller chunks of rubble as best they could. Kerry shifted a large piece of sheetrock and caught a glimpse of pink. A bit of ribbon protruded from under a section of a couch.

Pulling it out, she shouted. "I found something."

Ryan rushed toward her.

She handed it to him, saying, "Even though it's dirty from the explosion, it looks fairly new. I bet it belongs to the girl Tristan heard crying."

"You're probably right. I'll send a picture to Nicki. Maybe the parents can identify it."

They continued their search, but when nothing else turned up, they headed back to Kerry's vehicle.

Once in the truck, Kerry asked, "What's next?"

Ryan looked at his watch. "Let's get cleaned up. Then I want to go to the county courthouse and research the title."

"That's not a bad idea. Some of the outlying counties don't have their records computerized and ..." eyeing the wound on his head, added, "You need to clean that cut."

The fog had lifted, and she made good time on the return to the ranch. Cindy and Luke were on the front porch when they drove up.

"You and that security system. Saw us coming, didn't you?" Kerry said as they exited the vehicle.

"Yep, best damn system in the county," Cindy replied.

Luke grinned, then said, "I can tell you with absolute certainty—it is. Did you find anything?"

Kerry pulled the ribbon from her pocket. "Just this."

Cindy gasped. "Oh, my god! Then it's true. There was a little girl in the house along with Tristan."

"Yes, there was," Kerry said as she and Ryan followed the two into the house.

Inside, Cindy said, "I have breakfast ready if anyone is hungry."

Kerry glanced down at her filthy clothes. "Let us get cleaned up first."

When Ryan entered the bedroom, his clothes, clean and folded, were on the bed. At least, he wouldn't have to raid Cindy's brother's stash of clothes again.

A tap on the door and Luke walked in. He dropped a first aid kit on the bed and eyed the gash on Ryan's forehead. "It doesn't look serious, but if you need any help let me know."

Ryan examined the wound in the mirror. It had stopped bleeding. A shower and an application of antibiotic cream should take care of the problem.

In the kitchen, Cindy had bacon and eggs warming in the oven. Everyone filled a plate. Kerry asked about Tristan and was told he already had breakfast and was watching a video in his room.

In response to a question from Luke about their plans, Ryan said, "We're headed to the courthouse to research the property, then back to Austin. I have to meet with Senator Murdock."

Kerry looked at Cindy and Luke who sat across from her at the table. "Are you certain it's okay for Tristan to stay here?"

"Absolutely," Luke said without hesitation.

The courthouse was an impressive building with gargoyles mounted on the miniature towers at each corner of the roof. Inside, a clerk directed them to the office that contained the archived history of land titles. While they found several land records that referenced the lease of mineral rights over the last several years, the only useful detail was the owner's name, a corporation, on the tax rolls. Ryan texted the information to Nicki.

"Well, it wasn't a complete dead-end, but close to it," he said as they left the building.

"What now. Do we head to Austin?"

Glancing at his watch, Ryan said, "This took longer than I expected, and it's getting late. We might as well wait and leave early tomorrow morning."

The burner phone she had stuck in her pocket vibrated. "Probably my boss." Stopping on the sidewalk, she answered.

"Kerry, someone broke into your house. The silent alarm was triggered, and I called 911, but by the time the police arrived, the burglar was long gone."

Kerry lived outside of Austin. Working for a security company meant she had access to top-of-the-line security systems. When she moved into the house, Mike had a dedicated line installed for the system. Only the BSI personnel knew about the setup.

"I'm at the house now. The phone line was cut, and the kitchen door busted open. It appears all that is missing is the computer in your office. This wasn't your ordinary break-in."

"It has to be connected to the kidnappings, but how the hell did they know who I am and where I live," Kerry said.

"Can they get anything from your computer?"

"I doubt it. The password is protected on three levels."

"I'll get your door repaired and make sure the house is secured. What is happening on your end?"

Kerry quickly filled him in on the latest events, then added, "Mike, this is not your typical kidnapping, something else is going on. All we know so far is that two children are missing, and someone wants Tristan back."

"Cooper called, and he is threatening to issue an arrest warrant if you don't bring in the Murdock boy."

"What! How crazy is that? Well, that will never fly. I'll let Ryan know. His boss seems to have a lot of pull."

"Keep me posted. I'll hold off the wolves on this end."

Suddenly, a thought occurred to Kerry and sent a surge of fear racing through her. "Mike, check my office. Next to my computer was a wooden holder for envelopes and notes. See if it is still there?"

Footsteps sounded over the phone as she waited.

"No, it's gone. All that's on your desk is a cup with pens and pencils. Is it important?" Mike asked.

"Oh, my god, yes. Cindy sent me a note about my visit. I stuck it in the holder. They have her address, and will know I spent the weekend here and … it's where I've stashed Tristan."

Six

D*ear god!* We left Cindy and the two children alone this morning. Complacent in the belief the kidnappers couldn't connect the Shelton ranch to Tristan, she hadn't considered the danger to them. Panic clutched and clawed through her at the thought of an attack on the house and her friends.

Ryan, reacting to the fear on her face, asked, "What happened?"

"They … they have to leave," she stammered. "Yes, they've got to get to a safe place!"

"Kerry, slow down. Who has to leave? You're not making any sense."

She took a deep breath, then said, "That was my boss. Someone broke into my house. My computer and several letters I had on my desk are gone. One was from Cindy. They have her address and know it's where I stayed over the weekend. They could attack the house."

"Stop and think. You said there wasn't anywhere safer than Luke's house."

She realized he was right. Fear had caused her to overreact. Logic pushed aside the distress and cleared her thoughts. "That's not all. Cooper told Mike he would issue a warrant for my arrest if I don't bring in Tristan."

"I'll take care of it. Coop is probably blowing hot air, hoping to scare you, but let's make sure." He pulled his phone from his pocket and called his boss. "Cooper is raising a ruckus over Tristan and is

51

threatening to arrest Kerry. Plus, someone broke into her house. If it's related to Tristan's abduction, they know she spent the weekend at the Shelton ranch."

He listened, then said, "We're staying the night. Tomorrow, we'll head to Austin. As aggressive as the attempts have been to get Tristan back, I expect they will try again." He paused, then added, "Hold off on the reinforcements. It would only provide confirmation of Tristan's location."

Disconnecting, he looked at Kerry. "Don't worry about the warrant. If Cooper is stupid enough to pull that kind of stunt, Scott will handle it. Let's get back to the ranch."

When they pulled in front of the house, Kerry shoved the gear shift into park and rushed inside. Luke sat on the couch with a book in his hand, and Tristan next to him.

She gave the boy a hug, then looked at Luke. "I need to talk to you and Cindy."

At her tone of urgency, he said, "Tristan, why don't you take your book up to your bedroom. We'll finish reading it later."

Once Cindy was seated beside Luke, Kerry went over the details of the break-in and her fears of a possible attack on the house.

"If they do attempt something, they'll get more than they bargained for," Luke said.

"Scott offered to send a Seal team to provide additional protection if you think we need it," Ryan said.

Both women burst out laughing. Even Luke had a wry grin on his face.

"Okay, how'd I miss the joke?" Ryan asked.

Kerry answered, "Luke, Seth, and Butler are all ... former Seals."

He grinned and said, "Ah, hell. Good thing I told him to wait."

Luke called his brothers to get them back to his place. "As soon as they get here, we'll work out a plan. If necessary, Cindy, the baby, and Tristan can go to the underground bunker. No one can get to them there."

Luke headed to his office, and Cindy to the kitchen to take a batch of cookies out of the oven. Ryan, whose ears had perked up at the mention of cookies followed, hoping to snag one or two.

Kerry grabbed a notepad and pen from her backpack. Settled on the couch, she began to sketch the face of the little girl in her vision. When finished, she nodded in satisfaction and set it aside, then started on the man, certain he was the one who shot at her.

Upstairs, Tristan sat on the floor in his bedroom watching a group of happy dinosaurs singing and dancing on the TV screen. He looked up as she walked in. A smile lit up his face.

"Hi, Kerry. Want to watch my dinosaur movie?"

Kerry sat next to him and laid the sketches alongside her. "I don't think I've seen this one. They're funny. Can you sing and dance like that?" she said as she lightly tickled his ribcage.

He giggled, squirmed away from her fingertips. "Nope, I only watch."

"Tristan, have you seen this man?" she asked and held up the sketch.

A look of fear crossed his face as he stared at the paper. In a whisper, he said, "The bad man. Is he here?"

"No, and you don't need to be afraid. You are safe here. But we need to find him, and I wanted to know if this was the man you saw at the house."

A solemn look on his face, Tristan gazed at her. "He was scary, and I didn't like him."

Kerry picked up the second sketch. "Do you remember seeing her?"

He shook his head no. "She's pretty. Is she the one crying?"

"I'm not sure."

"I hope she's okay," Tristan said.

Kerry wrapped her arm around the boy's shoulder and gave him a kiss on the top of the head. "So, do I, sweetie. Do you want to come downstairs with me?"

"Nope. I want to watch my movie." His grin popped out again as Tristan hugged her back.

Downstairs, Kerry laid the two drawings on the coffee table. When Ryan walked in, he motioned toward the sketches with a hand that held three cookies. "Who's that?" he asked before popping one he held in his other hand into his mouth.

Eyeing the cookies, she asked, "Did you leave any for the rest of us?"

He mumbled, "A couple for Tristan, didn't want to eat his share."

She glared at him. "Don't you know it's not polite to talk with your mouth full of food?"

"You're just upset because you didn't get one," he quipped, then grinned. "So, what's up with the drawings?"

"I drew them. Tristan said this was the 'bad man' as he refers to him. I think the girl is who he heard, though, he didn't see her."

Astonished, Ryan stared at her. "How did you come up with these drawings?"

"Long story, and it's not important now. Send them to Nicki. It shouldn't take long to confirm if the girl is Wademan's daughter. With the Bureau's facial recognition program, she might get a match on the man."

Laying the cookies on the table, Ryan snapped a picture of each sketch with his cell phone and shot them off to Nicki. He'd already sent her a picture of the ribbon.

When his phone rang, it was Nicki. In response to her question, he replied, "It's one of the kidnappers and possibly the Wademan girl. Tristan identified the man."

Nicki said, "I can tell you it is Wademan's daughter. Who drew the pictures?"

"Kerry."

"How did she find out what they looked like?"

"Uh … well … I don't have an explanation …yet. I'll let you know when I do."

Luke stepped out of the kitchen to say his brothers had arrived. Grabbing his cookies, Ryan followed Kerry, and reminded himself, again, that he needed to research her.

Luke had a map of his ranch spread out on the kitchen table. Kerry bent over it studying the layout of the buildings and the road leading into the property.

"It will be impossible for someone to approach from the rear unless a helicopter drops them. Any breach of the perimeter fence line and the sensors would alert us to the location," Luke said.

Kerry asked a few questions about the security system and soon realized it was state-of-the-art. With the line underground, it couldn't be disabled.

"We know there are at least three, and it's possible they have added reinforcements. What do you have in the way of weapons?" Ryan asked.

"More than enough to handle anything they throw at us, though I want to stop them before they get close to the house," Luke said.

"What happens if they don't hit tonight?" Seth asked.

Ryan said, "I get a sense of urgency in their actions. If they don't, then it's a good chance everything will be okay, and I should be able to leave tomorrow. I have to get to Austin and talk to Murdock."

The brothers left saying they would be back before sunset. Luke told Cindy to check the bunker in case they needed to use it.

"I'd like to go with you. I've never seen it," Kerry said.

Ryan said he'd also like to see it.

In Luke's office, Cindy removed a book from the bookcase and pulled a lever hidden behind it. A section of the wall on the opposite side slid open, and a set of stairs led downward.

"This is not on any blueprint of the house. The only ones who know it's there are family members. The original purpose was in case of a tornado, but of course, Luke got carried away with the design."

Cindy hit a light switch at the top of the stairs. At the bottom was a large, metal door. Opening it, she walked into a room with a small sofa, two chairs, a wall-mounted TV on one side, and a kitchen on the other. A hallway led to several smaller rooms. Kerry opened the doors as they peeped inside to see bedrooms equipped with bunk beds, a bathroom with a shower and even a small utility room, complete with washer and dryer. Shelves held boxes of canned and dried food.

"We could live down here for several weeks if we had to. There is even an emergency exit, a tunnel leads to the barn." Cindy checked the refrigerator and cupboards. "I'll bring down milk and a few other items," she said as they walked back upstairs.

"Some setup you have down there," Ryan said as they walked into Luke's office.

"It didn't start out that large, but when I began the construction, I decided to equip it with everything we might need. We figured, if nothing else, any kids we had would enjoy it. We should all get some rest today as we may be up most of the night," Luke said.

Moore waited for the callback.

"Did you receive the location?" his boss asked.

"Yes. If the package is there, I will have it tonight."

"Don't leave any witnesses."

Seven

R yan headed to his room where he planned to spend the next
couple of hours on research, but this time it was Kerry who was
his subject.

As he scanned the first article that popped up, he was surprised to
learn she'd been a homicide detective with Austin PD before hiring on
with BSI. Kerry had been investigating a series of armed robberies at
convenience stores that had BSI security systems installed. When she
arrived at one of the stores, a robbery was in progress, and a kid was
parking his bike on the sidewalk. As the gunmen exited the store, she
shoved him to the ground, saving his life, but in the exchange of gunfire,
she was shot in the head.

The next series of articles dealt with her involvement in the
investigation and arrest of a high-profile Austin businessman for
insurance fraud and murder. A few weeks later she was involved in the
Ravine Killer case. Nicknamed by the news media because he dumped
his victims in ravines, the killer broke into Kerry's house and died under
mysterious circumstances.

Interesting lady. She was an enigma, a riddle he itched to solve. At
times, when he looked into her eyes, a wariness crept in, as if fearful
someone would get too close.

Kerry sat on her bed and pulled her laptop from her bag. She wanted to learn more about the Senators whose children were abducted. Murdock and Wademan were two of the top politicians on Capitol Hill. For the last several months, Murdock's name had circulated in the media as the leading candidate for the next presidential election. Even President Arthur Larkin had come out in support of his candidacy in the upcoming primaries. The latest articles dealt with Murdock's involvement in contract negotiations with the Chinese. Several major American companies had gone on record opposing the contracts. *Hmm, I wonder if he has received any threats because of the controversy over the contracts?*

Senator Wademan was from Oklahoma and another whose name had been touted as a possible candidate. The first photo she pulled up was of him standing on the steps of a house, his wife and small daughter next to him. That's her, the girl she saw in the bedroom of the old farmhouse! Jennifer Wademan, age six, her long blond hair curling over her shoulders, stared into the camera with a mischievous, engaging smile.

Picking up the laptop, she headed down the hall to Ryan's room. When he opened the door, she pushed past him. "I found a picture of her."

He turned, and his gaze raked her backside. Tight, black jeans encased long legs and a small, but very muscular butt. When she stretched to put the computer on the bed, a faint outline of nipples was visible against her t-shirt. A surge of desire shot through him. *This isn't good.* She might be a fascinating puzzle, but Kerry Branson wasn't the type of woman he gravitated toward. Besides, just yesterday she had pointed a damn gun at him.

Perched on the bed, she pointed to an image on the screen. "The girl in the farmhouse is definitely Senator Wademan's daughter." Not getting a response, she looked up.

His hand still on the doorframe, he stared at her.

"Hey, did you hear what I said?"

"Yeah. Nicki has already confirmed her identity," he growled, irritated by his reaction.

"Well, maybe so, but I wanted to know for my own satisfaction," she said in a snippy tone.

Grabbing his laptop from the desk by the door, he said, "Let's go downstairs where we'll have more room," and walked out.

As she followed him out the door, she muttered to herself. "Now, what's got him in a tizzy?"

Ryan wasn't about to enlighten her.

Seated on the couch, Kerry set her computer on the coffee table and searched for more images. "This picture was taken last week." She turned the computer so he could see the screen. "It must be the Senator's Oklahoma home behind them."

The picture Kerry had drawn was an uncanny resemblance to the little girl holding her mother's hand. *How had she come up with a sketch?* Ryan wondered. His mood had improved as his condition subsided.

"I found a couple of interesting items on Murdock and Wademan. Both are strong possibilities as candidates in the next presidential election. I didn't find much on Berkstrom. Murdock has come under fire from several companies and labor unions over the Chinese negotiations. Is it possible that's the motivation? No, it can't be since the other two aren't involved."

When Ryan's phone rang, he looked at the caller ID. "It's my boss. Let's run your idea by him."

"Scott, putting you on the speakerphone. Kerry, Scott Fleming."

"Kerry, nice to meet you even if it is over the phone."

"Any possibility the abductions are tied to the disagreements over the Chinese contract discussions?" Ryan asked.

"So far, none. The senator has received several threats, but nothing that would link to a kidnapping. Also, Berkstrom and Wademan are not involved. Nothing connects the Senators other than all three have been mentioned as presidential candidates," Scott said.

"Kerry spotted the presidential issue, and we were discussing it. It certainly seems to be a remote connection. Anything on the owner of the farmhouse?"

"When the owner died, it was in his estate for several years. The daughter finally sold the house and land to the company you found on the tax rolls. Nicki says it's a front for another company. She is still digging to find the actual owner. As soon as she has something, I'll let you know," Scott said.

"The person must be buried deep if it is taking her this long," Ryan said.

Scott replied, "Yes, and makes it even more suspicious."

"Have you found any suspects for our leak?" Kerry asked.

"Not yet. Blake and Adrian are still running full background checks on every agent in the Austin office."

When he disconnected, Kerry asked, "Who are the others Scott mentioned?"

"Adrian Dillard and Blake Kenner, two of the other agents in my unit."

"I've not heard about a Trackers Unit."

"It's new, only formed a few months ago. Our primary targets are criminals who stay under the radar and elude detection. Nicki and Scott have been working on a new software program, TRACE, for local agencies to enter the details of unsolved homicides. The computer will search for patterns in the crimes. I am sure from your experiences as a homicide detective, you know a murder is not always connected to a common killer because there's no link between the killer and victim. It makes it difficult to apprehend this type of criminal."

As Ryan talked, Kerry was reminded of the serial killer dubbed the Ravine Killer. Until Kerry's strange visions brought his crimes to light, he had been one of those Ryan had described, flying under the radar with his kills.

Luke walked in and said, "It's getting dark. Let's move the vehicles to the back."

Cindy had fixed a light supper of soup and sandwiches. Seth and Butler slipped in the back door as they finished eating. Both were dressed in fatigues. This time, streaks of camouflage paint smeared their face.

Kerry and Ryan left to change clothes. Dressed in a pair of black cargo pants, black t-shirt, and the hiking boots, she pushed her hair underneath a black ball cap. Walking out of the bedroom, Luke hollered at her.

"Hold up a minute." Stopping in front of her, he smeared a streak of the black paint across her cheekbones.

Ryan walked out of his room similarly attired. The black ball cap he'd borrowed from Luke covered his blond hair.

In the living room, Luke went over the plan one more time. He handed each a radio and headset, saying, "I wish we had night goggles, but the moonlight should be sufficient."

With a headset in place, Cindy would watch the security system and radio them of any intrusion. Tristan and the baby were already in the bunker, sound asleep.

Outside, they split to reach their designated spots. Kerry stretched out between two pine trees with one of Luke's scoped rifles. She rested her chin on the stock as she surveyed the landscape and realized it provided another element of protection. When Luke cleared the land, he left a section of trees a couple of hundred yards wide between the fence and the house. The trees added to the rustic look and obscured the view of the house from the roadway. But it also meant anyone coming through the fence had to cross the stretch of open land before they reached the edge of the trees.

Occasionally, someone would make a comment on the radio. Seth's voice echoed in her headset. "Look to your right."

She chuckled. An armadillo, its snout close to the ground, lumbered in front of the fence.

The radio crackled. Cindy's voice echoed. "Alarm, west side of the entrance."

Several men had crawled out of the creek bed near the fence, and one was cutting a section of the wire. Each had a rifle slung across their back. As she shifted to take aim at the intruder stepping across the downed fence, Luke fired. The man fell backward. The intruders dove to the ground and popped off several shots as they retreated.

Kerry fired, and several more shots erupted from the trees, but the men had moved back into the creek. Even the one Luke had shot was dragged back and out of sight. A few minutes later, vehicles could be heard racing away from the house.

Luke stood. "Well, I don't believe we'll see them again. We got at least one. Let's fix the fence line."

Kerry headed to the house. Inside, Cindy leaned against Luke's desk, her face pale and drawn. Kerry walked to her and wrapped her arms around her. "I'm so sorry, I brought all this down on your family."

Cindy drew back and looked at her friend, her voice stern and fierce. "Don't you dare be sorry. I'm so thankful we can help and protect that little boy. I shudder to think how I'd feel if it was my baby at risk. So, don't even think of apologizing again. You hear me?"

Kerry grinned, then replied, "Yeah, I do, loud and clear."

Upstairs, she washed the greasepaint off her face. The images of the assault circled in her mind and added to her sense of foreboding. Why was Tristan so important they were willing to kill to get him?

What the hell had happened back there? It sure wasn't a hick farmer, and now, he had a dead man. Since it was Sanford, the other guard who let the Murdock boy escape, it wasn't a loss that would affect the operation. Still, he could have used the extra help for a few more days. Too bad, it wasn't Boyd.

Moore tapped the number, let it ring twice, then hung up.

When he answered the callback, the voice on the other end said, "Do you have the package?"

"No. We experienced an unusual level of interference. One of my staff has departed."

"I don't give a damn about your employees. Was it the right location?"

"I'm not certain. It will require another approach."

There was a short silence before his boss said, "I'll get you access, don't make another mistake."

The calm, menacing voice sent chills down his back. Moore had survived as a mercenary for most of his adult life and not much scared him until he started working for this man. He soon learned his employer could reach deep into the criminal underbelly of society as well as the federal government and was not a man he wanted as an enemy.

Eight

When the men returned, they gathered in the kitchen. Kerry and Cindy had brought the children upstairs, and they were back in their beds. Cindy had made a pot of coffee, and a tray of sandwiches sat on the table.

"Those weren't street thugs, they were professionals. A coordinated withdrawal and they didn't panic when a man got shot or leave him behind; that's military training," Butler said as he grabbed sandwiches, passing one to Seth behind him.

"It ties into our conclusions on the kidnappers. The abductions were meticulously planned and executed," Ryan said.

Pouring a cup of coffee, Luke added, "I don't believe they'll be back. They didn't expect what happened, and it probably spooked them. If I were running the operation, I wouldn't."

As the two brothers turned to leave, Seth glanced at Ryan, then Kerry who leaned against the counter. "If you need any help, let us know. I'd like another go at those guys."

Ryan's phone rang, and he walked into the living room to answer the call.

"Mrs. Wademan braided her daughter's hair and tied it with a pink ribbon the night she was kidnapped," Scott said.

"Confirms what we suspected. We made the right call to stay here. A group of armed men tried to attack the house. We injured or killed at least one before they pulled back. They took him with them."

"Well, there goes another piece of evidence. Do you think they'll return? Do you need to move the boy?"

"No, I don't think they will make a second attempt, and it's also Luke's opinion. Besides, moving Tristan isn't a good idea. It would be more dangerous to transport him than to leave him here. This place is a fortress. And ... Luke and his brothers are former Seals."

Scott chuckled, then said, "So much for my offer of help. What is your next step?"

"Back to Austin to talk to Murdock. Oh, one other observation," and he explained the ex-military theory.

"If that's the case, it adds another layer of complications. I've another call," Scott said.

Washington, D.C.

Scott hung up the phone, leaned back in his chair and ran his hand over his face. This was the third call from the President. Three abducted children, and he had no answers. Already short on sleep, he didn't see much rest in the near future.

When the Bureau's Director, Paul Daykin, informed him the Trackers Unit would assist in the investigation of the Murdock abduction, Scott sent Ryan and Nicki to Austin. They were the closest having completed a case in Mississippi. As the unit profiler, Ryan's extraordinary insight into a criminal's thoughts and motivation would be invaluable in this type of crime.

The head of the Austin division, Will Cooper, hadn't been happy when two Trackers walked into his office. Scott pacified the agent by assuring him they were not taking over the case. Now, it had all changed. With the specter of a mole in the Bureau, the President had just put the Trackers Unit in charge of the investigation.

He might not have any answers, but there was one element of which he was certain—the capability of his team. Handpicked from his search of the Bureau's field agents, each had demonstrated unexpected skills. Since they were experts at hiding their abilities from their co-workers, he was confident he was the only individual aware of their unique talents. He smiled, amused at the notoriety his unit had already acquired as the rumors on the bureau's grapevine swirled over the mysterious team.

Picking up several folders, he walked into a large open area filled with desks. Nicki Allison, his research guru, was busy on her computer. High cheekbones, dark eyes, and coal-black hair that streamed down her back hinted at her native American heritage. Though petite, her muscular body reflected the regular trips to the gym on the first floor of the building.

Adrian Dillard and Blake Kenner were on the phone. Lean with a whipcord frame, Adrian's auburn hair curled over his collar and framed a face with deep-set eyes and a rough stubble of a beard. Tilted back in his chair, his long legs encased in black jeans were propped on the desk.

Blake was just the opposite. Stocky of build, he carried himself with a military air. Short hair, clean shaven, his gray eyes held a look of determination. Spit and shine was his style and the only one who had not taken advantage of Scott's elimination of the Bureau's dress code. His other two agents, Cat Morgan and Kevin Hunter, were on their honeymoon and out of the country.

"Everybody, conference room. Time to compare notes."

Chairs squeaked as calls were ended, and the agents followed him down the hall. Once they were settled, Scott said, "Ryan called. A group of armed men stormed the Shelton ranch. They successfully repelled the attack, but one of the intruders was shot. Ryan doesn't know if the man was killed or just injured."

"Why is this kid so important? Usually, kidnappers cut their losses if they lose their victim," Blake said.

"I don't know yet. Nicki, where do we stand on your research?"

"I'm still sifting through a pyramid of companies. Whoever owns the property has cleverly concealed his identity. I have a program running on the financials of all the agents involved in the investigation. So far, I've not found any red flags. Will Cooper appears to be clean though adamant the boy should be brought back to Austin. I'm not sure why— maybe it's only for personal reasons. He doesn't like the fact a child was kidnapped on his watch," she said.

Scott asked, "Any luck on the drawing of the man Ryan sent?"

"No, nothing yet from the facial recognition program. Any speculation on how the Branson woman came up with a drawing of the Wademan girl and a suspect?"

"A few suspicions, but I'd rather not say right now," Scott replied. He looked at the other two agents. "Anything from your research."

Blake answered, "We haven't found any unusual or suspicious activity for any of the Austin agents or their immediate families. I have to agree with Nicki's assessment that so far Cooper is clean."

"Okay, here's where we stand. The President has turned the investigation over to us. Cooper won't like it, but he'll have to live with it. If he can't, I'll have him removed," Scott said.

Stunned, the three agents stared at him, then glanced at each other. Unusual didn't even begin to describe the President's actions.

"Adrian, any unusual details in the kidnappings?"

"No, and I've examined all the reports," Adrian said. "All were professional hits. Security systems disabled, and they knew the location of the child's bedroom. A fast in and out. No one even knew someone had been in the house until they found the child missing, Chloroform was detected in the Murdock boy's bedroom. It was probably used in all the kidnappings. No evidence, no fingerprints, and still no ransom demands."

"Other than the fact all three senators hold powerful positions in the Senate, is there anything else that ties them together?" Scott asked.

Blake said, "I pulled the background of each one. As to their Senate activity, I cannot find any link unique to these three, any more than to any other senator. Murdock is front and center in the news with the contract negotiations with the Chinese. A lot of people don't like the idea of us getting further in bed with them. But Wademan and Berkstrom aren't involved. The only common factor I found and is extremely remote, are the rumblings over the next Presidential race. All three are mentioned as possible candidates."

"Kerry and Ryan brought that up when I talked to them on the phone." Scott turned his head and stared at the darkness that pressed against the office window and began to tap the table with his pen. The agents had learned this was a habit when Scott was deep in thought.

After several minutes, he asked, "Who else has been mentioned as possible candidates?"

"Senators Barker and Pittman are the only two I've seen in the news articles," Blake answered.

"Do we know their location?" Scott asked.

"Yes, they are both in Washington?" Blake said.

"Are their families with them?"

"I don't know, but I'll find out." He left the room.

"Are you thinking the kidnappings have something to do with a possible run for the Presidency?" Nicki asked.

"I'm not sure, right now just throwing out ideas," Scott replied.

Blake walked back in. "Their families are here in Washington."

Scott pulled his phone and punched in a number. "Director Henley, this is Scott Fleming," paused, then said, "I am requesting a Secret Service detail be dispatched immediately to protect the families of Senators Barker and Pittman. Yes, this is related to the kidnapping cases."

In disbelief, the agents eyed each other again. Their boss had called the Director of the Secret Service, not only called him but got him on the phone in the middle of the night.

Scott listened, then said, "Yes, it is possible there is an imminent threat, and even if not, I would rather err on the side of caution." He paused, thanked the man and disconnected the call.

The agents, unsure what to say, stared at him. This level of interaction with high-ranking officials had always been above their pay grade. Evidently, they had stepped into a new stratosphere.

Tap, tap, tap, Scott's pen hit the desk. "No contact, no demands for money, which tells me they have no intention of returning these kids. Two high profile children, and repeated attempts to get the third back. They have a plan, and it's not to get money from the parents," Scott mused.

Blake was the newest member of the team, and early in his career had worked with the Bureau's Human Trafficking Task Force. "Blake, do you still have any informants from your days on the task force?"

"Yeah, I do."

"I want you and Adrian to shift your focus. Concentrate on finding intel on any new activity on the black market for children. Nicki, keep digging to find the owner of the property and the identity of our suspect. They are the only leads at the moment."

"What is happening in Texas?" Nicki asked.

"Right now, the Murdock boy is safe. Ryan believes the Shelton ranch is the safest place for him. He and Branson are headed to Austin for a conversation with Senator Murdock which should prove to be an interesting meeting."

Nine

Texas

Kerry repacked her overnight case. At least, thanks to Cindy, her clothes were clean as she hauled the suitcase downstairs. Footsteps sounded behind her. It was Ryan with his backpack over his shoulder.

"I'm ready when you are," he told her.

In the kitchen, Luke had his property map spread across the table. "I think you should go out the back entrance. Anyone watching the front won't see your truck leave. Behind the barn is a dirt road that leads to the gate at the back fence. It has an electronic lock. Call me when you get there, and I'll disable it."

From the gate, he showed them what roads to take to reach the main highway. After Kerry finished jotting notes on a small notepad, he looked at Ryan.

"I've been thinking about what has happened. There is no doubt these men are ex-military. The precise placement of the explosives at the farmhouse and their actions last night, all show specialized training. One more element you need to consider. What I observed last night was a team operation, not a bunch of ex-soldiers. I believe you are up against a highly trained and experienced group of men, who have been working together for some time. There is only one way it could happen— mercenaries," Luke said.

"As my boss so eloquently stated last night, it does add another layer of complications," Ryan said.

"Yeah, it does. Both of you, especially you Kerry, watch your backside. If ordered to kill, these men will do so without hesitation."

"Thanks for the warning," Kerry said as she hugged first Luke, then Cindy. "I can't think of anyplace that would be better for Tristan." She'd already said goodbye to the little boy playing in his room upstairs.

"Use this phone to call me." She laid one of her remaining pre-paid phones on the table. "I've already programmed it with Ryan's and my number."

Cindy handed her a large thermos filled with coffee and an insulated bag.

"What's this?" she asked.

"Sausage and egg taquitos. They're wrapped in foil and will stay warm for several hours. At least you won't have to stop to eat."

Ryan lugged the cases outside and set them in the backseat while Kerry toted the food and coffee. Her phone rang as they drove out the gate. It was Mike's burner number on the screen.

"What's your status?" he asked.

"We're headed back to Austin, though we had more trouble last night. Several gunmen tried to raid the ranch to get Tristan," she answered and explained what happened.

"Have you come up with any answers?"

"Not yet, though Ryan's boss and his team are working on it. We are leaving Tristan here. I would be afraid to transport him. We could end up in another firefight."

"Call me when you get to Austin. Are you staying at your house?"

Luke's warning flashed in her mind. "No … I don't think so. I'll stop by, though, to pick up a few clothes and check the damage."

Ryan's phone was the next to ring. "Nicki, anything new?"

"Oh yeah! The President turned the investigation over to us. Holy hell, can you believe it?" Nicki said.

"Jeez, no I can't. The President, damn!"

"And … that's not all. The boss man picks up the phone and calls Henley, Director of the Secret Service to request a protection detail for Senators Barker and Pittman and gets it without any argument from the man. Damn impressive."

"Why the two of them?" Ryan asked.

"Right now, the only common link between Murdock, Berkstrom, and Wademan is their potential candidacy. Barker and Pittman have also been mentioned. Last night, Scott did his tap dance with the pen, then calls Henley. He also tossed out another theory. The boss man doesn't believe the kidnappers plan to offer the parents a chance to get their kid back. He told Adrian and Blake to start running down any leads they can find on black market activity. Are you still in East Texas?"

"Yes. We just left the ranch, though, and are headed to Austin. I want to talk to Murdock. What about Cooper? Bet he's ticked off over this whole deal. Is he going to be a problem?"

"Nah, not according to Scott. The Trackers are now in charge, and per our boss, if Cooper doesn't like it, he's out. I haven't found the owner of the property yet. Oh, by the way, you still have your room at the hotel in Austin."

When he hung up, Kerry asked, "The President. What's that all about?"

Ryan quickly filled her in on Nicki's information.

"Dang, I'm running in a lot heavier company than I realized," Kerry said.

"Hey, shocked me just as much. I had no idea my new boss had this much clout. Somehow, I think we'll need every bit of it before we're done."

Kerry had no difficulty finding her way to the main highway, unlike the night she found Tristan. The roads looked a lot different in the bright sunlight instead of a murky fog.

Turning south, she glanced at Ryan. His laptop was open.

"What are you searching for?" she asked.

"Every bit of information I can find on Murdock. I want to be prepared before we talk to him. I also want to see what I can find on black market rings."

"Your boss certainly came up with a disturbing theory."

"Yeah, he did. Damn! If he is right, and I think he is, do you have any idea how difficult it will be to find the two girls?"

Cindy and Luke stood on the back porch and waved as Kerry drove away. Once the truck was out of view, Luke said, "I'm going to check the fence line again, make sure the repairs from last night will hold. I won't be gone long."

As he walked down the porch steps, his phone rang. The display showed 'unknown.' Tapping the answer key, he answered, "Shelton."

"This is Scott Fleming with the FBI. Ryan informed me of the attack last night. Is there any assistance I can provide?"

"Thanks for the offer, but at this point, we should be okay. I don't expect the kidnappers to make another attempt. Last night, they walked into a firefight I'm certain they didn't expect."

Scott chuckled and then said, "Ryan mentioned your military background, so I have to agree. I'm texting you my private number. Call at any time if there is a problem."

Luke had stepped back inside the house as he talked. Disconnecting, he told Cindy the details of the call. As he turned to walk toward the door, the speakerphone on the alarm panel buzzed. Two sheriff cars were parked at the gate. Generally, it was left open, but with Tristan's arrival, he had kept it locked.

"What are they doing here! Get Tristan into the bunker along with anything that would show he's been here." Luke wasn't sure why he felt the urgency to hide the boy, but he had learned not to ignore a gut instinct.

Cindy raced upstairs. Tristan was playing on the floor. His room was clean, and the bed was made. Other than the few toys there was no sign the room had been occupied. She scooped up the boy and the toys and said they would go downstairs to play.

Another buzz, then a third, but Luke waited until he saw her and Tristan on the stairs before tapping the keypad to open the gate. He stepped outside to wait.

The cars pulled in front of the house. The sheriff, along with three deputies exited the vehicles.

Luke called out, "Morning, Sheriff. What can I do for you?"

Sheriff Anderson nervously ran his hand over his face as he approached the porch steps. Even though the temperature was cool, sweat stained the armpits of his shirt. A large, overweight man in his early fifties, broken blood vessels covered the nose and cheeks of his puffy, florid face. His belly hung over the gun belt strapped around his hips. A black cowboy hat and black cowboy boots rounded out what the man evidently believed was the look of a Texas lawman. Luke had met him at different county events and had never been overly impressed.

The deputies took a position behind Anderson. With legs spread, a hand rested on the butt of their gun. Two were slightly overweight, dressed on the sloppy side like their boss. The third had a hard look on his face and a brawny build. His uniform looked a size too small. A long-sleeved shirt stretched tight across broad shoulders, and pants hugged muscular legs that needed to be an inch or so longer. The man's eyes scanned the terrain before returning to stare at Luke. A sense of uneasiness flowed over him. Something about the deputy didn't set right.

The sheriff's voice shifted his attention. "Luke, … I … uh … well, I've got a serious problem and hope you will cooperate. A child is missing. We are checking all the houses in the area to make sure he hasn't snuck in somewhere to hide."

"Sheriff, I don't have any idea what you are talking about. There's no one here other than myself, my wife, and our baby."

"Well, okay. I understand, but you know kids. They're slippery little devils." His nervous laugh bordered on a giggle. "Look the other way, and they are gone or hide in places that wouldn't even occur to you. This is only a quick search to make sure he hasn't slipped in somewhere. It's a case of crossing off all possibilities. I hope you understand. I ... uh, just need to make sure."

The man was even more stupid than Luke had realized. He wondered who thought up such an absurd excuse to get inside the house. Anderson had either been bribed or blackmailed.

After several seconds of watching the man wipe the sweat from his face, he asked, "Do you have a search warrant?"

"Now, it's nothing like that. I'm not accusing anyone of a crime. I'm only trying to find a missing boy. It's why I'm asking for your cooperation."

He knows he can't get a warrant. Unless they were also corrupt, there wasn't a single judge who would grant it. If he let them search, it should convince them Tristan wasn't in the house.

Luke glanced at the three deputies. Two slouched, looking down at the ground as if embarrassed by the Sheriff's demand. The third's unwavering gaze was still fixated on Luke. His instincts told him the man was watching for any suspicious behavior.

The door opened behind him, and Cindy stepped out.

Anderson tipped his hat as he said, "Morning, ma'am."

"Sheriff Anderson. What's going on?"

Luke answered. "He wants to know if we have a missing child in the house. It seems he's checking all the homes in the area." Even though he was angry, Luke kept his voice neutral. He didn't want to give the deputy, if indeed he was a deputy, any reason to wonder at his reaction.

Astonished, Cindy said, "You want to search our home! Is that what you're asking?"

Anderson's face turned a deeper shade of red at her soft voice of protest.

"Now, ma'am, nothing to get all upset over. We only want to look through the rooms. Imagine if it was your child missing."

Luke said, "I don't like it, though I'll cooperate. If you are tied up here in a useless search, the less chance you have of finding the boy," and stepped back, motioning for the men to enter the house. He noted the name tags as they walked in—Taylor and Hawkins. The deputy with the attitude didn't have a tag.

"Sheriff Anderson, our baby is asleep upstairs. I hope you won't cause a ruckus and wake her." The concern in Cindy's voice was evident.

Luke hadn't believed Anderson's face could get any redder, but it did. It only took a few minutes for the men to walk through the downstairs, searching any space large enough for a child to hide before heading to the second floor. Luke told Cindy to wait in the kitchen as he followed them.

The one he labeled bad-ass, lingered in the bedrooms, searching the closets and even looking under the beds. When he extended his arm to open a closet door, Luke noticed the tattoo. It was unusual, the head of a snake on the back and wrist of the hand. It suddenly dawned on him, this was the only one wearing a long-sleeved shirt. Was it to hide the tattoo?

Downstairs, they trooped out the door. When the deputies strode around to the back, he assumed they planned to check the garage and outbuildings. Anderson stopped at the bottom of the porch steps. Cindy had followed her husband.

His large-brimmed hat in his hand, he said, "Mrs. Shelton, Luke. I apologize for any inconvenience. Once again, I'm sure you can understand if it was your little girl missing. You would want me to conduct a thorough search of any building to find her."

"Sheriff, what are the names of your deputies?" Luke asked.

Surprised, the man stared at him for a few seconds before saying,

"Uh … Deputy Taylor and Hawkins."

"That's only two."

"Oh, yeah, the other is Harris, Deputy Harris."

He turned to walk to his car. Sweat stains covered the back of his shirt. When the deputies came around the corner, Harris gave Luke a long, hard stare as he got into the patrol car. Luke watched the cars exit his driveway before walking back inside. He called each of his brothers to warn them of the impending visit and to come to his house once the Sheriff had left. He used the burner phone to call Fleming.

"I had a visit from the local sheriff wanting to search the house. Since we had Tristan well hidden, I let them look."

Scott asked a few questions as Luke filled him in on the details. Luke then added, "There was one officer who was suspicious. He looked out of place, a hard, aggressive stance, and his uniform didn't fit. The name tag was missing. Anderson said his name was Harris."

When Scott asked for a description, he replied, "Around forty, six-foot, a solid muscular build, maybe two-twenty. Short dark hair and a scar on the left cheek. His face was weather-beaten like he had spent too many hours in the sun. Heavy lids over his eyes, thin lips, and a crooked nose, it may have been broken at one time. The head of a snake was tattooed on the back of his hand."

He hesitated, then added, "The deputy could be connected to a possibility I discussed with Ryan. The kidnappers are a team of trained mercenaries."

Kerry was at a truck stop waiting for her tank to fill when her phone rang. Ryan had gone inside. She recognized the number of the phone she had given to Luke.

"What's happened?" Her voice terse at the unexpected call.

"We had a surprise visit from the sheriff and three of his deputies wanting to search the house. He was looking for Tristan, though he had a bullshit story made up," he said as he covered the details of the search and his suspicions of the deputy.

Luke then added, "It's an election year. I expect someone made a hefty donation to his campaign fund though I may never be able to prove it. I called Fleming to let him know. Until you two figure out what the hell is going on, my brothers and I plan to rotate shifts for night patrol."

"If you need anything, let me know," Kerry said.

Ryan slid into the truck as she hung up. She relayed what had happened, and Luke's suspicions of the deputy.

"How did they get the sheriff involved?"

"Luke thinks he was bribed."

They had switched places, and Ryan pulled out. Kerry poured a cup of Cindy's coffee, grabbed a taquito, and settled back in the seat with her computer on her lap for some research of her own. She had a name, Harris, and a tattoo.

He glanced at her a couple of times. With her head bent over the computer, the long ponytail pulled through the back of her ball cap had slid over her shoulder. In the sunlight, her dark auburn hair had tints of gold. Kerry was tougher than she looked. She was quick and intuitive in her thought process—all attributes of a top-notch investigator. Still, there was a paradox, an underlying ability he didn't understand and defied his profiling skills.

"How did you come up with the drawing of Wademan's daughter and the suspect?"

Startled by the question, she said, "What!"

"The drawings. How did you do that?"

"Hmm ... well. It's a long story, and this is probably not a good time to explain. Let's just say ... um ... sometimes, I get a hunch, and it pays off."

Her answer further piqued his interest; a secret she doesn't want to discuss. Ryan was familiar with secrets and the difficulty of hiding the source of the information. He'd experienced the same problem throughout his law enforcement career. He also got it—Kerry didn't trust him.

Uncomfortable with his questions, she picked up the coffee cup from the console holder and took a sip, then said, "I've been pondering this presidential angle. Why kidnap the kids over something which may or may not happen? And even if it is the reason, how could anyone use the kids to influence a process that's months down the road? None of it makes any sense. Did Nicki have anything else to say about the demands?"

"Just there still haven't been any." He grabbed his phone from his pocket and hit the speed dial. When she answered, he tapped the speakerphone button.

"Nicki, you did say there hadn't been any demands, right? Oh, by the way, Kerry is listening."

She greeted Kerry, then said, "No contact at all from the kidnappers. I hear there was a bit more trouble at the Shelton place this morning."

"Yeah, interesting development. How did someone get to the sheriff so fast? Luke thinks he was bribed."

"I do too. I'm pulling the Sheriff's financial records. I'm also searching for anything I can find on the deputy."

"Nicki, whoever is behind this has money and influence," Ryan said.

"Yes, it's the same conclusion we've come to here. Adrian has been analyzing the abductions. Somebody had to pay for the information, and it wouldn't have come cheap."

"Anything more on the angle of the presidential campaign?" Kerry asked.

"It's still the only common link we've found. The Senators interaction with each other isn't any more connected than it is to the rest of their colleagues. Right now, I can't see where it would be an issue. Getting the presidential nomination is only a possibility, it might not even happen, so how does it tie into the kids? Doesn't make sense to me though Scott didn't hesitate to beef up the security on the other two senators. I don't think he's holding back on us, but this whole deal is weird, just plain weird."

"That's basically the gist of what we have discussed as well. I'll get back to you later," Ryan said. He glanced at Kerry. Her head leaned back against the seat, and a frown marred her forehead. She was deep in thought. He wondered what swirled around in that quick mind of hers.

His phone rang again. It was Cooper.

"Glad you finally decided to answer your phone. I understand your boss has taken over the investigation."

"That's what I was told. By order of the President," Ryan said.

"What the hell is going on?"

"I can't say right now," Ryan said.

"Dammit, this was my investigation, and President or no President, I want to be kept in the loop."

"Coop, it's not up to me. It's Scott's call. I suggest you talk to him."

"Where is the Murdock kid? Why are you keeping him under wraps? Don't you realize his parents are desperate? When I told the Senator, I was off the investigation, and why, he said he would contact the President. You'd better come up with the kid and fast is all I can say."

"Not my call. Talk to Scott," Ryan repeated.

As the call was disconnected, he said, "He is one furious and unhappy man."

He tapped the speed dial again. "Scott, I got a call from Cooper. He's livid. He indicated Senator Murdock planned to call the President."

He listened, then said, "We're an hour from Austin. I can head straight to his residence."

Washington, D.C.

Scott wasn't worried about Murdock's call to the President. Earlier, he had briefed Larkin on the new developments. Leaning back in his chair, he pondered his next step. Even as a kid, he had an exceptional ability to detect patterns in seemingly unrelated facts and excelled at games that required an analysis of each move. He was the state champion in chess his senior year. He even remembered the first time he picked up a Rubik's cube. Solving the enigma of the colored panels only took a few minutes. When he joined the Boston Police Department, Scott soon learned he could unravel the twists and turns of criminal behavior. What he always referred to as connecting the dots led to an unprecedented number of arrests.

There was a master plan behind the abductions. In time, he would have the pieces assembled and be able to see the pattern. It wasn't much different from solving the Rubik's cube. The first step was to set the first layer, then move the other layers or pieces into place. His instincts told him, the run for the presidency was his first layer.

Texas

Another unscheduled call. Moore knew his boss would be displeased.

"Did you find the package?" the man asked.

"No. The locations were searched, but it wasn't there."

"Are you sure?"

"Yes."

"How do you know?"

Irritated by the implication he was incompetent, he said, "I helped with the search. The woman's truck was gone. She must have taken the package with her."

"Find her—get her to talk. I don't care how you do it, but locate the shipment, then dispose of her."

Disconnecting, he leaned back in his chair and stared out the window at the Austin skyline. Anger pulsated through him. A damn private investigator wasn't going to ruin the plans it had taken him a year to build. He had to have the Murdock boy.

A knock on his door, and it opened. His secretary said, "Sir, your meeting is ready to begin."

"I'll be right there," he answered, sliding the phone into his pocket.

Ten

Barriers blocked the street and prevented vehicles from approaching the Murdock residence. News vans lined the roadway. Reporters and camera crews milled around their cars.

"Well, I guess the cat is out of the bag. The news hounds will be in a feeding frenzy," Kerry said as Ryan pulled in front of the barrier.

Parked on the other side was an Austin PD squad car. Two officers leaned against the trunk and watched the circus in front of them.

When Ryan exited, an officer approached and said, "Sir, no through traffic is allowed. Unless you live on this street, you will have to go another direction."

Ryan pulled his badge case and handed it to him. "We're here to see Senator Murdock."

The other officer walked up, looked at the ID, then strolled to the end of the barrier to move it back and allow Ryan to drive through.

A news reporter stood on the sidewalk and watched the interplay. When he realized Ryan would be allowed to pass, he ran into the street shouting questions about the abduction. Other reporters heard the ruckus, rushed up and added more questions to the din.

Ryan ignored them and strode back to the truck. A cameraman stepped up and snapped a picture of his face. Another camera crew approached on Kerry's side. She turned her head, so they couldn't get a clear view of her face.

Ryan watched the crowd in his rearview mirror as he drove away.

The barricade was back in place, and the two officers once again leaned against their car.

At the gate to the Murdock residence, he buzzed the speaker. When a voice requested identification, he held his badge case up to the camera and said, "FBI Agent Ryan Barr and Kerry Branson."

The gate slid open, and Ryan drove up the driveway and stopped on the circular drive in front of the house. Similar to the old-style plantation homes, it was two-story with a large front porch and white columns across the front.

Two armed men immediately approached the truck. Holding his hands away from his body, he stepped out of the vehicle. "I'm Agent Ryan Barr. This is Kerry Branson."

Kerry had exited in the same manner.

"Let me see your identification," the agent demanded.

Ryan pulled his badge case, flipped it open and held it out. The man glanced at it before holstering his gun. He said, "I'm Benson, and this is Tedford," nodding at the other agent who had checked Kerry's I.D.

"We're here to talk to Senator Murdock," Ryan said.

"He's expecting you."

The door opened. One of the most influential men on Capitol Hill filled the doorway.

His voice abrupt, the man asked, "Are you, Agent Barr?"

"Yes, sir, I am. This is Kerry Branson. We need to talk to you and your wife."

Murdock stepped back into the entry hall.

Kerry had only a moment to absorb the beauty of the graceful staircase and marble floors before a tall woman, standing behind her husband, cried out, "Do you know where our son is?"

Under normal circumstances, Catherine Murdock was beautiful. Slim with long blonde hair, she was the perfect foil for her husband's stocky build and dark, brooding appearance. Now, her hair hung dull and limp around a haggard face.

Sympathy for the woman flowed over Kerry. She couldn't imagine the emotional turmoil a mother must feel over a missing child.

"Yes, ma'am, we do. He is safe, but we need to talk to both of you in private."

Relief from Kerry's words caused the woman to collapse against her husband. Slipping his arm around her shoulders, he murmured in her ear. His wife stared into his eyes and hope lightened her face. He lightly kissed her forehead, then turned his head to look at Ryan and Kerry. "We'll talk in my study."

With his arm still around his wife, they led the way to a large office off the main living room. Ryan asked the two agents who had followed to wait outside and closed the door.

Kerry caught a glimpse of anger on their face. They didn't like being excluded, but at this point no one could be trusted.

Murdock turned and angrily demanded, "Why haven't I been told where my son is? All I know is your boss called to tell me you would give us the details."

"As Kerry said, he is safe. She found him alongside a road and has kept him out of the hands of the kidnappers."

Murdock and his wife looked at her, the anger and distress diminished as gratitude appeared.

"Is he … all right?" Mrs. Murdock asked, her voice faint.

"Yes, his only injuries are a few scrapes on his feet. The last time I saw him he was laughing at dancing dinosaurs on TV," Kerry said.

Mrs. Murdock's hands covered her face, and she choked back tears.

"I think you had better explain," Murdock said as he guided his wife to the couch, then sat next to her, their hands tightly clasped together.

Kerry and Ryan sat in the two chairs that faced the couch.

Ryan nodded for her to take the lead in the conversation. She covered the events that had happened since she picked up Tristan on the roadway. The only part Kerry left out was the Sheltons identity. She and Ryan had agreed Tristan's location needed to be kept a secret even from his parents. There was too much at stake to take a chance on someone overhearing a conversation.

"Why can't you bring him home?" Murdock asked.

Ryan said, "We believe there is a leak somewhere in the investigation. With four attempts by the kidnappers to get your son back, his location needs to remain a secret until we know who is involved in the plot."

"I talked to President Larkin. He informed me he had turned the investigation over to the Trackers Unit. Is this leak the reason?" Murdock asked.

"I expect it is one of them. We weren't involved in the case until after your son was kidnapped. I was on the plane sent to pick up Tristan in Mt. Pleasant."

Murdock said, "I was angry over the treatment of Agent Cooper. I like the man, but I understand the problem. Everyone gets tainted. Damn!" he exclaimed, pounding his fist on the arm of the couch. "Why was our son abducted? What did they want, and why didn't we hear from the kidnappers?"

"We don't know yet, but two other children have been kidnapped, Berkstrom and Wademan's daughters," Ryan said.

Stunned, Murdock and his wife stared at them.

"We hadn't heard. I haven't left this house, and communication with my office has been limited since Tristan was taken. This is unbelievable," he said as he rose and paced around the room.

"Has there been any ransom demands for the two girls?" Mrs. Murdock asked.

"No, nothing from the kidnappers," Ryan answered.

"Agent Barr, do you have any idea why?" the Senator asked.

"We are searching every possible avenue for a reason," Ryan said.

Kerry asked, "Mrs. Murdock, may I see Tristan's bedroom?" She caught the surprised look Ryan gave her. *He's probably wondering why since we already know the kidnappers didn't leave any evidence behind.*

Puzzled over the request, Mrs. Murdock stared at Kerry for a few seconds, then stood, saying, "Why, yes, of course, you can see the room."

They followed her up the stairs to a bedroom that faced the front of the house. For a few seconds, Kerry stood in the doorway and gazed into a room that was all boy. The walls were blue with white trim. A small bed was against one wall, a desk with a computer under the window, and shelves and a dresser on the opposite side. The bedspread was printed with images of dinosaurs. A T-Rex poster covered an entire wall. Shelves held models of the beasts, along with cars, a couple of fire engines, building blocks, and other toys. A large toy box sat alongside the desk.

Stepping into the room, she said, "Wow, when Tristan told me he liked dinosaurs, I didn't expect this degree of interest."

Mrs. Murdock's voice trembled, and tears shone in her eyes as she said, "He's crazy over them. It started when he was three, and we keep thinking he will move on to something else, but so far, he hasn't. If you ask him what he wants to be when he grows up, his answer will be, a paleontologist."

Kerry walked around the room, occasionally stopping to examine a toy. She glanced at Ryan who had followed her. He stood by the bed, motionless, with his hand on the bedpost. He seemed mesmerized by the sight of the bedspread as he gazed intently at it.

When she stepped beside him to see if something on the bed had engaged his attention, he turned his head and said, "If you're ready, let's go back downstairs."

As she left the room, she took one last glance over her shoulder. She had hoped to see what happened the night Tristan was abducted. Nothing, but then, she never knew when her bizarre gift would kick in. Walking down the stairs, she pondered Ryan's odd behavior. *What was that all about?*

"What now, Agent Barr?" Murdock asked as they returned to the

Senator's office.

"We'll continue our investigation. My team in Washington is following several leads, and for now, Kerry and I will be in Austin. I do have a few questions. Have you received any threats in connection with the Chinese contract negotiations?"

"Yes, but they were not unusual for this type of interaction with another government. There is always someone who is dissatisfied. My office keeps track of any abusive phone calls or letters. I gave the file to Agent Cooper when Tristan was kidnapped."

"Have you been involved in any activity with either Senator Berkstrom or Wademan?"

"We have co-chaired a few bills, but that's all."

"Do your families visit, or have any ongoing activity outside of your job," Ryan asked.

"We are friends and meet at social functions. Occasionally, my wife is involved with their wives, but nothing out of the ordinary."

"There has been publicity over a possible run for the presidency. Berkstrom and Wademan have also been discussed. How have you been involved in the process?"

Stunned, the man stared at Ryan for a couple of seconds. "The presidency, what connection could there be with something that won't happen until next year?"

"We don't know if there is one, but we are looking at every possible link between the three of you. Right now, it seems to be the only connection," Ryan said.

"I have had a few meetings with party officials to discuss strategy, but I haven't decided whether to make a bid or not. I know there have also been separate discussions with other senators. But this is all still in the planning stages."

"Here is my card. If you think of anything, no matter how remote, please call me."

Mrs. Murdock looked at Kerry, tears trickled over her cheeks.

"Thank you for saving our son. We will forever be in your debt."

Kerry felt the tears clog her throat. She nodded as she followed Ryan out the door.

Washington, D.C.

Scott's boss, Director Paul Daykin, had called to warn him the news media had the story of the Murdock kidnapping. So far, the reports only dealt with the one abduction, but Daykin said it was probably a matter of hours before the reporters learned there were two more missing children. Scott would have liked to know who leaked the story, but the chances of finding that bit of information were slim to none.

"I found it!" Nicki's voice rang through the office. Adrian and Blake spun their chairs to look at her.

She sat in front of her computer while a look of unholy glee spread across her face.

"What did you find?" Scott asked as he rushed out of his office.

"The owner of the property in East Texas. It is the Del Rio Oil and Gas Company, headquartered in Austin. The owner is Mitchell Harmon. Wow, this guy has money and power. LPJ Inc., the company on the tax rolls at the courthouse, is a shell corporation. LPJ is connected to another shell company that is linked to another. You get the idea, multiple layers of companies."

Stunned, Scott said, "Harmon owns the property!" He was very familiar with the individual. Over the course of the last couple of years, he had attended several social functions where the man was present. Harmon was one of the most influential individuals within his party as well as an advisor to the President. If he gave the nod to a candidate, it meant money in the campaign coffers.

"LPJ bought the farm a little over a year ago, allegedly for oil exploration purposes, though nothing has been done with the property since the purchase," Nicki said.

Scott sat in the chair at one of the empty desks as he pondered Nicki's disturbing information. "Nicki, I want a full background run on Harmon. Everything you can find on his financials. Adrian, check his business and social activities. Give me a report as soon as you can."

He headed back to his office, pulling his phone from his pocket. Hitting the speed dial for Ryan, it rang several times before rolling to voicemail. He left a message to call. Seated behind his desk, he picked up his pen, tap, tap, tap. *What possible connection could there be between Mitchell Harmon and the kidnapped children?* The possibility was beyond the realm of reality. Yet, he couldn't deny the fact Harmon's company owned the house used by the kidnappers. This was going to get very, very sticky.

Nicki's computer beeped. She glanced at the screen. The word 'match' pulsated in red letters. Clicking on the icon, a mug shot popped up. It was the suspect from Kerry's drawing.

"Bingo, I've got a match." She hit the print button as she studied the background information listed on the screen. "Geez, this is one, shady dude." Picking up the printed copies, she dropped one on Adrian and Blake's desk, then walked into Scott's office.

Handing him the printout, she said, "Our suspect is Ray Boyd, better known as Bullman. He lives in Austin and has been arrested on charges of aggravated assault, drug distribution, and arms trafficking. The cases were all dismissed by a judge for lack of evidence."

Glancing over the document, Scott said, "Start digging into his background. I'll let Ryan know when he returns my call. Since Branson is an ex-homicide detective with Austin, she might have come across this guy."

His phone rang. It was Ryan, and he motioned for Nicki to have a seat.

Ryan said, "We just finished meeting with Senator Murdock. We had to run a gauntlet of news reporters when we arrived. I wonder how they got the story?"

"I doubt we'll ever find out. Anything come out of the visit?" Scott asked.

"Not really. The Senator confirmed nothing connected him to Berkstrom or Wademan. He is as confused by all of this as we are. Oh, he's not happy with Coop being taken off the case, but understands the need for caution."

"Nicki is in my office. You're on the speakerphone. She found the owner of the house in East Texas. I'll let her tell you."

"Kerry is listening on my end."

Nicki said, "LPJ, the company you found, is a front for several other companies owned by Del Rio Oil and Gas. The CEO is Mitchell Harmon."

A gasp could be heard in the background. "Harmon! My god, the man is a billionaire, an icon in Texas. Why would he be involved?" Kerry asked.

"Kerry, we don't know that he is. All we have is the property is owned by one of his companies," Nicki said.

"His headquarters are in Austin," Kerry responded. "We need to talk to the man."

Scott warned them. "Tread lightly until we have more information. Harmon is close friends with the President."

"We will," Ryan responded.

"I also found your suspect. His name is Ray Boyd, and he lives in Austin," Nicki said.

Kerry's astonished voice rang out again. "Bullman! That's his nickname, and he's one ruthless individual. After I left the PD, my ex-partner, Tim Baker, dealt with him on a couple of cases. I'll contact Tim and find out what I can."

"Nicki, did you ever get anything on our leak? Is it Cooper?" Ryan asked.

"So far everyone has come up clean, including Cooper. I am running all the Bureau employees who work in the Austin office, even the janitors."

"When Luke called about the sheriff's visit, he mentioned mercenaries and a possible link to the deputy," Scott said.

Ryan explained Luke's theory and added, "His supposition makes sense. I would be interested in what you dig up on Deputy Harris."

As he disconnected, Scott said, "He may be on to something. Expand your search to look at Harmon's security force. His company has overseas operations that would require protection. And get Blake involved."

A tap sounded on the door. Scott looked up as Blake walked in. "I received a call from an agent I worked with a couple of years ago. His informant said there is chatter over an upcoming auction and believes it is to sell a large shipment of drugs. The agent is trying to run down more information. So far, it's the only rumor of anything out of the ordinary."

"Auction, … hmm, interesting. Keep on it. Ryan suggested the kidnappers could be mercenaries. Work with Nicki on Harmon's security force. Find out if anyone falls into that category."

As Nicki and Blake walked out, Scott smiled to himself. His agents had handed him another piece of the puzzle.

Eleven

Texas

When Kerry pulled out of the driveway, she turned to exit on the other end of the street which also had a set of barricades and a police car. There weren't as many news vans. "I don't want to pass the same reporters on our way out."

Once they had gone by the horde, Kerry asked, "Where to now?"

"FBI office. Time to talk to Cooper. What do you know about Bullman? God, how did he get a name like that?"

"He likes to keep pit bulls. Tim had a run in with him a year or so back. Had a search warrant and when they got to the house, there were several pit bulls in the front yard. They had to shoot a couple of them before they could serve the warrant."

"So, what's he into?"

"He's bad-ass. Drugs, prostitution, assault, weapons, you name it, and he's involved. The problem is nothing seems to stick. Tim was complaining about it not long ago. Said the man must have friends in high places. We need to swing by the PD and talk to him."

"We'll make it the next stop once we're done at the Bureau."

Kerry pulled into the parking lot of the office building for government agencies. Looking up at the multi-story building, she said, "It's been awhile since I've been here."

Exiting the elevator, Ryan led the way down a long hallway lined

Anita Dickason

with offices. "Do you know Will Cooper?" he asked.

"No, so far he's been a voice on the other end of the phone. He moved to Austin after I left the PD." She sent a smirk his way before she added, "As a P.I., I don't usually associate with heavy-footed federal agents."

Stopping in front of a door, he looked at her and said, "This is one heavy foot he'll want to shove in your face."

"I faced worse than a pissed off FBI agent."

Her confrontation with the Ravine serial killer crossed Ryan's mind. She was right.

He tapped on the door before opening it. The man seated behind the desk looked up at the sound. When he realized who stood in the doorway, he leaned back in his chair, and a look of anger crossed his face.

"Son-of-a-bitch! Look who finally showed up? What the hell are you doing in my office?"

"We need to talk. Coop, this is Kerry Branson."

The agent's eyes raked her from head to toe with a look of disdain. "I won't say it's good to meet you since it isn't. The two of you royally screwed me."

"It wasn't intentional or personal. The lives of children are in jeopardy, and I don't make apologies for anything I do," Kerry shot back.

He snorted and swiveled his head to look at Ryan. "Since I've been cut out of the loop in the Murdock investigation, why don't you clue me in on what there is for us to discuss."

Ryan shut the door and pulled out a chair to sit down. Kerry leaned against the wall, arms crossed in front of her, and a scowl on her face. Cooper was in his late forties, with a few touches of gray in his short, buzz style haircut. From what she could see of his build, he had kept himself in good shape.

"There is a leak somewhere in your office," Ryan said.

"What! Did you have to make up some bullshit excuse to take over my investigation! How the hell did you come up with that idea?" His voice sputtered in anger.

"Not an excuse, fact," Ryan said. "Kerry, why don't you explain."

She quickly reviewed the events that happened in Mt. Pleasant. "Someone told them I was at the hospital and then the airport. You were the only person who knew I would be at both places."

Stunned, the agent's eyes flicked between Ryan and Kerry. "You ... think it was me!"

"Everyone is a suspect. Who did you talk to?" Ryan asked.

"It was common knowledge in the office. Everyone involved in the investigation was here that night. God damn, I don't know what to say."

"Well, it's why the Trackers unit took over. Everyone in this office is under scrutiny."

Cooper shifted his head to stare out a window, his anger replaced by dismay and uncertainty. Kerry and Ryan stayed silent as they watched the battle of emotions flick across his face.

Turning back, he said, "I don't know how to convince you that I'm not your leak. I've been friends with Senator Murdock for several years. Since before his son was born." Emotion caused his voice to break. He took a deep breath before continuing. "There isn't anything I wouldn't do to make sure Tristan is safe. His kidnapping has eaten at me. Tell me what I can do to help, it's all I'm asking. Does Senator Murdock know?"

"Yes, and it is why Tristan is not coming home. There have been four attempts to get him back."

"Four! How did that happen?" He stopped and shook his head, then said, "Since I'm under suspicion, I won't ask any questions. If I can help, let me know."

Ryan nodded and stood up. He had always liked Cooper, but until he knew for sure who was involved, he couldn't take a chance and trust the man.

As they walked out of the office, Kerry glanced over her shoulder at the agent, slumped in his chair. He looked tired and older than when they first walked into his office.

In the truck, Kerry said, "Let's swing by the PD and check with Tim. If he knows where Boyd is, we can put a tail on him."

Walking into the PD, the desk sergeant seated at the front desk gave her a broad grin. "Well, look at what came dragging in. Decided to come back and slum with the real cops."

She chuckled, then said, "Murphy, if it meant I had to slum with you, I'd walk back out the door. Good to see you again."

"You too. Big Mike been treating you right? Cause if he hasn't, he'll have to answer to me."

"Yeah, I'm doing fine at BSI though I must admit, I sometimes miss this place. Murphy, this is Ryan Barr. He's a fed."

"Well … I guess we'll let you in the door seeing who you are with," he quipped.

Ryan smiled as he shook the sergeant's hand.

"Is Tim in the back?" Kerry asked.

"He came in a few minutes ago, and he's ticked off. Got in a foot chase with a suspect and lost the race. I told him he was getting too damn old to be running after the bad guys. They're getting younger, and he's getting older."

Kerry led the way to a door that opened into a large room filled with desks. An aroma of stale coffee mixed with sweat hung in the air. A low buzz of voices hummed in the room. A whistle rose over the noise, as one of the detectives shouted, "Look who walked in, the crazy woman herself." Several catcalls rang out.

Kerry grinned and said, "Hey, play nice. This is Ryan Barr. He's FBI."

Another voice rang out. "She's hit rock bottom, running with the feds now."

Ryan grinned at the good-natured taunts. He was used to dealing with local police agencies.

Kerry walked to a desk at the back of the room. "Tim, what's this I hear about you chasing after some suspect." Pushing fifty, he looked ten years younger. He still hit the gym on a regular basis and watched his diet.

"Yeah, not one of my finer moments. Needed you with me, and we'd have caught the bastard." He walked around from behind the desk and grabbed her. "God, it's good to see you though you look tired. What's up?"

Kerry had partnered with Tim for most of her time as a homicide detective, and they had developed a deep friendship. "Tim, meet Ryan Barr. He's FBI. You have a few minutes? I thought maybe we could grab a cup of coffee at the Bakery."

Tim gave Kerry a questioning glance, but only said, "Barr, pleased to meet you," as they shook hands.

The Bakery was a deli located across the street and a favorite hangout for most of the cops. Kerry walked to a corner booth. She wanted privacy for this conversation. It wasn't she didn't trust the detectives she had worked with, but the more who knew, the easier an offhand comment could happen.

Once the waitress had their orders, Tim said, "Okay, what's going on? I know you didn't ask me over here because you missed my rugged good looks."

Kerry gave a quick glance at the surrounding tables before she began her explanation. She stopped when the waitress brought the coffee, then picked up with the story.

As Tim listened, shock and concern flashed across his face. It hadn't taken Ryan long to realize the relationship between these two people was close, and Tim's concern was not only for the abducted children but also for Kerry's safety.

"Geez, Kerry, when you step in it, you don't do it by small steps. I hadn't heard any rumors Murdock's son had been kidnapped until this morning when one of the news channels broke the story."

Ryan had kept silent, letting Kerry do the talking, but at this comment, he said, "The FBI has kept a tight lid on the kidnappings, which makes the leak even more serious." It stuck in his craw, but he had to say it. "It has to be in my department."

"What can I do to help?" Tim asked.

"First, anything you do to help us has to be on the QT. Will it cause you a problem?" Ryan asked.

"Nah, the chief pretty much lets me handle my cases my way. He knows I'm too close to retirement to take any grief he might dish out."

"What do you know about Ray Boyd? He is one of the kidnappers. Tristan Murdock identified a sketch of the man," Kerry said.

Amazed, he asked, "How'd you get a sketch?" He shook his head. "No, don't answer. All I will get is one of your bullshit answers. Bullman is one individual I would like to get off the street before I walk out the door. He's into everything. Pimps for several prostitutes, but none of them will talk. He's running drugs and weapons. Been arrested several times, but the D.A. can't make the case. Witnesses have a way of disappearing."

Tim took a sip of his coffee, then said, "He's a low-level enforcer, Kerry. I can't see him being the one in charge. He does what someone else tells him. We've never been able to identify who is yanking his chain. Bullman wouldn't be able to pull off a kidnapping like this. He doesn't have the smarts."

"Can you find him?" Kerry asked.

"If he's in town, yes. What do you want me to do if I locate him?"

"We need to put a tail on him," Ryan responded.

"How do we do that, if we can't use any of the Bureau personnel here in Austin?" Kerry asked.

"I could do it, but it would take the chief's approval," Tim said.

Ryan pulled his phone and keyed a number.

"Scott, if we can locate him, I need to set up a tail on Boyd. I don't want to use the Bureau's personnel or Austin PD." He listened and then disconnected.

"Scott Fleming is my boss. He'll call back. There is one other detail

Kerry skipped over. The President has assigned the investigation to my unit."

"Dang … woman. I take back my comment about steps. You dived headfirst on this one," Tim said.

"Ryan, I want to get my boss, Mike, involved. We have two investigators, Dan Carter and John Davidson who can help. We also need a base of operations and can use BSI's offices."

"I don't have a problem with it," Ryan said. When he researched Kerry's background, he had also run the company.

Ryan's phone rang. "It's Scott." He listened, then said, "I plan to set up operations at BSI and use their personnel to help. They know Austin."

Disconnecting, he explained, "Adrian Dillard is an agent in my group and is on his way to Austin. He'll be here late this evening."

Grabbing a napkin, she jotted her number. "Tim, see if you can locate Boyd. Call me at this number, it's a burner phone. Even though it won't take long for anyone to find out I'm in town, I don't want to advertise my whereabouts."

Folding it, he stuck it in his pocket. "Where will you be? Are you planning to stay at your house?"

"No, I would rather get a room at a hotel near the office."

They stood in the doorway and watched Tim cross the street to the PD.

"I need to set up hotel reservations. I'll get three rooms. Which hotels are close to BSI?"

Kerry mentioned two within a few blocks and added, "I'll call Mike. It's getting late, and I'd like to meet with him before he leaves for the night."

Since Ryan was on the phone with the hotel, she walked a short distance along the sidewalk to call Mike. When he answered, she said, "Hey, it's Kerry. I need your help. Are you still at the office?"

"Just getting ready to leave. Where are you?"

"At the police department. Ryan and I drove in today. Have Dan and John left?"

"A few minutes ago. Do you need them?"

"Yes."

"I'll call them. See you in a few minutes."

Kerry walked to the truck and climbed behind the wheel. As Ryan got inside, he asked, "Everything set at your office?"

As she pulled away from the curb, she said, "Mike is calling Dan and John to get them back to the office. Dan is our security system expert and is one of the best in the country. John is the computer guru."

"They should get along with my team, especially Nicki since she is our resident computer expert."

Focused on the conversation, neither one noticed the dark car that pulled into the street two blocks behind them.

Twelve

Kerry parked in front of an office building with Bradford Security and Investigations over the double glass entry doors. They entered an impressive reception area. Two couches and several chairs were positioned in front of a large glass window that overlooked a small garden.

An older man exited an office and greeted them. Based on his walk and buzz haircut, Bradford was probably ex-military. He appeared to be around fifty or so, and his six-foot-three-inch frame was trim and fit, no extra body fat. Ryan liked his looks as he introduced himself.

"Let's go to the conference room. Dan and John should be here in a few minutes."

As they walked in, Mike motioned to the coffee pot on a side table. "Help yourself."

"Ryan?" Kerry asked as she headed to the pot.

"No, thanks, I'll pass for now." He had already learned the woman had a serious love affair with coffee.

Footsteps sounded in the hallway. "What have you gotten yourself into this time?" the man asked. He took a seat and stared at Ryan.

"A frigging mess, Dan, and I don't expect it to get better," and introduced Ryan. She added, "We'll wait until John gets here to explain."

"Explain what?" a second man asked as he walked into the room.

Kerry went through the introductions again. Taking a seat next to

Dan, John repeated his question. "Okay, what do you need to explain? I have a hunch you are up to your neck in something. And with a fed in tow, it can't be good."

Ryan had quickly assessed both men. They had been included in his research of BSI and had impressive backgrounds. Dan was six-foot, with a wiry, thin build. Shaggy brown hair flowed over his shirt collar and framed a narrow face with high cheekbones. John was shorter with a sturdy build and probably outweighed Dan by a good twenty pounds. Black hair was cut short, though not the buzz cut his boss had.

Once again, Ryan sat back and let Kerry explain. This was her boss and team. They needed to hear from her, not him.

"You're right. First, what we discuss must stay in this room. You'll understand why in a few minutes." Kerry went through the events that had occurred since she first spotted Tristan alongside the road. Looks of amazement turned to anger as they listened.

"Do you have any idea what or why?" Mike asked.

Ryan picked up the conversation. "At this point, we don't have a clue, but we do know there is a leak. I'm assigned to the Trackers unit. It's new, formed a few months ago. The President pulled the investigation away from the bureau personnel in Austin and assigned it to my team. I expect there were two reasons. The first is my boss is evidently highly thought of within the Bureau. The second is the leak won't be in my team."

"Kerry glossed over the part where she picked you up in Mt. Pleasant. How did you get off the plane?" Dan asked.

"Jumped when it turned on the runway. The men waiting to ambush us couldn't see the door."

"Excellent timing," Mike said in approval.

"There's more," Kerry said.

"Hell, how much worse can it get," John asked.

Kerry proceeded to tell them as she explained Mitchell Harmon's ownership of the house.

"Damn!" was John's only comment, as the three men assessed the latest information.

"Why would he be involved?" Dan asked.

"We don't know he is. At this point, it could be the kidnappers used the house because it was vacant and have no connection to Harmon," Kerry said.

"If he is in town, I intend to meet with him tomorrow," Ryan said. "What do you know about him? I haven't had a chance to research him."

Mike answered, "He's one of those larger than life personalities in Texas politics. He owns two refineries on the Gulf coast, plus oil and gas wells across the U.S. and the Middle East. His wife died a few years ago, I think from cancer. He's never remarried and has no children."

John added, "He's also close friends with most of the high-ranking officials in the state. I saw a picture of him playing golf with the governor and attorney general a few weeks ago. It was for some charity event."

"What do you need from us?" Mike asked.

"We need a base of operations. Until we can find out who leaked Kerry's whereabouts, I can't trust any of the personnel in the Bureau's office here," Ryan said.

"Consider it a done deal. This office is yours for as long as you need it. What else?" Mike asked.

Kerry said, "We have to locate Boyd. Tim is trying to run down his location. If we find him, I want to set up surveillance. Another agent from Ryan's team is on the way, but he doesn't know Austin. We do. I am hoping Boyd will lead us to the girls."

Ryan added, "John, Kerry said you are the computer expert. I'll have Nicki Allison contact you. She is our research guru. I would like the two of you to coordinate your research. Concentrate on Boyd and Harmon."

John nodded his head in agreement as Mike said, "I see why you don't want to stay at your house. Based on what I've heard, it wouldn't be wise. Oh, your door has been replaced. I also had all the locks changed, and a new set of keys are in my office."

"Thanks for taking care of it. I'll be at the Patio Suites. Ryan has already obtained rooms for the three of us."

"You know you can stay with Maria and me."

"Thanks for the offer, Mike, but staying at the hotel allows more flexibility to come and go. I would hate to disturb your household by dragging in late from somewhere."

Mike turned to Ryan. "I'll show you how to operate the alarm system and give you a key to the front door."

The two men rose and left the room. Dan and John looked at Kerry.

"Whatever you need, let us know," John told her.

Dan nodded his head in agreement.

"If I get in a bind, I'll call. I bought a pre-paid phone, so I couldn't be tracked," she said, giving them the number for the burner and Ryan's phone.

Kerry gathered up her material and followed them, stopping in Mike's office to get her new house keys.

Leaving Mike to lock up, they headed to Kerry's truck.

"Where to now?" he asked.

"A pass by my house. I want to see what is missing and pick up more clothes."

Ryan said, "I need to stop at the hotel where I stayed when I first arrived in Austin. I'll check out and get my gear."

It was dark when Kerry turned onto the county road that led to her home. She glanced in her rearview mirror. The same vehicle had been behind her for the last several miles. When the car went straight, she thought, *I'm getting a bit too paranoid.*

"Not many houses out here," Ryan said.

Turning into her driveway, she said, "There are a couple on down the road."

The headlights illuminated an old style, single story farmhouse with an enclosed porch. She parked in front.

"Come on in. I won't be long." She pulled her suitcase from the backseat.

Inside, she deactivated the alarm on the panel beside the door and flipped the light switch. The entryway led into the living room, where a large couch with two matching chairs faced the fireplace. Several pictures depicting Texas landscapes hung on the walls. A kitchen was visible through an arched doorway on the left, and a hallway was on the right.

"Make yourself at home. There are sodas in the frig." She scanned the kitchen before heading down the hall.

Ryan glanced in the kitchen. A small table was positioned against one wall. A large window overlooked the backyard. Whatever mess the burglars made had been cleaned up. Wandering back into the living room, he examined each of the pictures. On the mantle were a couple of family photos with a much younger Kerry positioned between her parents.

The sound of rolling wheels echoed on the hardwood floor. Dragging a large suitcase, Kerry headed to the front door. "They made a mess of my office and bedroom, but I'll clean it up later. Ticks me off my computer is gone. I hate breaking in a new one."

"Let me take the suitcase," Ryan said, stepping to grab the handle. His fingers slipped over hers. The warmth of his hand sent a jolt of anticipation sliding through her, dispelling the irritation.

Startled, she stared into his face. The gleam in his eyes intensified the magnetism the man exuded. She stopped herself from leaning toward him. *Good, lord, this is not a good time for my hormones to kick into high gear,* and quickly pulled her hand away, hoping he hadn't noticed her reaction.

He pulled the case out the door. With a few quick taps on a wall monitor to activate the alarm system, she followed. "Next stop, your hotel," she said, glad the darkness hid the heat of a blush on her face.

Pulling onto the main highway, she kept an eye on the rearview mirror.

Ryan noticed her quick glances. "A problem?"

"I don't think so. A vehicle stayed behind me for several miles on the way to my house, though it didn't turn when I did. Probably nothing to it."

At the hotel, Kerry told him she'd wait in the vehicle while he picked up his suitcases and checked out. Using the burner phone, she called Cindy.

"Hey, girl. I'm checking in to see if everything is all right."

"No new excitement, thank goodness. Luke and his brothers have set up a schedule to patrol the perimeter at night. They decided not to wait for an alarm to alert them. So far, the sheriff's visit was the last attempt to find Tristan. Who, by the way, has bonded with Luke over a couple of games. Cutest thing you'll ever see. He tags behind Luke whenever he can, though he still asks for his mother and father. I explained it would be a few days before we could take him home. What's happening on your end?"

"Running down leads. We still don't have a clue why this is happening, but a lot of people are working to find the answer. If you need to call, be sure to use this number. I am keeping the burner phone with me along with my regular one."

"Are you staying at your house?"

"No, I'm at the Patio Suites along with Ryan and another member of his team who will be arriving in a few hours."

"Hmm ... you and the sexy Ryan together at a hotel. Girlfriend, sounds like fun," Cindy quipped.

"It's not the reason I'm staying there, so get that tone out of your voice. It's close to the BSI offices which we are using."

"Right! Good excuse. All I am saying is, you can't work twenty-four hours a day. You do have to take a few hours to eat and sleep. Maybe even a little sex time to relieve the stress."

"Even if I was interested, which I'm not saying I am, the sexy agent hasn't expressed an interest."

Cindy's laughter caused Kerry to snort in protest, "Humph," then added, "Not happening, so shut up."

"Hey, I saw how he looked at you. Better listen to me, the man is definitely interested."

"Well, I still say it's not going to happen. You know how I feel about relationships. It works for you and Luke, but I consider you the exception, not the rule. I'm the rule."

"You've been telling me this for years, it's only a rule because the right guy hasn't come along."

Ryan opened the passenger door. "Ryan's here, we need to go. I'll talk to you later."

"When you do, I expect to hear all the juicy details."

Her chuckle was the last sound Kerry heard as she disconnected.

"I called Cindy to find out if they had anyone else interested in them. The sheriff was the last incident."

"How is Tristan doing?"

"Luke and Tristan have evidently become best buds," she replied.

"I don't know about you, but I'm starved. Cindy's taquitos and the snack we grabbed at the truck stop didn't last long," Ryan said.

"Do you want to eat first or go to the hotel?"

"Let's grab takeout, then head to the hotel. I want to research Harmon. I'm the unit profiler and want to get a feel for the man before we meet him."

Startled, Kerry glanced at him. *Profiler! That accounts for his flashes of intuition.*

"If pizza sounds good, there is a place close to BSI. We can take it to my office, and it will be more convenient than trying to work out of a hotel room."

"Then make the hotel our first stop."

Ryan's phone rang as they pulled out of the parking lot. He listened, then said, "We are headed to the hotel, then to pick up pizza. Do you want any?" After a pause, "I'll text you the address for Kerry's office. It's where we will be."

Disconnecting, he glanced at Kerry. "Adrian's at the airport and is picking up a rental car. He wants a large, all meat pizza."

The phone rang three times. When the man answered, his voice demanded, "Report!"

Moore replied, "I've located the woman. My men are in place to pick her up, but she is traveling with an associate."

"Remove anyone who gets in the way. Have you taken care of the man who lost the package?"

"It's been handled."

"Excellent! I expect your next call will be to inform me you have recovered my shipment."

Thirteen

They'd laid the boxes of pizza on the conference table when a knock sounded from the front door.

"It's probably Adrian," Ryan said and walked out. A few minutes later he returned followed by another agent who didn't fit the typical appearance of a fed.

Dark, deep-set eyes under thick brows picked up the reflection of auburn hair that flowed over the collar of a leather jacket. Slipping out of his coat, tight jeans and a black T-shirt covered a lean, whipcord body.

As they shook hands, Kerry smiled when his gaze that held an engaging twinkle, skimmed over her. *Odd, when I got the same look from Ryan, it sent my pulse racing. With Adrian, not even an extra beat.*

"Help yourself." Ryan motioned to the food and drinks on the table. As they ate, Ryan updated Adrian.

At the mention of mercenaries, Adrian said, "Blake and I discussed it before I headed out the door. It makes sense and would account for the expertise in the abductions."

Kerry's phone rang. It was Tim. She held up a finger to stop the conversation as she answered.

"Bullman's body was found in an alley," Tim said.

"Hell! Do you know what happened?"

"He was shot. So far, it looks like a mugging gone wrong."

"Where was he killed?"

"Behind the Cantina Bar and Grill. We're canvassing the area, but haven't found any witnesses who saw or heard anything."

"I want to look at the crime scene. Is anyone still there?" Kerry asked.

"Yeah, Austin PD is still on site, but the M.E. has already picked up the body. I'll meet you there," Tim said.

Disconnecting, she pushed her paper plate away in disgust. "Someone just killed our only lead," and relayed Tim's information.

"I want to see the body. Is it still at the scene?" Ryan asked.

How odd? Why would he want to see the corpse? Not wanting to question his motives, she said, "No, it's on the way to the morgue. I'll give you the directions and you two head there. I'll meet Tim."

She parked behind one of the squad cars that filled the street in front of the Cantina, Exiting, she greeted Tim who waited on the sidewalk. Together, they walked to the back of the building.

"He was killed with a single shot to the chest. His body had been stripped of anything of value. It's why the responding officers thought it was a robbery. Jerry Sawyer is the detective who was called out. He recognized Bullman and knew I was looking for him," Tim told her.

A man standing by the crime scene tape that stretched across one end of the alley greeted them. "Kerry, don't tell me our vic is into something you're investigating?"

Since she didn't want to stir up the department's rumor mill, her response was low-key. "Yeah, I've got an incident that might involve Bullman. What do you have?"

"Right now, not much, not even a shell case. A dishwasher came outside to smoke and found him in the middle of the alley. No money or identification."

"Hmm … you mind if I look around?"

"Nope. We're done here. I was getting ready to leave when Tim called and said you were on your way."

Kerry stepped over the tape and surveyed the parking lots with large metal dumpsters that lined the sides of the alley. The odor of rotting garbage hung heavy in the air. The light shimmered, and the empty alley disappeared. Instead, she saw two men who faced each other. One—arms outstretched, and the other—a gun in his hand, his face hidden by a black ski mask. As Bullman cried out that it wasn't his fault the kid got away, a shot echoed. The vision vanished, and Kerry stared at the empty alley.

Harris! Luke said the deputy who searched his house had the head of a snake tattooed on his hand. Bullman's killer had a tattoo of a snake that coiled around the arm.

When she turned, Sawyer gave her an odd look. She shrugged her shoulders and stepped back over the tape. "Guess this was a wasted trip," she said and along with the two men, headed to the street.

Tim stopped on the sidewalk as Jerry continued to his car. "Do you think it was an execution and not a robbery?"

"I do. I've got a hunch our killer is one of the kidnappers." What she didn't add was the information she had learned from her vision.

Tim eyed her with suspicion though his only comment was to ask if there was anything else he could do.

"Check your street contacts for any rumblings of mercenaries operating in Austin."

Surprised, he said, "Mercenaries, now that's an interesting development."

When he headed to his car, Kerry pulled her phone to call Ryan. The call rolled to his voice mail. She assumed he was still at the morgue and left a message she was headed back to BSI.

A few blocks from her office, she noticed a car rapidly approaching from behind. Then it moved into the oncoming lane. Though Kerry sped up, the car still pulled alongside her. A man leaned out the window, gun in hand, and took aim at her front tire. A quick spin of the wheel and she swerved, slamming into the side of the vehicle. The car veered to the left and over the sidewalk.

Kerry's foot stomped the accelerator, racing down the street. *Damn, they're still coming* as she watched the car pull back onto the road. Tires squealed when she turned on a side street, fighting to keep control of the wheel as the truck skidded. This was her turf, she knew the streets and soon lost her pursuers as she weaved through the surrounding neighborhood before heading to the hotel.

Grabbing the phone, she tried Ryan again. This time, he answered.

"Someone tried to run me off the road. I think I lost them, but I don't want to take a chance on returning to BSI."

"Where are you now?" Ryan asked.

"Headed to the hotel. I'll park in the covered garage."

"We're on the way. Stay with your vehicle until we get there."

Inside the garage, she backed into a space near the elevators. Gun in hand, she exited, scanning the area for any movement before she examined the damage to her truck. Just what she didn't need—another explanation to the insurance company. The sound of an engine sent her spinning to take a position behind the truck. She sighed in relief when she recognized Adrian's rental car.

When the two men exited, Ryan shouted, "Kerry!"

She stuck her pistol in the back of her pants and stepped out. "Here, I'm okay, though my truck took another hit."

Ryan knelt to look at the damage as she explained. "Black paint, but it doesn't tell us much. Anything else you remember?"

"No, it all happened fast."

"They're after you so they can find the boy," Adrian said.

"I agree, which means you need to be with one of us at all times," Ryan said.

Her body tensed, and she bristled at the thought they didn't believe she could take care of herself.

Ryan eyed her, and in a conciliatory tone said, "Two guns are always better than one."

He's right, though Kerry hated to admit it.

"We need additional weapons. Since you and Kerry are headed to

Harmon's office in the morning, I'll stop at the Bureau's office and pick up what we need," Adrian said. He grinned, then continued, "It should make for an interesting conversation around the office coffee pot."

Adrian checked in while Kerry and Ryan headed to their rooms. Kerry wanted to call Mike, and Ryan intended to call Scott. They agreed to meet in the bar.

"Are you planning on sleeping tonight?" Mike quipped when he heard her voice. When she explained, his tone turned serious. "You need to take every precaution not to be caught alone."

"I agree. Adrian Dillard arrived tonight, so between Ryan, Adrian, Dan, and John, I should be safe."

Disconnecting, she wondered, *why is this child so important?*

The distinct odor of the morgue still filled Ryan's nostrils as he walked into his room. It clung to clothes, skin, and hair. Instead of the shower he desperately wanted, Ryan had to be satisfied with splashing cold water on his face while he pondered what he'd learned.

When he and Adrian had arrived at the morgue, the autopsy was underway. Bullman's nude body was stretched out on a metal table, and the Medical Examiner had already cracked open the chest cavity. Wearing disposable scrubs, face mask, and booties, they had stepped up to the table. The M.E. eyed them through his glass face-shield as an attendant introduced the two agents.

When Ryan's gaze skimmed the face of a corpse covered with multiple scars and tattoos, he was astounded by the likeness to Kerry's sketch. Her drawing was eerily accurate. A reminder he still had to find out how she did it.

While Adrian questioned the doctor about the bullet, Ryan managed to touch the body. During the contact, he picked up on two emotions—rage directed at Kerry and fear of a man named Moore.

Ryan had an exceptional ability to tap into a criminal's thought process. It was why he was the profiler in the Trackers Unit. Even his boss had commented that Ryan seemed to have a direct link to a criminal's mind. He chuckled. If Scott only knew how accurate his statement had been, but then … maybe he did. Since joining the team, Ryan had spent considerable time analyzing the possibility. There was something inexplicable about Fleming and for that matter, the entire team.

Wiping his face with the hotel towel, he debated how to insert the name Moore into the investigation. He was convinced it was one of the kidnappers and probably the man who had shot Bullman. He'd keep it simple and allude to a vague source. Tapping the speed dial, Ryan leaned against the counter and waited for his boss to answer. "Boyd was shot tonight. The police believe robbery was the motive."

"Hell! He was our best lead. Are you sure it was a robbery?" Scott asked.

"No, I don't. I think Bullman was executed because Tristan escaped. I heard a name mentioned, Moore. He may be the killer and one of the kidnappers. If he is ex-military, Nicki might be able to find his records. Also, there was an attempt to kidnap Kerry. A car tried to run her off the road."

"Is she okay?" Scott asked.

"Yeah, she rammed the car when a passenger tried to shoot her tire."

"Have you set up protection for her?"

"Yes. She's staying here at the hotel, so it makes it easier. Adrian or I will be with her wherever she goes. Since we are using BSI headquarters, her associates can help."

"Do you need anything from my end?" Scott asked.

"A couple of items. I would like Nicki and Blake to coordinate their activities with the BSI investigators, John Davidson, and Dan Carter. John is the resident research guru, and Dan is their expert on security systems. Adrian is picking up weapons at the Bureau in the morning along with a bureau vehicle. I'm not sure how Coop will react to the request."

"I'll make sure Cooper understands he and his personnel are to give you their full cooperation on any request. If he doesn't like it, I'll have the Director contact him."

"One more question, has Nicki come up with any information on Harris?" Since he left the morgue, his intuition had tingled, a sure sign there was a critical connection he had missed.

"Yes, she has. It seems Deputy Harris has been on vacation for the last two weeks, and his description doesn't match Luke's description of the deputy."

That was it—the missing connection. He was sure the bogus Deputy Harris and Moore were the same man. "So ... someone did get to the sheriff. Do you plan to confront him?" he asked.

"No. I don't want to draw attention to the Shelton ranch. There are other ways to find out what prompted Sheriff Anderson to allow a man to impersonate an officer."

~ॐ∾

Downstairs, Kerry and Adrian sat at a table at the back of the room. It was late, and there were only two customers seated at the bar. They had ample privacy, and the bartender graciously agreed to fix a pot of coffee. When Ryan arrived, the man brought three cups along with a bowl of chips to the table.

Kerry asked, "Anything on the bullet."

"Just that it was a 9 mil and hit the heart," Adrian replied.

"A shell case wasn't found at the scene, so the killer must have taken it. Not typical for a robbery, which I don't even for a split second, believe was the motive for his death." Picking up a chip, she waved it in the air. "I think he was killed because he let Tristan get away."

"I suspect you're right," Adrian replied. He glanced at Ryan who had been acting strange ever since leaving the morgue.

Ryan was preoccupied with another problem as he took a sip of the hot brew. His explanation about the man's name had worked with Scott, but would it work with these two. It was always one of the downsides of his gift—how to explain information he shouldn't know. He suddenly realized Adrian and Kerry had stopped talking and looked at him with an expectant expression.

"What!"

"Jeez, Ryan, where did you go? I asked if you had any contacts on mercenary activity, and you're enthralled with the table," Kerry said, gesturing with another chip.

"Pondering Bullman's death and the reason for it."

"Yeah, well, buddy, that's what we've been discussing if you decide to tune back into our conversation," Adrian joked.

"I don't think he was killed because of a robbery. It was because Tristan escaped."

At the sound of the laughter that erupted, he stared at them with an amazed expression. "What now?"

"Kerry said the same thing while you were in never, never land," Adrian responded.

His expression changed to a blush of embarrassment. "Uh … well … okay. Sorry, I missed it."

"At least, we agree," she said.

"I talked to Scott and found out our mysterious Deputy Harris was an imposter," he said, adding the details he had learned. He took a sip of his coffee, then added, "His real name might be Moore, and is probably Bullman's killer."

Stunned, Kerry leaned back. *How did he make that connection and come up with a name?* She wasn't buying the implication he heard it from Scott and was beginning to believe they needed to have a serious conversation—just the two of them.

"How did he get set up with the sheriff? We need to contact Anderson," Adrian said.

"No, Scott said he'd handle it."

"Then what's the next step?" Adrian asked.

"First on the agenda is still the visit to Mitchell Harmon," Ryan responded.

"Any idea how you plan to play this one? The man has some serious stroke and won't hesitate to use it if he thinks he is in danger," Adrian said.

"I'm not sure yet. Once I meet him, I'll have a better idea."

Pushing back his chair, Adrian stood and pulled out his wallet. He tossed a few dollars on the table. "I don't know about you two, but I'm headed to bed. I have a feeling sleep will be in short supply before we finish with this mess."

Ryan turned to Kerry. "You ready to head upstairs?"

Kerry watched Adrian walk out of the bar. "Hmm ... not yet. Think I'll warm up what's in my cup. Do you want a refill?"

Carrying the two cups to the bar, she mulled over the questions she wanted to ask. Unsettled by Ryan's comments, maybe it was time they put the proverbial cards on the table. Kerry had never explained the strange visions that had become a barrier in her business and personal relationships. The fear she would be seen as a crazy person by friends and associates had kept her silent. Even Cindy didn't know the secret she held tight in her mind. *Can I trust him? No, it doesn't matter whether I can or not. Some secrets aren't important when it comes to the life of a child.*

Fourteen

The hair on Ryan's neck had prickled at Kerry's serious demeanor when she asked about a refill. She was up to something, and the coffee was an excuse, but he didn't have a clue as to what. Well, he'd stick around. He might find out how she came up with those damn drawings.

Setting Ryan's cup on the table, she settled in her chair and took a sip. The heat felt good as the liquid slid down her throat. Staring at Ryan over the rim of the cup, she took a second sip, then said, "How did you come up with Moore's name?"

The question wasn't a surprise, but hopefully, he could avoid the explanation. "Hmm ... a hunch. Someone mentioned the name, and it seemed to fit the Harris imposter."

Kerry thought, *what a crock. He's using the same kind of answers I do when I can't explain how I know something.* "Nope, I'm not buying that answer. What is it you don't want to tell me?"

Perturbed by her persistence, Ryan fired back. "How did you come up with the sketches?"

"Fair question. Since I believe we both have issues we don't want to discuss, I would like to propose an ... alliance, for lack of a better word. The only rule is this discussion stays between the two of us. Considering the risk to our careers, I think it is a fair resolution to our individual concerns."

Chagrined, Ryan had to admit she was right. He was reminded of a similar conversation with one of his team members that had ultimately saved two lives, one being his fellow agent. "Agreed. So … let me ask this. Do you believe some people have extraordinary perception or abilities, to be able to see, hear or feel what others can't?"

Kerry propped her elbow on the table, rested her chin in the palm of her hand and stared down as a finger idly traced a circular defect in the wood. "If you had asked me a year ago, I would have said no. But now …" she sighed, her mind slipped back to the previous summer.

She'd saved the life of a boy during an armed robbery but had been shot in the head in the process. During the long weeks of recovery, she had struggled to make sense of a strange voice she heard as she lost consciousness. *"The power you have been given, yours to hold, as the Keeper of the Gift."* Then, she began to experience strange visions.

First, an old woman had appeared with a cryptic message. *"From faerie to mortal, for the life you did save, a powerful gift I do give. Keeper of the Gift, justice you will serve. Evil cannot hide from the power to see, and when evil walks, all will be revealed. When the banshee's wail is heard, in death's sweet slumber, the gift will be held, and when courage acts, the power will pass."*

Then other visions occurred, momentary flashbacks in time, and always at a crime scene. At first, Kerry wanted to believe it was all due to the head injury until she discovered an archaic legend. The old woman was her great-great-great grandmother. She had acquired a gift passed down through the women in her family whenever there was a feat of bravery. Her action in saving the life of the boy at the robbery had triggered the transfer of the gift from the old woman to her. She had become the Keeper of the Gift.

When Kerry's eyes fixated on the table, her face lost all expression. Ryan sensed her thoughts were in another place and time. He settled back in his chair and studied her. From the first moment he saw her, she had pulled at him, unlike any other woman he had met. Maybe it was the secrets in her eyes. Dark and mysterious, they shimmered like a liquid pool when she was angry. Would he see the same hypnotic gleam in the heat of passion, sucking him deep into their mysterious depths? His groin tightened at the thought. To ease the sudden discomfort, he shifted his body.

At the scrape of the chair leg on the wooden floor, her lashes swept upward, and she blinked. "Oh ... uh, sorry, was wool-gathering. Sometimes, it's a bad habit of mine. Didn't mean to fade out on you," she said, embarrassed by her lapse into the past. "I didn't answer your question. Yes, I believe it's possible."

"Is the change in your opinion based on personal experiences?" Ryan asked.

Her lips narrowed into a cynical smirk. "I guess you could say that. How about you?"

Well, so much for the subtle approach. They still danced around the topic. Time for total honesty. Ryan said, "Oh, it's definitely personal experiences. Occasionally, I can tap into thoughts and emotions of the dead. In this case, it was Bullman. In his final moments, he was terrified of a man named Moore and enraged at you."

Flabbergasted, Kerry gaped at him. She wasn't sure what she expected, but it wasn't this revelation. "Dang, just how does that work?"

"By touch. Very useful in profiling though it's a talent I have managed to keep a secret from all but one of my fellow agents."

"Jeez, I can see how it would be handy. So, if you were to touch me, would you know what I'm thinking?"

"Well, now, let's see." He reached across the table and picked up her hand. His gaze locked onto her eyes as he stroked the back with his fingers.

The sensation caused a tingle to trickle down her back. Startled, Kerry realized she had never felt such a powerful attraction. She abruptly sat back, pulling her hand away. *Maybe Cindy was right.*

A broad grin had split his face at her response. "Nope, not a single clue."

"When did you learn, you had this ... uh, what do ... you call it?"

"Hmm ... connection always seemed appropriate. After I joined the FBI, I was involved in a drug investigation, and one of the gang members was killed. When I touched the body, suddenly, I sensed inexplicable thoughts. They weren't mine. Scared the hell out of me."

His fingers drummed the table as he remembered the fear of that moment. "Somehow, and don't ask me to explain because I don't know, I had linked to what happened at the time of the murder. The details I picked up led us to the killer. He was the leader of the cartel, and we shut down his operation. Since then, I have found that on rare occasions I can extend the connection to objects or even a living person."

"Are you saying you talk to dead people?" she asked with a tone of skepticism in her voice.

"No, not at all. It's only emotions and thoughts I'm able to discern. Animals can sense, smell and hear what humans can't. I've often viewed my ability as a similar level of awareness."

"The bedroom," she exclaimed. "That's what you were doing in Tristan's bedroom, trying to pick up something from the kidnappers."

Smiling at her perception, he drank the last of his coffee and pushed the cup aside. "You're right, but nothing was there. Your turn."

Despite her sense of trepidation, Kerry explained what had happened when she was shot and the strange words she had heard. "I soon discovered, I could see events that happened at a crime scene. The first time was an abandoned house near my home. I had a time shift to when a woman was killed in the house. I saw it happen. Since then, I have had several of the same types of visions. When I looked in the bedroom at the old farmhouse, I saw a little girl lying on the bed crying. A man walked in and told her to shut up, and it's how I came up with the sketches."

For a few seconds, Ryan was silent as he contemplated Kerry's comments. "Did you see anything in Tristan's bedroom or the alley?"

Surprised at his swift uptake, she hesitated, then said, "Like you, nothing from the bedroom, but I did see the killer in the alley. He was wearing a ski mask, so I can't identify him other than the tattoo of a snake around his arm. I heard Bullman say he didn't mean to let the kid escape."

"Which brings us back to our imposter, Harris. We've got a good description of him from Luke," Ryan said.

"You're right! I need to make a call." Tapping her phone, she said, "It's Kerry. Yeah, I know it's late. No, Cindy, don't you go there," she protested as her friend started to tease her about Ryan. "I need to talk to your hubby." As she waited for Luke to answer, she glanced at Ryan. He nodded as if to agree with what she was doing.

"Luke, our lead suspect was shot tonight. The killer had a snake tattoo on his arm. We believe he is the man who posed as Deputy Harris who, by the way, has been on vacation. His real name is Moore. If he is ex-military, is there any chance you could come up with information on him?"

"Do you have any other details?" Luke asked.

"No, only the snake tattoo and the name Moore. Give me a description of the deputy." She jotted notes in her small notebook as he talked.

When she disconnected, she said, "I'll type this up on my laptop and do a sketch of the tattoo. Tomorrow, I'll make copies for everyone."

"It was a good idea to call Luke. He might get a lead on him." Glancing at his watch, he said, "We'd better get some sleep."

As Kerry scooted her chair back, images of Ryan, naked, crawling into her bed floated in her mind. She wondered what it would feel like to be curled in his arms, the heat of his body pressed against her.

Fifteen

Washington, D.C.

When Scott received the disquieting news of the attack on Branson and Bullman's death, it was a disturbing setback in a troubling day. Walking out of his office, he watched Nicki manipulate the two computers on her desk. The devices were linked, and she had already informed him she needed another computer. He grinned at the image of her marching into his office, fisted hands on her hips and demanded a new system. Scott had already decided whatever she wanted, she got, and a new one would be delivered in a few hours.

Blake was making calls to what seemed an endless list of contacts.

They looked up at his approach. Blake told whoever was on the phone that he'd call back.

"There was an attempt to kidnap Kerry," and detailed the circumstances of the attack.

Nicki said, "They get her, they can find the Murdock boy. And ... we still don't know why the kid is so damn important. Do you plan on sending us to Austin?"

"No, you're more valuable here," as Scott explained Ryan's setup at the BSI offices. He also passed on the names of the two investigators and Ryan's request for coordination between the two teams.

"We also lost our lead, he was killed tonight in Austin."

"What happened?" Blake asked.

Scott explained the police version and then Ryan's theory. "He came up with a name, Moore. See if you can find any military records or ties to mercenary activity."

"Any idea how Ryan came up with the name?" Nicki asked.

"No, he was rather ambiguous in his explanation. Nicki, dig deeper into Bullman's background. Let's see if he has any military experience. Also, find the attorney who represented him and run a background check."

"Anything, in particular, you want me to look for?" Nicki asked.

"Nope, let's just see what pops up."

Ryan is not the only one who gets ambiguous in their explanations as she turned to her computer.

Scott looked at Blake. "Any new intel on the auction?"

Blake sighed. "No, only the one comment. I did find out there is an increase in the chatter between members of several drug cartels in Mexico and Bolivia. A friend in the NSA said the only odd bit of intel dealt with a package. He thinks it's a large shipment of drugs on the way into the U.S. I asked for any details they hear."

Scott had decided to stay in his office. Earlier, he had returned to his apartment long enough to take a shower and fill a suitcase with a change of clothes. His two agents had done the same. Tilted back in the chair with his feet propped on the desk, his mind manipulated the information they had received, searching for the patterns that would reveal the motivation behind the abductions. Somehow, he dozed off. The shrill ring of the phone startled him, and he almost landed on the floor because of the precarious position of the chair. Grabbing the receiver, he answered, "Fleming."

His face turned grim. "I need the agent's report as soon as possible." Hanging up, he ran his hand over his face and silently cursed.

When he stepped out of his office, Nicki and Blake had turned their chairs to face his doorway. He realized they had overheard his comments. "Another child has been abducted—the son of Utah

Governor Simpson."

"Damn!" Blake said. "What connection does a governor have to this mess?"

"That's what we need to find out. Blake, get me everything you can on her background. Nicki, how soon will you have a report on the properties owned by Harmon."

"I should have something in the next couple of hours. At least, a partial list."

His phone rang a second time—caller ID—the White House. Since Mitchell Harmon was a close friend of the President, it was an awkward conversation. If there was a possibility Harmon was involved, what the President knew could also mean Harmon knew. Scott didn't want to bring the man's name into the conversation, not until he had evidence of a connection to the abductions. The best he could do was caution the President they still hadn't identified the leak and request he not discuss the details with anyone other than Secretary Vance Whitaker of Homeland Security and FBI Director Paul Daykin.

He looked at his watch. His instincts said Texas was the epicenter of the conspiracy. Punching a number on his keypad, he waited for Ryan to answer.

Texas

The ring of the phone brought him out of a deep sleep. The caller ID told him it would not be good news.

His boss's voice was abrupt as he said, "Ryan, another child's been kidnapped—the son of the Utah Governor. I don't have any details yet. As soon as I get the report, I will forward it to you."

"A governor, what's the connection?" he asked, voicing the same concern Scott had heard from Blake.

"We don't know yet. But we need to come up with some answers fast," he added, then disconnected.

Ryan sat on the edge of the bed and pondered the new information. How did a governor fit into the picture?

Kerry's voice was alert when she answered, though she couldn't have gotten any more sleep than he did. He relayed the news of the latest abduction and asked how soon she could be ready to head to BSI. Then made the same call to Adrian.

When they pulled into the parking lot, Ryan was surprised to see the lights on in the office since the sun was only a brief glimmer in the sky.

Seeing the astonished look on his face, Kerry explained, "I called Mike. He said he would have Dan and John meet us at the office. I also called Tim. If he is not already here, he soon will be."

Walking in the door, Mike greeted them, and she introduced Adrian.

"Kerry said another kid has been abducted. Anything new on the investigation?" Mike asked with a note of despair in his voice.

"There have been developments. Once everyone is here, I'll go over them," Ryan answered.

"Dan and John are in the conference room." As they started down the hallway, the front door opened, and Tim walked in.

Kerry was surprised to see computers on the large conference table as everyone took a seat.

At her questioning look, Mike said, "I figured this would be better than trying to work in the individual offices."

Once Adrian had met the BSI investigators and Tim, Ryan said, "Another child was kidnapped in Utah last night, the governor's son. We still have no idea as to the motivation behind the abductions, and there has been no communication from the kidnappers. The only lead we had was killed last night."

Tim asked, "Any connection between the parents?"

Ryan answered. "The only link we've found is Murdock, Berkstrom, and Wademan are the front-runners for the next Presidential election. I don't have any information on the governor."

"It seems pretty far-fetched as a possible motive," Tim said.

"I can't disagree. The rest of my team in Washington are searching for other connections," Ryan said.

"Whoever set this up must have money and connections," Kerry said. "Obtaining the security system details and layout of the house would have been expensive."

Mike agreed. "Yes, it would have been very costly depending on how the information was acquired."

"What about Harmon, is that one going anywhere?" Dan asked. "He's one of the most powerful men in the state."

"Kerry and I are headed to his office this morning. It will be interesting to see the man's reaction to our questions," Ryan said.

"What can we do?" Mike asked.

"A couple of avenues we can pursue. Luke Shelton is a former Seal and was suspicious of one of the deputies who searched his property. He had a snake's head tattooed on his hand. We've since learned he was an imposter, and his real name is Moore. I've received intel he is Bullman's killer. What's more important is that he is one of the kidnappers, and we need to focus on finding him. Kerry has a description and drawing of the tattoo."

Tim leaned forward, glanced at Kerry who handed out the copies, then directed a glare at Ryan. "How did you get his name, and have you informed Jerry Sawyer, the detective in charge of the homicide investigation?"

Ryan had anticipated Tim's reaction. "Tim, how I got the name isn't important. I can't release it until we know who is involved in the conspiracy."

Tim glanced at Kerry again. He raised his eyebrows in question, but she just shrugged her shoulders. The irony of the situation had not escaped her. She had become an accomplice to the 'national security edict' that had always irritated her in previous dealings with the FBI.

"How are the criminals moving so quickly? Kidnappings in other states, and we know the Wademan girl was brought to Texas. Moore killed Bullman here in Austin after he was involved in the search at the Shelton ranch. What are they using for transportation?" Ryan said.

"Good point, what are they using?" Kerry sat back and considered the timelines. "It could be by car, but it would make more sense to use a private plane or even a helicopter."

Nodding in agreement, Ryan looked at Mike and his two investigators seated across the table. "Since we know Moore is in Austin, check your sources for any leads. We need a list of planes Harmon owns, where they are based, and any recent flights. Nicki is working on a list of Harmon's holdings. If he is connected, and it wasn't a fluke the kidnappers decided to use his property, he would likely use another one he owns. John, as soon as she has the list, it will be sent to you."

Ryan paused as if to gather his thoughts, glancing at each of the individuals around the table. "We need to use extreme caution in the questions we ask. If Harmon is involved, and he believes his operation is in jeopardy of discovery, everyone connected, including the children will disappear before we have a chance to find them."

Sixteen

After the meeting broke up, Adrian and Dan paired up. Dan planned to track down some of his informants, and Adrian wanted to stop at the Bureau. John said he'd stay to research airfields in the area. Mike headed to his office to start making calls. He still had friends in the military and would run Moore's description by them.

It was too early to leave for the meeting with Harmon, so Kerry and Ryan continued their conversation with Tim.

"Finding a motive is critical," Tim said. "If we know why, we can narrow the focus of our search. But, this isn't your typical kidnapping. I've never worked one where there wasn't a demand of some type."

"You're right, but I'm not sure how to find the motive without more information," Kerry said.

Tim leaned back, a thoughtful look on his face. "I've been thinking about this mercenary angle. I've come up with an idea to trace Moore. Kerry, do you remember a case we worked when you were first assigned to the detective division, the Brewster kidnapping?"

"I do. Mom was carjacked, and the boy kidnapped. What does that have to do with this case?"

"We found an informant, a prostitute who gave us a lead on the boy's location. One of her johns had run his mouth about the kidnapping. I think we should talk to a few prostitutes."

Excited, Ryan said, "You may be on to something. If we are dealing with mercenaries, they could be involved with the local prostitutes.

129

Male egos like to impress."

"I'll talk to the Vice guys. They should be able to give me a list of who is working the streets."

Kerry glanced at her watch. "Time for us to leave as well."

On the way, Kerry asked, "How do you want to handle this?"

"On this one, let me do the talking. You watch his reaction to my questions. And, I want to get us into his office without identifying you. Let's see what happens when I introduce you."

The headquarters of Del Rio Oil and Gas Company was an impressive, multi-story building on the loop that extended around Austin. An armed security guard stood inside the front door. His neatly pressed uniform stretched across a muscular body. A cold expression on his face, his eyes raked them from head to toe as they entered.

Inside, a receptionist was seated behind a large semi-circular desk and greeted them as they approached. Ryan handed his badge to her and said he would like to speak to Mr. Harmon.

Flustered, the woman looked at his ID as she said, "Uh … oh, I … not sure, let me check."

The security guard had followed them and stepped behind the desk. He held out his hand for the ID case. He studied it for a few seconds, snapped it shut and gave it back to Ryan. Apparently, an FBI agent standing in the lobby asking to speak to the head of the company was not a typical occurrence.

"This is Brandy. There are two FBI agents here to see Mr. Harmon. Yes, I'll send them up." Her assumption Kerry was an FBI agent was what Ryan had hoped would happen.

Harmon's office was on the top floor. Stepping off the elevator into a luxurious reception area, furnished with numerous couches, tables, and chairs, the ceiling to floor windows provided a spectacular view of the Austin skyline. One wall was lined with artwork, and on the other, was a double set of doors. An older woman, with perfectly coiffed gray hair, in an expensive black, pin-striped suit, was seated behind a metal and glass desk equipped with a monitor and elaborate phone system.

"I am Mrs. Wells, Mr. Harmon's personal assistant. How may I help you?"

Ryan produced his badge case again and handed it to her. "I am FBI Special Agent Ryan Barr. We would like to speak with Mr. Harmon."

"I am sure I can answer any questions if you would tell me why you are here."

A pompous tone in his voice, he said, "This is a matter of national security, and it is imperative we speak to Mr. Harmon."

Mrs. Wells stared at them for a few seconds before picking up the phone. "Mr. Harmon, two FBI agents are here. They insist on talking to you." She carefully replaced the receiver and pushed back her chair. Rising, she said, "Mr. Harmon agreed to meet you," and walked to open one of the double doors.

Entering, Kerry realized the luxury of the outer office was nothing compared to Mitchell Harmon's office. The wall-to-wall windows afforded the same view, but it was where the similarity ended. Lush, thick carpet, a rich golden brown emphasized the warm auburn tones of the furniture. A bar stood against one wall with a variety of glasses and decanters. Two sofas faced each other on the other side, with swirls of gold and green. Chairs in the same color scheme were on each end, and a large coffee table was in the middle. The focal point of the room was the large desk, with a monitor and bronze accessories. Positioned in front were two chairs in the same green and gold motif.

Kerry quickly scanned the pictures on the walls and had no doubt she was looking at originals, not reproductions.

When the man behind the desk stood, Kerry suddenly felt gauche and uncertain. She had seen pictures of him, but they failed to convey the power and arrogant confidence he exuded. Just shy of his sixtieth's birthday, his gray suit with a patterned shirt and dark red tie fit snug over his trim, six-foot frame. Silver hair brushed back from a high forehead was as thick as the carpet. Deep-set eyes, high cheekbones, and a bronzed face added to his rugged good looks. *I bet that tan came from a tanning booth.*

A smile crossed his face, but his eyes held a hard, penetrating gaze as he held out his hand. "Mitchell Harmon."

Ryan shook his hand as he introduced himself, then turned to introduce Kerry.

She saw the slight widening of the eyes at her name. If she hadn't been watching closely, she would have missed it. *He recognized my name* as she shook his hand.

"Are you an agent as well?" he asked.

You know damn well, I'm not, but said, "No. I'm a private investigator."

"How interesting, an FBI agent and a private investigator. How may I be of service?" he asked as he motioned for them to take a seat.

"This is a bit awkward, and we appreciate your cooperation. We need to ask a few questions regarding a piece of property your company owns," Ryan said.

Surprised, his eyes flicked between Kerry and Ryan, before he said, "Property? I don't understand."

"It is a ranch in East Texas. It was purchased by ... uh," Ryan stopped to pull a notebook out of his pocket, thumbed through the pages, and then continued, "Here it is, LPJ Inc., which I understand, is one of your companies."

"I do own LPJ, but I'm not familiar with any property in East Texas. Can you tell me why you are investigating the ownership?"

"Well, as I said, this is awkward, as I am sure you are not involved, and I don't mean to imply you are. We believe the house may have been used in the commission of a crime. Before we could investigate, someone blew it up."

Anger vibrated in Harmon's voice. "I can assure you, I certainly don't allow anyone to use my property for criminal intentions."

"Uh ... yes, sir. I understand, and that's not the issue. What we are attempting to determine, uh … well … was the property rented to anyone or did the criminals luck into finding a deserted house?"

"What was the criminal activity?"

"Oh … I'm afraid I can't disclose any details." With a pacifying tone in his voice, he added, "I'm sure you understand."

If the purpose of the conversation didn't have such deadly implications, Kerry would have been amused at Ryan's performance. He was playing the embarrassed, bumbling law enforcement officer to perfection.

Harmon's body language had changed as he listened to Ryan. Instead of his upright position, elbows resting on the desk, he had relaxed and leaned back in his chair. His eyes held a look of disdain as he gazed at Ryan. The only sign of tension was the occasional flick of his eyes at Kerry.

"I would need to make a few phone calls as I am not always informed of every transaction concerning property I own. Where did you say it was located?"

Ryan provided the address.

Noting it on a pad on his desk, he asked, "Would that satisfy you?"

"Oh, yes sir, it would. If it's rented, I would appreciate a contact name so we could interview the individual. I'm surprised you weren't notified the house had been destroyed."

"It wouldn't be unusual. I'll have my staff check into the matter. I am curious about one issue. Why is a private investigator involved with the FBI in an investigation of my property?" At the question, his eyes shifted to Kerry. The force of the emotionless gaze sent frissons down her back.

Her tone neutral, she calmly said, "I work for Bradford Security and Investigations, and we're assisting the FBI in their investigation."

Harmon stared at her for several seconds before turning his attention back to Ryan. Internally, she breathed a sigh of relief. For a moment, she had the sensation she was pinned to the chair.

"You said the house was destroyed before you could investigate?"

"Yes, we were on our way there when we heard the explosion."

"If you have a business card, someone will contact you if there is any information that might assist your investigation."

"Yes … right, a business card," he mumbled, patting his pockets, before removing one.

Harmon studied the card, laid it on his desk, then stood, signaling the meeting was over.

Extending his hand, Ryan said, "I appreciate your time."

There was a slight hesitation before he reached to shake Ryan's hand.

As they walked out the door, Kerry felt another tingle of disquiet brush her neck. Certain that Harmon continued to stare at them with his lifeless gaze, she resisted the urge to look back over her shoulder.

Seventeen

Exiting the elevator, the chime of a phone echoed in the vast expanse of the lobby. The receptionist answered, then handed the receiver to the security guard. A scowl crossed his face as he listened, and his gaze fixated on Ryan and Kerry as they strode across the marble tile. Handing it to the woman, the guard crossed to the door, giving them another hard look as they walked out of the building.

Sliding behind the wheel, she leaned against the seat and breathed a sigh of relief. "That was one … very … very, scary man, and Harmon's guilty as hell!"

"I feel the same way. He recognized your name," Ryan said, closing his door.

"Yes, he did. I'm not sure what he expected when we walked into his office, but the question about the property caught him off guard. His body language changed once he realized that was all we wanted to ask. That was quite a performance you put on."

"I was hoping it would allay any suspicions he might have. I guess it did the trick."

Kerry glanced at the lobby doors. "That guard is still watching. I bet the phone call was from Harmon."

"He probably wanted information on our vehicle. Let's get out of here and get back to BSI."

"Did you pick up on anything when you shook hands?" she asked as she started the engine.

Still uncertain whether she believed his explanations in the hotel bar, Ryan gave her a sideways glance. Was she serious, or was it a joking comment? Her grim look belied any hint of humor.

Oddly relieved at her acceptance, he said, "He believes no one can touch him and was amused the FBI was in his office. The second handshake was different. Anger and hatred had replaced his condescending contempt, and—it was focused on you."

Ryan's words increased her sense of foreboding. "I felt the rage, though I wasn't certain it was directed at me."

"Well, it was. It's even more important someone is with you at all times."

Damn, she hated someone hovering over her shoulder. It was one of the reasons she resigned from the PD. "Humph," she grunted, checking her rearview mirror as she merged onto the freeway.

"I'm serious, Kerry. You're a target, but not to kill you. The thought of what they would do to get you to talk sends chills down my back," he said and tapped the speed dial on his phone.

"I know and am not disagreeing. So, now the big question is why? What would a man, in his position, have to gain by kidnapping children?"

"I wish I knew," he replied as he waited for his boss to answer. "Scott, we just left Harmon's office. Enlightening visit."

"What's your opinion?" Scott asked.

"Guilty. Kerry and I agree he's behind the abductions," Ryan said and explained what they had garnered from the contact.

"Hmm, that just moved him to the head of the list," Scott replied. "What's your next step?"

"We're going to chase prostitutes," Ryan told him.

"What!" Scott responded.

"Tim Baker, Kerry's ex-partner at the police department, suggested we talk to prostitutes. They may have interacted with the kidnappers which is a polite way to reference their activity. We are headed to the police department to pick up a list of names."

"Good idea, let me know what you find."

Disconnecting, Ryan's thoughts reverted to the interview with Harmon and the impressions he had gained. When he shook hands with the man, he sensed the disturbing intensity of emotions hidden behind the hard facade. His first impression was of absolute superiority. The man is convinced he is invincible. He had been amused by their visit as if they were only children playing a game. When he learned Kerry's identity, it changed. She became the focus of intense hatred.

The icon on the screen told him the call would be a problem. Moore had hoped to have Branson and not have to explain another failure.

"Why don't you have the woman?" The voice was harsh and angry.

"We made a try for her, but she managed to escape. I have another plan and should have her this evening."

"I won't tolerate another mistake, Moore. What is the status of the next package? Did it arrive in good condition?"

"Yes, I received it this morning. There were no problems," Moore said.

"And the next one, is it set for tonight?"

"Yes, everything is in place. I should have it by tomorrow."

"There is a change for the last one. We won't attempt to acquire the package. Schedule the auction. Have you received confirmation from the buyers?"

"Several groups have confirmed their interest," Moore answered.

A nasty chuckle echoed. "You should make a nice profit, but I must have the missing package by then, do you understand?"

As he disconnected, Moore wondered what had changed with Senator Pittman, and why the abduction of his son had been canceled.

Washington, D.C.

Scott leaned back in his chair, his fingers tipped together as he mulled Ryan's information. He trusted his agent's instincts, and if Ryan believed Mitchell Harmon was behind the abductions, then he was their prime suspect. Now, he had to figure out why.

Nicki walked in with a stack of papers in her hand and said, "I have the list of his holdings. It is extensive, and many are overseas," and handed the documents to Scott.

"What does he have in Texas?"

"The first ten pages are the Texas locations. They are scattered across the state. Most are land only, but several do have a house. I highlighted those."

"Tell Blake to come in, I want to talk to both of you." While he waited, he scanned the list of several hundred pieces of real estate. An appalling uncertainty pervaded his thoughts. The kids could be anywhere, from Texas to the Middle East. Checking every location would be impossible. *Am I placing too much reliance on my instincts they are in Texas?* If he were wrong, the results would be catastrophic. He laid the list on the desk as he pondered his next course of action.

When Nicki and Blake were seated, he said, "Send the Texas locations to John at BSI. I want a physical check of each property."

She nodded. "I also found our mole. Beth Moreland is a clerk in Cooper's office who was hired six months ago. Her grandfather works for Harmon and manages one of his ranches. I'm running his financials, but the report hasn't come back. The rest of the employees are clean, no significant deposits, none are in any financial difficulty or have medical issues."

"Cooper's in the clear?" Scott asked.

"I haven't found anything and would say yes."

"God, that's good to know. We need his help. I'll call him and then let Ryan know. What do you know about Moreland?"

"She's single, lives in an apartment with a roommate who works for a real estate agent. She doesn't have a criminal record, not even a traffic ticket. I didn't find any unusual deposits. She is either an unwilling participant—blackmail, or an unwitting one and is passing on information she believes is gossip."

"We need to find out which it is. I'll give that task to Ryan. He and Kerry met with Mitchell Harmon this morning. Based on their observations and conversation with the man, they believe he's behind the abductions."

A whistle escaped from Blake. Scott nodded in agreement, and continued, "From now on, both of you concentrate on learning every aspect of his life. Dig into every dark corner. We have to discover his motive."

"I have another piece to add," Blake said. "The attorney of record for LPJ's purchase of the East Texas property was Bullman's attorney. I also found a sizeable contribution has been deposited in Sheriff Anderson's campaign fund. Want to guess who is the donor of record … the attorney."

Scott said, "Another connection. Find out what other clients the attorney has represented. Anything on Moore yet?"

Nicki and Blake both shook their heads no.

"Blake, how about your contacts? Anything new?"

"Only one, another rumble over an upcoming auction. The agent said his source was vague on the specifics. I told him to follow up and get me every bit of available information. I haven't heard back."

Scott leaned back in his chair and looked at the ceiling. Tap, tap, tap, his pen against his desk. He stopped and looked at Blake. "Where is the agent located?"

"The El Paso office, which is why I told him to follow up."

"Texas again. What is the latest from the teams assigned to the parent's residence? Any contact with the kidnappers?"

Blake said, "I called the agents at each location an hour ago, and nothing. Not one single phone call or demand."

Tap, tap, tap. "If there were going to be a call, it would have happened by now which confirms our theory there is another plan for the children. What if those plans were to auction them off?"

Nicki said, "You would get a lot of money for the kids, but why take a risk when you don't need the money? Harmon certainly doesn't. His financials are extremely healthy, no money problems."

"She's right, the money wouldn't be worth the risk," Blake said.

The pen tapped again as Scott frowned at his desk, deep in thought.

"Who would be the buyers?" he asked.

"I expect every badass drug dealer and terrorist would crawl out of the woodwork for an auction like that," Blake said.

"Exactly! It's who these kids are that creates interest. Imagine owning the son or daughter of an influential U.S. politician. You might even think you could control the parent's actions if you have the child."

"They might believe it, but it wouldn't be realistic. All that would probably happen is the person would quit," Blake said.

"You and I would know that, but would a drug dealer or terrorist realize it. Especially, if they have been sold a bill of goods on what to expect if they have the high bid."

"You could be right," Nicki exclaimed. "Besides, they might not care. All they would want is to get control of the child and use them to suck the parents dry."

"I still have a few untapped resources in the DEA and NSA. I'll find out if there is any more chatter on an auction," Blake said and bounded out of his chair.

"I still don't get what is in this for Harmon," Nicki said.

"I have an idea, but I want to think about it before I say anything," Scott said.

Picking up the phone he called Agent Cooper.

When the man answered, Scott asked, "Are you in your office?"

"Yes."

"Is your door shut?"

Cooper's voice was surprised as he said, "Uh, no, hold on," A few seconds later he said, "It is now."

"We believe we found the mole in your office. It is your clerk, Beth Moreland." He heard a deep sigh and could empathize with Cooper's apprehension. Trust once lost was hard to gain back.

"You can't know how relieved I am to hear it is not one of my agents. How did you find out?"

"I'll let Ryan fill you in on the details. For right now, nothing is to be said to her or any of your personnel. Ryan is on his way to Austin PD to meet with Tim Baker. I suggest you head over there to sit in on this conference. We need your help."

"Scott, that is music to my ears. I appreciate your call."

Ryan was next.

"Where are you?"

"Kerry and I are pulling into the parking lot at the police department."

"Put me on the speakerphone. I want Kerry to hear this. We believe we have found the leak, Beth Moreland. She's a clerk. Her grandfather manages one of Harmon's ranches. I contacted Cooper and told him the news. He's on the way to meet you at the police department. I also told him not to discuss this with anyone in his office."

"I'm glad it has been resolved. When we met with Coop, it was obvious he was devastated by the kidnapping, and then to be under suspicion added another heavy burden," Ryan said.

"I told him you would give him the details of where we stand in the investigation. We need to find out Moreland's role in this. Has Adrian been to Cooper's office yet."

"I don't know. Hold on, Dan is with him. I'll have Kerry call."

Kerry quickly grabbed her phone. When Dan answered, she asked, "Where are you?"

"A couple of blocks from the Bureau's office. Why?"

"Hold up, don't go in yet. I'll call you back."

Ryan resumed his conversation with Scott. "She caught them before they arrived. What do you have in mind?"

"I want to set up a sting using Adrian. Moreland won't know him, and she is single. He might be able to get her to talk."

"We'll handle it," Ryan said.

"One more item. Blake has been picking up rumors about a high dollar auction for a big drug shipment. We believe it's going to be the children, not drugs. A sale like this will have the drug cartels and terrorist groups fighting to get the high bid," he said and disconnected.

Ryan stared at Kerry. "Damn, didn't think this could get worse, but it just did."

Eighteen

Texas

Stunned by Scott's last comment, they sat silent for several minutes, assessing the unthinkable.

Ryan broke the silence. "He's right. Why the abductions if you aren't going to demand a ransom. There had to be another plan."

"The bastard! That goddamn bastard! He plans to sell those kids!" Kerry exclaimed. "But why? It doesn't make sense. Harmon sure as hell doesn't need the money."

"Difficult to imagine someone of his stature as the instigator of such an insidious plan," Ryan said.

Kerry picked her phone from the console. "There has to be something we are missing, a huge piece of this puzzle. I think we should regroup at BSI. It has the privacy we won't have at the PD."

When Tim answered, she said, "Can you meet us at BSI. We have new information, and it would be better to discuss it there. Good, bring your list."

Ryan called Cooper and caught him as he was leaving his office and passed on the change in plans, then called Adrian.

As they pulled into the BSI parking lot, Dan and Adrian were behind them.

"You've got news?" Adrian asked as he got out of the car.

Ryan said, "Yes. Let's get inside."

Adrian glanced over his shoulder at a man exiting a vehicle parked next to his. "Will Cooper is here."

Quickly, Ryan said, "He's been cleared."

"Well … that's damn good to know. When did you find out?" Adrian asked.

"A few minutes ago. I had Scott on the phone when Kerry called."

As Cooper approached the group, his face held a look of uncertainty. When Ryan said, "Glad to have you back on the team," his body straightened as he glanced at the group.

Ryan made the introductions, and they headed inside the building. Mike and John were seated in the conference room talking to Tim.

As everyone grabbed a chair, Ryan started the briefing.

"First, Agent Will Cooper is the latest addition to our team. We believe we found the leak in the bureau's office. It's a clerk, Beth Moreland."

Cooper held up a finger to stop Ryan. "When Scott called, he insisted the information was to be kept confidential, even from my team," he said with a sideways glance at the civilian BSI personnel and APD detective.

Ryan recognized the implied criticism in Cooper's comment. Why would these people be told when his agents were excluded?

Since there had been no opportunity to bring Cooper up to speed on the details, for now, a brief explanation would have to suffice. "Until we identify her contact, no one in your office can be involved. We can't afford to have a conversation overheard, and we can't move her out of your office. We located the house where Tristan Murdock and Jennifer Wademan were kept. The property is owned by Mitchell Harmon. It's what raised the red flag on Moreland. Her grandfather is the manager of Harmon's ranch. Everyone else in your office was clean."

Cooper leaned forward, a look of shock on his face. "Mitchell Harmon!"

Ryan said, "Yes. Kerry and I met with him this morning and are convinced he's behind the abductions."

A buzz broke out as everyone started to comment. Mike's loud ex-marine voice won out. "What could possibly be his motivation?"

"We don't know yet, but it gets worse. Based on intel my boss and the rest of my team have found, we believe the children will be sold at an auction on the black market, and it changes the focus of the investigation."

Stunned silence met this remark.

Adrian recovered first and asked, "Why did you stop me from going into the Bureau's office?"

"You get to play lover boy," Ryan said.

Adrian's eyes narrowed as he stared at Ryan. "You're kidding, right?"

"Nope. And, before you blame me, this idea came from Scott." Ryan had no problem throwing his boss under the bus on this one.

"I think ... you had better explain," Adrian said, an ominous tone to his voice.

"Beth Moreland is single. If you can meet her, add in a bit of romance, we might find out who is on the receiving end of her information and why."

As Adrian glared at Ryan, Cooper chuckled, then said, "This shouldn't be difficult. Beth is attractive and likes to party. I can fill you in on whatever you might need to know, at least up to a point," and chuckled again.

A frown crossed Adrian's face. "Ryan, why can't you do it? That male model persona of yours is a chick magnet, a hell of a lot better than me."

"She's seen me, but she hasn't seen you. That's why."

"Ah, hell!" Adrian said and sat back in his chair.

Continuing where he left off, Ryan said, "It will be the drug cartels and terrorists that will be the bidders. Tim, we need to add any drug informants you have to your list of prostitutes. Someone might have heard about an auction."

A phone rang. It was John's. Excusing himself, he stepped out of the room. "Davidson," he answered.

"John, this is Agent Nicki Allison. I'm sending you two files. I'd like your help in researching the background of a local attorney, Stuart Lane."

"I know him. What's the connection?" he asked.

"He was Ray Boyd's defense lawyer and the attorney of record for the purchase of the property in East Texas. We need to find out who are his clients."

"Okay. What else?"

"The second file is the list of Texas properties owned by Harmon. The ones with asterisks have houses that need to be checked. Have you talked to Ryan yet?"

"We're in a meeting, and he's covering the details of the latest activity. Difficult to believe a man of Harmon's professional stature would be involved in a nefarious plot to sell kids."

"I agree. I'll keep you posted on any new details I find."

John walked back into the room. Conversation stopped as all eyes looked at him expectantly. "That was Nicki. She handed us another link to Harmon—Stuart Lane, a local attorney. He represented Bullman and handled the purchase of the property where Tristan was held. We need to identify his clients. She's also sending a list of the Texas properties Harmon owns, and we need to take a look at them."

Tim snorted, saying, "Lane ... he's a dirtbag. Several cases on Bullman were dismissed when the witness either disappeared or recanted their statements."

"Tim, can you find out who he has represented?" Ryan asked.

"Yeah, I can, but I'm getting stretched pretty thin here. We've got the prostitutes along with the drug informants and now need to add the research on an attorney."

Cooper said, "Let me work the attorney angle. The district attorney and I are golfing buddies. I can get the information."

Ryan said, "Coop, we also need weapons and a vehicle. It was the reason Adrian was headed to your office this morning, a requisition mission," which elicited a chuckle from Mike.

Cooper glanced at Adrian and smirked. "Since we don't want Adrian coming to the office, I'll have the vehicle delivered here. I'll load the trunk with whatever you need. You can leave the rental car, and I'll have it picked up."

Tim looked at Cooper. "If we're going hunting, we need undercover vehicles. It would be helpful if those cars didn't scream 'fed.' These people get spooked real fast when they see a cop car coming their way. We also need money to sweeten the pot. Give them a reason to talk to us."

"The cars won't be a problem, and I'll handle the money. How much do you need?" Cooper said.

Tim thought for a few seconds, before saying, "At least two grand. I'll keep a record of the payoff's if you need it."

"Don't worry. We'll take care of the recordkeeping when this is done."

"Let's split the list. Since Adrian will be, uh ... tied up on his undercover assignment." Ryan stopped and grinned at Adrian before continuing, "Kerry and I will team up, and Dan with Tim. That lets John work on the files from Nicki?" Ryan glanced at Mike. "Anything from your military contacts?"

"Not yet. John came up with a hanger Harmon owns at an airport on the west side of town. I'm headed there to find out what type of aircraft he uses," Mike added.

After Cooper made a call to have the money and cars delivered to BSI, Ryan pulled him aside to get him on board with all the details.

Kerry divided Tim's list of contacts that included mug shots of each one. Prostitutes routinely lied about their name, hoping to avoid an arrest for outstanding warrants issued under another fake name. When she worked in patrol, she had carried a 'hook book.' It contained the picture of every prostitute she either arrested or contacted. Each time she stopped one and was given another fake name, it was entered in the book. When she left patrol some of the prostitutes had dozens of aliases. As she scanned the list, she recognized familiar faces.

Armed with a stack of twenty-dollar bills, Ryan and Kerry headed to a section of town, with cheap motels that rented rooms by the hour. Kerry had opted to stay with her truck.

Dressed in jeans and t-shirt, with her ponytail pulled through the back of a ball cap with a tractor on the front, Kerry hoped she wouldn't be recognized from her days as a beat cop.

Ryan was dressed in similar attire that only added to his elegant good looks. The man could wear bib overalls and still be sexy as hell. Distracted by the sharp quiver of desire that twisted through her, she stared at the long fingers deftly turn the wheel as she envisioned his hands running down her body. Vexed, she shook her head to clear her thoughts. *What's the matter with me? I've only known him a few days. This is crazy.*

Ryan's voice broke into her thoughts. "Check out the woman on the sidewalk. Looks like a candidate to me."

"Uh ... don't recognize her," she said.

He pulled to the curb. Kerry lowered her window and signaled to a woman dressed in three-inch spike heels, skin-tight leggings, and a crop top that barely covered her ample breasts. Coarse blond hair was pushed into a knot on top of her head. Heavy makeup covered her face, eyes were outlined in black and lips sported a bright orange-red color. The woman stared at her in suspicion, then decided they were a safe bet and strutted to the car.

Their cover story was Kerry was searching for her brother. Since this was her turf, she'd do the talking. It should work unless they encountered someone Kerry had arrested.

The hooker put her hand on the side of the car, leaned over and gazed at Ryan. Breasts rolled over the top. Fascinated, Ryan waited for them to completely pop out.

"Hello, darling. Aren't you a yummy one. Looking for a little action? Well, baby … you came to the right person. I'd love to help you out."

Kerry slid a twenty-dollar bill on the window sill, and partially covered it with her hand. The woman's eyes darted to the money.

"We're looking for someone. I'm hoping you might have seen him," Kerry said.

The woman looked at Kerry, then back to the money. "I may or may not. Depends on who you're looking for."

"My brother. He just got out of the military and has been having problems. He up and left the house a few days ago, and I haven't seen him since." Kerry went on to add the description of Moore. She watched the woman's face carefully, but there was no sign of recognition.

"Nah, not seen anyone like that. I for sure would remember the snake."

"This is my number. If you see him, please call. There's a substantial bonus," she said and wrapped a note with the burner number around the money.

The woman slid her hand over it and tucked it into the top of her leggings. Bending over, she looked at Ryan and pursed her lips in a kissing gesture before turning and continuing her stroll along the sidewalk.

As they drove off, Kerry looked at Ryan with a smirk on her face. "She liked you … a lot."

"Yeah, well, definitely not my type, so get that goofy grin off your face."

Five contacts later and a hundred dollars gone, none of the women had seen Moore.

The next one, Kerry immediately recognized as one she had arrested several times, though she couldn't remember her name. Quickly scanning the list, she found her picture.

"This one will know me," she said.

As the woman approached, Kerry's gaze scanned her from head to toe. Prostitution was a rough business, the abuse, and drugs aged the women at an abnormal pace. She remembered the first time she had encountered Sandy. She had been young, around eighteen, and attractive. Dismayed at the young girl working the streets, Kerry had talked to her several times about returning to school and getting her GED. The girl would listen and agree, then go back to turning tricks. Kerry finally realized she was wasting her time and effort.

The woman walking toward her looked drastically different. The bleached hair, coarse and dry, hung around a thin-lined face. She looked years older than her actual age. Wearing a crop top, tight jean shorts, and high-heeled shoes, she was the typical street hooker.

Using the woman's real name, she said, "Sandy, how are you doing these days?"

Her eyes widened in alarm as she recognized Kerry. "I ain't done nothing wrong, and got no warrants," she protested, easing backward, ready to run.

"I'm not here to arrest you. I'm looking for information," Kerry said and held up the twenty-dollar bill. The woman eyed it, glanced inside to look at Ryan, then shifted her gaze back to Kerry.

"Yeah, what kind of information?"

"Have you heard any rumors of missing children?"

"Huh!" she exclaimed.

"Any of your johns making odd comments about kids?"

"Nope, nothing like that. Why are you asking about kids?"

"It's a case I'm investigating. Thought you'd want to pick up a little money and help me out. Have you seen a man with a snake tattoo around his arm? Military type."

"I ain't seen him. If I do or hear something, what's it worth to you?"

"Depends on how good the information is." Kerry pulled another piece of paper from her notepad and wrote on it. "Here's my number.

If you hear anything, day or night, call me."

Sandy folded the paper, along with the money and stuck them inside the snug top she wore.

The scenario was repeated numerous times over the next several hours as they drove up and down streets, handing out more bills.

It was evening when her phone rang. It was Tim. "Any luck?" she asked.

"Nada. I've talked to at least twenty informants on my list and nothing. What have you found?"

"The same. I left my number with all the ones we've talked to. Hopefully, one of them might hear something."

"I'll drop Dan off at BSI, then head back to the office to pull a few more case files," Tim said.

Discouraged, they headed back to their hotel for a quick break and meal before continuing their search. As they walked into the lobby, Adrian exited the elevator. Ryan's whistle resulted in a look of disgust on Adrian's face.

"Damn, dude, don't you look slick," Ryan said, then grinned.

"Shut up, or I may have to remove that shit-eating grin from your face."

Adrian was spiffed up in tight black jeans, a snug western shirt with opal snaps, and a pair of black alligator boots.

Kerry even felt the attraction of the man as she said, "I have to agree with Ryan. You look downright dangerous. The women are going to be all over you. Maybe ... one of us ought to go along for protection," then laughed.

"I'm glad you both think this is so funny. I need to get going. Coop found out the target is attending a big party at one of the local clubs," he growled.

They both grinned as they watched the man stroll out of the lobby.

Nineteen

U ncomfortable, he ran a finger around the collar of his shirt. *I don't like this assignment.* Adrian had gone undercover a couple of times in his career, but it was never a role he embraced, unlike several of his friends. They relished the undercover assignments. But like it or not, the endgame was to identify Moreland's contacts. The lives of children were at stake, and his discomfort wasn't a factor to even consider.

Coop said Moreland had talked about a birthday party at a local club for the last couple of days. He also said Adrian wouldn't have any trouble spotting her, look for a woman with coal black hair and a streak down one side. Evidently, she routinely changed the color and this week it was red.

The beat of western music poured out as customers streamed through the front door of a club in the shape of a barn. Inside, the large dance floor was surrounded by tables and a bar that stretched across the back of the room. In one corner, a live band played. The dancing had already begun as rows of people, all dressed in western attire, line-danced.

As he strolled to the bar, he scanned the tables for his target. It didn't take but a few seconds to spot her. Two tables had been pushed together, and several women faced the dance floor. Beth sat in an end chair.

At the bar, Adrian eased onto a stool and ordered a glass of beer.

When the bartender slid the glass toward him, Adrian pushed a twenty toward the man, and waved his hand over the bill, to indicate he didn't want any change. It was the best way to get on the right side of a bartender who could be a wealth of information. Plus, it set him up as someone willing to spend money. He took a sip, then asked, "Big crowd, is it always like this?"

The bartender, a young man in his middle twenties palmed the twenty as he looked around. "Yeah, pretty much so. It's a popular place. You're not from around here?"

"No, in town on business and was told this was a good place to get some Austin atmosphere and maybe meet a woman, someone who likes to dance."

A lecherous smirk crossed the man's face at Adrian's comment on dancing. "Well, you came on a good night. It's ladies' night which means all their drinks are half-priced."

"I noticed a number of groups were only women. A good way to draw in the men."

"We get a lot of all-women parties on ladies' night, birthdays, showers, that type of stuff. Then there are the ones just out to have a little fun."

The bartender walked off as another customer sat down. Adrian took a sip, then spun on the stool. Elbows on the bar, he leaned back and glanced around the room. Beth was still seated at the table, her hand tapped to the beat of the music. Adrian had to agree with Coop's assessment, the woman was damned attractive. He knew she was twenty-five. The black hair was short and framed an oval-shaped face. Ruby red lips drew his eyes.

She must have sensed his perusal as her gaze flicked toward the bar and met his. Adrian let a smile slowly build as he stared at her, then lifted his beer glass in acknowledgment. She smiled back and turned to the woman next to her. After a short conversation, the second woman swiveled her head to look at him.

Adrian turned back to the bar. *Okay, I've got your interest, let's see how I can build on it.* The bartender walked towards him, wiping the top with a towel.

"You doing okay?" he asked, glancing at Adrian's half-filled glass.

"Yeah," he said and took another sip. "The woman in the group behind me, the one with black hair and a red streak, do you know her?"

The bartender looked toward the table. "Oh, yeah, that's Beth Moreland. She's a looker. They come in here a couple of times a month. One of her friends is having a birthday."

"Really! Good reason to celebrate. I'll buy the table a round of drinks," Adrian said. He pulled his wallet from his pocket and removed a hundred-dollar bill and slid it to the bartender.

The bill was whisked out of sight. With another smirk, he said, "I'll let them know." He picked up Adrian's glass and replaced it with a full one, then filled a tray with a variety of mixed drinks and beer. When he walked to the table, Adrian spun to watch.

The young man set the tray on the table and began to hand out the drinks. Whatever he said, had the women turning their heads to look at Adrian. He smiled at the group, nodded his head and shifted his eyes to Beth. He stared at her for a few seconds, smiled and winked, then turned back to the bar. Adrian could see the table in the mirror that covered the wall. After a short discussion among the women, Beth got up, walked towards him and slid onto the seat next to him.

Her eyes met his in the mirror. Adrian swiveled to look at her as she said, "We wanted to thank you for the drinks." Her voice was soft with a slight lilt in the tone.

"You're more than welcome. The bartender mentioned it was a birthday party."

"Yes, one of my friends turned thirty today. She was depressed, and we decided a party was what she needed to cheer her up. I'm Beth," she said and held out her hand.

Adrian took it, stroking the back with his fingers. "Adrian. Nice to meet you, Beth. Do you come here often?"

"Yes, this is a fun place, and we always have a good time. Do you live in Austin?"

"No, I'm here on business. I live in D.C." he answered, letting her pull her hand back.

"What business are you in?"

"Oil and gas. My company is involved in the installation of pipelines."

Her eyes widened. "Your company. You own it?"

"Yes. So, Beth, what's your occupation, let me guess. Ah … a teacher. Yes, you look like a teacher." Leaning on the bar, his gaze slid over her face, stopping on the bright red lips.

"Not even close," she said and smiled.

"Hmm … okay. A real estate agent, you have a classy look that would sell houses."

"Nope." Laughing, she tilted her head back and flipped her hair. Under other circumstances, he would have enjoyed her company.

"Okay, I give up."

Her dark eyes sparkled as she said, "I work … in an FBI office."

"Wow, no kidding, I would never have guessed that. Hey, do you like to dance?"

"I sure do. It's the reason we come here."

"Well, let's get to it."

They joined the group on the dance floor, and for the next couple of sets, they twirled and swung to the beat of country western. When the second one ended, they were both out of breath. A slow tune started, and Adrian raised his eyebrows and opened his arms. She flowed into him as they began the steps of a waltz. Pulling her tight against him, he had to fight the sexual attraction he felt. *This is not the time, remember why you are here.*

At the end of the dance, he returned her to her table and met the other women before heading to his seat at the bar.

The bartender wandered back and handed him a cold glass of beer. "That was some fancy stepping for a D.C. boy," he said, which told Adrian he'd been listening.

He slid the kid another hundred bucks for a second round of drinks at the table. He waited, making casual conversation with the bartender whenever he wandered by until the band struck up another slow song. He walked to the table and held out his hand. He kept her on the dance floor for another waltz, then a round of line-dancing, before leading her back to the bar. Time to talk.

Signaling for a drink for Beth, he brought the conversation back to her job. "I don't think I've ever met anyone who worked for the FBI. How long have you worked there?"

"About six months," she said.

"Are you an agent or what?"

She giggled, and said, "No, I'm a clerk. But it is so, so exciting. You never know what kind of case the agents will get."

"I never considered it, but I can see where it wouldn't be boring. My job is rather mundane by comparison." He sighed. "All I deal with is metal pipes. Would you like to hear about problems with pipes?"

Another giggle erupted, and Adrian laughed with her. "See what I mean. Who wants to hear about pipes? Was this a lifelong dream to go into law enforcement?"

She took a sip of her drink, then said, "Not really. Actually, you were close to the mark on a teacher. It was my degree in college. But, I had a chance to hire on with the FBI, and who could resist that?" she said with enthusiasm.

"How does someone get hired? In my company, it's a complicated process. I can't imagine how difficult it must be for the FBI."

"Oh, it was. I had an in though. My grandfather knew someone. Still, I had to go through a complete background check, then take some tests, even ..." she waved her hands in front of her for emphasis, "a lie detector test."

"You're kidding, right?"

"Nope. They hooked a bunch of cords on me and asked questions." Her voice had a slight slur.

Adrian said, "It was fortunate your grandfather was able to help you. Mine helped me start my company though he died a couple of years ago."

"Oh, I am so sorry for you. It must have been hard to lose him. My grandparents lived a couple of miles from me when I was growing up. He's always been a special person."

"Sounds like it since he was able to help you get hired by the FBI. My grandpa didn't have that kind of stroke."

The bartender picked up their glasses and replaced them. Adrian took a sip of the beer and watched Beth. He was concerned at the effect of the alcohol and needed to speed up his questions.

"Hey, are you hungry?" he asked, signaling to the bartender. He placed an order for nachos, hoping the food would slow down the absorption of the alcohol. "Lie detector, how amazing. It would be hard to believe any cases could be more exciting than that experience."

"Nope, you're wrong. We have one working now, it is unbelievable." She stopped to look for the bartender who was at the other end of the bar. "It's a kidnapping, isn't that awful. It must be terrible for the parents."

Adrian let an expression of surprise show on his face as he sat back. "A kidnapping. I haven't seen anything in the papers. Wait a minute, I do remember something on one of the TV channels just before I left my room this morning."

"It's in the news now, but it was kept quiet for several days. They didn't tell anyone because it was the son of a senator."

"Isn't that unusual? I would have thought the news media would be all over that type of story."

"Seemed strange to me until my grandfather called. He'd already heard about it. So, I guess there was some reason the reporters didn't print the story."

Adrian slid his fingers over her hand on the bar, smiled, then asked, "How did your grandfather find out?"

"I'm not sure. I don't think he ever said, only that the case sounded intriguing and to call whenever I heard something. We had several conversations trying to figure out what was going on."

The bartender set the plate of nachos on the bar, and Beth pulled her hand back and picked up a cheese-laden chip. Adrian slid another fifty at him. *The kid made out like a bandit tonight* as he mentally added up the cost, sure most would end up in his pocket.

"Did they find the boy?"

Waving the chip in the air, she said, "Yeah, a woman, a private investigator here in Austin, found him alongside a road. But, that where it really gets weird," and took a bite of the chip.

Adrian took a sip of his beer, then picked up a chip before asking, "What happened?"

Beth looked around again, then said, "She was supposed to take him to the hospital, but something happened there. I never heard what, but then she was to take him to the airport. My boss sent a plane to pick up the boy, but she never showed. Everyone was talking about it in the office, and now he has disappeared again. No one knows where he is."

"With all the turmoil going on, it was probably difficult to talk to your grandfather that night."

"Not really. Granddad called several times. I think he was just lonely, wanted to know when I would be coming for a visit. Hearing what was happening with the kidnapping seemed to cheer him up."

Adrian had what he needed, but didn't want to abruptly leave. He stayed, continued to talk, shifting the conversation to other topics, while they crunched on the nachos.

"How long will you be in town?"

"I have to leave tomorrow." Adrian made a show of looking at his watch. "As much as I hate too, I really should go. I have an early morning meeting before I catch my flight. But, I'll be back in a couple of weeks. Maybe, I'll see you in here again."

She wiped her hands on a napkin, leaned over and pushed those beautiful ruby red lips against his. His hands gripped her shoulders as he deepened the kiss, then gently pushed her back.

"Let me take you back to your table. I want to say goodbye to your friends."

Walking to his vehicle, he rubbed his hand over his face. Undercover jobs always left him with a sleazy feeling, and this one was no exception.

He hit the speed dial for his boss.

"What did you find out?" Scott asked.

"She's an innocent dupe. It was her grandfather. The night Kerry found Tristan, he called several times, and Beth told him everything that happened. She believed he was just lonely and talking about the case cheered him up."

"Are you certain?"

"Absolutely." The touch of his hand on hers had told him she wasn't lying. "If Nicki's not already investigating the grandfather, he needs to be added to the list. He knew about the kidnapping before it ever went public. Beth didn't know how he found out. Here is another point, her grandfather knew someone who helped her get the job. I believe she was hired six months ago. It sounds to me like a plan was getting put into place."

"I agree. I'll be in touch as soon as we know more. Good work, Adrian. I know this was a repugnant assignment for you."

As he disconnected, he wondered about Scott's last comment. *How the hell did he know that?*

Twenty

Ryan's phone rang. "Well stud, how did the evening of romance go?"

Yep, I'll be the butt of jokes until something else comes along. "Yeah, yeah, okay, enough with the jokes. What are you doing?" Adrian asked.

"Been chasing prostitutes, not having near as much fun as you. We're headed to BSI. Everyone is meeting there. What happened?"

Adrian said, "I'll meet you there. I've already told this to Scott and only want to repeat it one more time."

As they walked into the office, Tim and Dan greeted them. Each held a cup of coffee. Kerry inhaled the aroma drifting through the air. "Did someone make a fresh pot?" she eagerly asked.

"Yep, Mike did," Dan said as he watched her head to the pot. Kerry's infatuation with coffee was a standing joke. "I'm surprised she doesn't have an IV, so she can inject the stuff straight into her veins," which brought a chuckle from Ryan.

As they gathered in the conference room, everyone looked at Adrian with an expectant expression.

With a grimace, he started his explanation, quickly recapping the information he had gained.

Coop picked up on the connection to Beth's hiring. "Was a plan to plant a mole in my office set up months ago?"

"I suggested the idea to Scott, and he seemed to believe it was possible. Do you remember anything about Beth's application?" Adrian asked.

"No, it went through the personnel department, but I can find out tomorrow."

"She said her grandfather knew someone who helped her get hired. It's another link we need to find," Adrian said.

"I'd like to get her the hell out of my office without raising suspicions," Coop said.

Ryan said, "No, it's better to wait. If you do, and word gets back to Harmon, he'll wonder why. We can't risk it. Tim, did you and Dan get anything? We didn't."

"No, a dry hole for us as well."

"Mike, anything on your visit to the airport?" Ryan asked.

"He keeps his jet at the airfield. I posed as someone looking for a place to park a plane and talked to a mechanic. The jet hasn't moved for a couple of weeks. Harmon also has a small plane and helicopter, which he keeps on his estate. He has an airstrip and hanger. I'll follow up tomorrow."

"Then we're at a dead end unless someone has another idea," Ryan said.

Kerry's burner phone rang. "Yes," and a look of excitement crossed her face as she jotted notes on her pad. "I'll meet you at the same corner."

When she finished the call, she looked around the table. "No, we're not at a dead end. That was one of the prostitutes we met today. She said a gang is in town looking for a kid." She looked at her notes. "One of them is six-foot, two-twenty, black hair, and a snake tattoo on his arm. I'm headed to pick her up. Who's going with me?"

Ryan and Adrian looked at each other and nodded. Ryan said, "We'll both go. Coop, did you get us any weapons?"

"Yeah, in my trunk, along with extra ammo. I wasn't sure what you wanted, so there is a selection of handguns, rifles, and riot gear."

"You do good work, I'm impressed," Adrian quipped.

Ryan drove Kerry's truck. Adrian was in the backseat, his feet resting on a case with the weapons pulled from Coop's vehicle.

Kerry's phone rang. She listened, then said, "We are a couple of minutes from you. Walk to the Suds and Bucket Bar. When we get there, get in the back seat."

Rounding the corner, Sandy stood in front of the bar nervously watching each car as it passed. When they pulled up, Kerry lowered the window and called to her. Sandy jerked her head toward the sound, then ran to the truck.

As soon as the back door closed, Ryan hit the accelerator. Adrian twisted to watch out the rear window. Kerry turned so she could see Sandy. "Who hit you?" The side of the woman's face was bruised, her eye swollen.

"The guy you're looking for."

"Do we need to get you to the hospital?" Kerry asked.

"No. I'll be fine."

"Anyone following?" Ryan asked as he passed a vehicle.

"Not that I can see," Adrian said.

"Do you know what kind of car he was in?" Kerry asked.

"It's a black SUV, three men inside."

A few seconds later, Adrian said, "We're clear."

"Tell us what happened," Kerry said.

"This car pulled up, and the one in the front seat asked how much. We talked for a few minutes. The driver got really pissed, said they had to find a kid and a woman. The other man told him to shut up, he wouldn't be gone long, then he got out, and we walked to the motel."

"Sandy, tell me exactly what was said, as close as you can remember."

"Uh ... 'Goddamn, Cal, we don't have time for this. We have to find the kid and the woman.' That's when the other man—Cal—told him to shut up, he wouldn't be gone long."

"Did you hear another name other than Cal?"

162

"No."

"What happened when you got to the motel?" Kerry asked.

Sandy glanced at the two men in the car. "I'm not going to get arrested or anything for this, am I?"

"No, you get a free pass this time," Kerry said.

"Well, we get inside, and, uh … we … you know, anyway, after he was done, I asked about the kid. Said I might be able to help him. He gets this vicious look on his face."

"Ryan, we have a tail. Two cars back. He has been keeping pace since we got on the freeway," Adrian said.

Ryan glanced in his rearview mirror. "I got him."

Kerry said, "Take the next exit. When you get to the light, turn right. We'll head to the PD. They won't follow us into the parking lot," and tapped her phone. "Tim, where are you?"

"Back at the station. What do you need?"

"We picked up the informant and have a tail. We'll pull into the parking lot in a few minutes."

"I'll have a couple of squad cars waiting," Tim said.

"No. I want to turn the tables and tail these guys ourselves."

"Coop and Dan are here. Hang on while we discuss it."

Kerry could hear the buzz of distant voices, then Tim was back on the phone. "They're going to follow the car. Do you have a description?"

"Hold on a minute."

"Sandy, tell me again everything you remember about the vehicle," Kerry said.

"It's four doors, black, an SUV type. Oh, it has damage on the passenger side. The guy had trouble getting the door open."

Kerry relayed the description. "Have one of them call me when they're in position." Turning back to Sandy, she said, "Finish telling us what happened."

"He wanted to know why I asked about the kid. I said I was just curious, thought I'd make a couple of bucks. That's when he slugged me. Told me if I wanted to live another day to keep my mouth shut."

Kerry's phone rang. It was Dan, and they were in place. "Stay on the phone," then said, "Ryan, take a left at the next light and straight for three blocks. You'll see the PD parking lot on the left side of the street."

A few seconds after they pulled into the lot, a dark vehicle matching Sandy's description raced by.

"Dan, our tail just passed the entrance."

"We got him. Looks like they're headed to the freeway."

Ryan parked and turned to look at Sandy. "Is your face the only place he hit you?"

"Yeah."

"Are you sure you don't want to have a doctor look at you?" Ryan asked.

"No. I've had a whole lot worse than a bruised face. So, what happens now?"

"I want to get you with a police artist," Kerry said.

Sandy didn't look thrilled at the suggestion. "Does it mean I have to go inside the police station?"

"No. I'll make arrangements to have the artist meet you."

Exhaling a sigh of relief, she said, "That's okay then."

Kerry hit the speed dial for Tim. "I need a police artist. How soon can you get one lined up?"

"I'd have to make a couple of calls. Where do you want her?"

"BSI."

"Call you back."

While they waited, Kerry said, "Do you have a place to stay where no one can find you for a few days?"

"Yeah, my old boss has a room over his garage. Sometimes he lets me hang out."

"Do any of your friends know you stay there? If someone came looking for you, would they be able to find you?"

"Nah, never told anyone. I didn't want to get him in trouble. He's a nice old man and doesn't have a lot of money."

"Where does he live?" Kerry asked. As she wrote down the address, her phone chimed.

"Megan's on her way to BSI. As soon as I wrap up a few reports, I'm headed there. I want to see if I know this guy."

Ryan glanced at Sandy in the rearview mirror. "Sandy, picture the man in your mind, and tell us everything you can remember."

"He's big, really muscular. He walked like maybe he'd been a soldier. Black hair that is cut short. His face had a rough stubble, and there's a scar on the cheek."

"What about the tattoo?" Adrian asked.

"They're on both arms, creepy stuff. One was the snake. It coiled around his arm, and the other was a skull's head. I didn't see them until he took off his jacket."

"How was he dressed?" Kerry asked.

"Those pants like the cops wear, black with pockets on the legs, a black T-shirt, and black jacket."

"Did you see a weapon?"

"Yeah, a knife tucked in his boot. I didn't know he had a gun until he left. When he undressed, he must have hidden it. But when he walked out the door, his jacket was caught on his belt, and I saw the gun."

"Can you describe the other two men?" Kerry asked.

"No. The driver was wearing a ball cap."

"Anything else you remember?"

Sandy shook her head no.

Adrian asked, "Did the tattoos have any writing?"

Sandy thought for a minute, then said, "I think so, but I didn't pay a lot of attention."

Parking in front of the office, Sandy was escorted inside.

Kerry motioned toward the coffee pot. "Help yourself."

Sandy filled a cup, then picked up a magazine from the large coffee table and sat in one of the chairs in the reception area.

Mike walked out of his office when he heard voices. His eyebrows raised when he saw the woman. Kerry smiled to herself. Probably the first time a prostitute had stepped foot in BSI.

"Want to explain?" he quipped in a joking tone.

"That's our witness. She had … oh … an encounter with Moore. A police artist is on the way, so she'll be our guest for the next couple of hours."

"How'd she get hurt?" Mike asked.

"He knocked her around before he left. She started asking questions he didn't like." She walked over and filled a cup with coffee, then picked back up where she left off. "On our way back, we picked up a tail that peeled off when we pulled into the APD parking lot. Coop and Dan are following it. I think it's the same vehicle I saw at the airport, and it's the same one I rammed. There is damage on the right side."

The door opened, and a woman in a police uniform walked in, followed by Tim. A smile lit up Kerry's face as she walked over to give the woman a hug.

"Tim said you needed help with a sketch."

Kerry was delighted Megan Renner was the artist. The woman had an uncanny ability to develop an image that was an absolute likeness of the subject.

Mike offered the use of his office, and within minutes, the two women were ensconced inside.

Taking a sip of coffee, she glanced at her watch. "I'm getting worried we haven't heard anything."

A few seconds later her phone rang. With a sigh of relief, she said, "It's Dan."

"We lost them."

Kerry tapped the speakerphone, so the men could hear. "What happened?"

"When you pulled into the parking lot, they hauled ass to the freeway. We managed to stay behind them as they headed south. We lost them outside of Lytton Springs," Dan said.

"Where is Lytton Springs?" Adrian asked.

"Thirty miles southeast of Austin," Tim answered.

Ryan asked, "Were you able to get the license plate number?"

"No, there wasn't a front plate, and something covered the back one, so we couldn't read it. It's the same vehicle you rammed, Kerry. Has a large dent in the side."

"Where they headed to a new hideaway?" Adrian said.

"I don't know, but we need to find out. We're headed back. What happened to your prostitute?" Dan asked.

"She's in Mike's office with a police artist."

A whistle was heard, then Dan's voice, "An intriguing picture. I would have liked to have seen the boss's face when she walked in."

Laughing, Mike said, "Hey, careful what you say, I'm listening."

Washington, D.C.

The display for the incoming call was Paul Daykin, Director of the FBI. This won't be good. "Fleming."

"Scott, there's been another kidnapping, Senator Thompson's son. Secretary Whitaker of Homeland Security has relayed a request from President Larkin for a meeting. Larkin is at a banking conference in California. As soon as he returns, Whitaker will notify us of the date and time," the Director told him.

"How soon will I have a report?" Scott asked.

"Within a few minutes," he replied and hung up.

Scott leaned back in his chair and stared at the ceiling as he contemplated the latest incident. Hell! Why Thompson? Nicki's research had included every senator, and Thompson had not popped up as a potential target. What was the link? Well, if one existed, Nicki would find it.

Walking out he looked at the mess of electrical wires, cables, and computers on Nicki's desk. She had run out of space and had pulled an empty desk next to hers. Scott made a mental note that when they moved to their new location, it would include a large office equipped for her computer needs.

Sitting at an empty desk, he waited for Blake to end his call, then said. "Another abduction, Senator Thompson's son. Nicki, where do we stand on the research on the Utah governor?"

At the mention of Thompson, a look of surprise crossed Nicki's face. "In a nutshell, I hadn't found any link to the presidential election. There is, however, one to Thompson. The Senator has sponsored a bill to stop construction of the Danver pipeline through Utah. The Governor has been very vocal about environmental concerns for the route of the pipeline and has been pushing the legislature to pass the bill. Harmon could lose millions if it happens."

A surge of adrenaline shot through him, another piece dropped into place.

Nicki continued, "There is one other item I found. A year ago, Harmon was considered as a possible candidate for the President's race. There were a couple of articles, then it died. I haven't found out why."

The last piece of the puzzle fell. Scott was positive he knew the motive.

Blake's phone rang. Glancing at the screen, he said, "It's the El Paso agent, Dave Jenson." Scott motioned for him to answer.

"Dave, anything new?" Blake asked.

"Yeah, and it's not good. I talked to a contact I have in Mexico. He heard there is an upcoming auction for some high-priced commodities. Whatever is up for sale, has the interest of the drug cartels in Mexico and South America. He is getting a lot of chatter from their wiretaps."

"Do you have a location or time?" Blake asked.

"Only that it will happen in the next couple of days, but I don't have a clue yet as to where."

"Any bit of information, I don't care how trivial it may seem, we need."

"Can you clue me in on why?"

"This is confidential and not to be discussed with anyone in your office. The children of several senators and a governor have been kidnapped. We believe they are going up on the auction block."

"Holy Hell! This isn't about drugs then. I have a couple of ideas. Let me get back to you," he said and abruptly hung up.

As Blake recapped the call for Nicki and Scott, their expressions turned to anger at the confirmation of what they had suspected.

"Nicki, have you come up with anything on Harmon's security forces."

"Not as much as I had hoped. He hires ex-military, and most are overseas. He has several working as guards at his facilities in the U.S. and as his personal security. There's no one with the last name of Moore. I did find out Bullman was dishonorably discharged from the Army for assault five years ago. He was never on Harmon's payroll."

Tap, tap, tap. The agents were silent as they watched their boss.

"Based on what we know, give me your assessment of Harmon's motive," Scott said.

The two agents glanced at each other, a look of uncertainty on both their faces. Scott was aware his request was unusual, but he had confidence in his team.

Blake was the first to comment. "Harmon is killing two birds with one stone. If he wants to be the presidential candidate, he's eliminating his competition. If we can't stop the auction, the children will disappear, and it will be nearly impossible to find them.

"It will have a demoralizing effect on the parents. The loss could even be used to discredit their political actions if the voters believe they are under the control of a drug lord or terrorist leader. At the same time, he has targeted a bill that is a financial disaster for his company."

Nicki said, "Blake's right. It also answers the question why Tristan is so important. Murdock is the number one candidate, his biggest threat to Harmon's presidential aspirations. Murdock has wealth, power, connections, and he is popular. My research identified Harmon as a cold, calculating individual driven by egomania. Given the differences in their personalities, Murdock would easily win out over Harmon."

Scott nodded his head in agreement. His agents had confirmed his conclusions. "Blake, we have to find when and where the auction will be held. Contact anyone who might have intel."

He stood. "I have a meeting with the President as soon as he is back in town. I need every possible connection between Harmon and the abductions. I've got to convince him that his best friend is our prime suspect."

Scott headed back to his office. It wasn't often he ever felt the sharp thrust of terror. It was biting at him now, tying his gut in a knot, as he envisioned the possible fate of the children if they couldn't stop the auction.

Twenty-one

Texas

Inside the conference room, a large Texas map had been tacked to the corkboard mounted on one wall. Red push pins covered the surface. John stood in front with a pin in his hand. He turned when Kerry, the two agents, Mike, and Tim walked in.

Motioning toward the map, John said, "A couple more, and I'll be finished marking the locations of Harmon's properties. How'd the meet with the prostitute go?"

"She's in Mike's office," Ryan answered, filling him in on what happened.

A look of amusement crossed John's face. Then, as the rest of the information sunk in, his face turned grim. "They were coming after you again."

"Yeah. Dan and Coop are on their way back," Kerry said as she looked at the map. A red pin was near Lytton Springs. She pointed to the location for the benefit of Ryan and Adrian. "John, what's at Lytton Springs? It's where Dan and Coop lost the trail."

John shuffled the papers until he found the property's description. "Fifty acres with a house. Purchased six months ago by LPJ, same as the property in East Texas. Lane was the attorney."

"We need to check the place tonight," Ryan said.

"We have a van, but it would be a tight fit. It would be better to take two vehicles," Mike said.

Ryan and Adrian looked at each other, an expression of uncertainty on their faces. "Mike, I appreciate your offer of help, but this could get ugly. I can get a team from Coop's office."

"There's six of us, eight counting Dan and Cooper. I figure we can handle anyone we find out there. Besides, you know getting another team together will take time, which we may not have," Mike said.

Dan and Cooper walked in. "What's the game plan?" Dan asked.

Pointing to the map, Ryan said, "Harmon owns a piece of property outside of Lytton Springs. As soon as everyone gets geared up, we're headed there."

Coop and Tim went outside to get vests and other equipment from the trunk of the bureau's car while the rest studied the map. John pulled up an aerial of the location to let Ryan and Adrian plan an approach to the site.

Surrounded by trees, the house was set back several hundred yards off a county road. There were several outbuildings on the back side. Ryan's plan would allow them to use the trees for cover until they could get close to the house.

A tap on the door frame and Megan walked in. She laid a sketch on the table. "I've never seen him," she said.

Kerry stared down at the face. The eyes were narrow-set under heavy brows, the nose crooked. It had probably been broken at one time. Thin lips added to the harshness. An arm drawn in the upper corner portrayed a snake tattoo coiled around the forearm, and the head resting on the wrist. A screaming skull was in the opposite corner. Kerry knew this was Moore. Looking up she saw everyone had gathered around her and were studying the picture. "Well, we have a first name, Cal. Does anyone know him? Tim?"

"No, I don't think I've ever seen him," he said.

Ryan pulled his phone and snapped a few pictures, then sent them to Nicki and followed it up with a phone call to explain.

"Send a copy to Luke," Kerry said.

"What about Sandy?" Megan asked as she looked at the preparations underway.

Concerned over getting to the Lytton Springs property, Kerry had forgotten Sandy needed a ride to her friend's house.

Tim grinned when he saw the blank look on Kerry's face, then said, "Megan, would you give her a ride on your way back to the PD?"

"Sure, not a problem," Megan answered.

Kerry said, "Thanks. She's staying with a friend who lives near downtown."

Sandy was waiting in the reception area. Kerry pulled the remaining twenty-dollar bills from her pocket and handed them to the woman. "Officer Renner will take you to your friend's house. You've got to stay off the street for the next few days. You can't call any of your friends and tell them where you are. These men may come looking for you. Do you understand?"

Sandy nodded. "I hope you get him."

Tim drove one vehicle with Kerry and Ryan. The rest were in BSI's van driven by Mike. As they wove their way along county roads, the darker it became, with only an occasional light in a house as they passed. Turning onto the road that led to the farmhouse, a reddish glow was visible in the distance.

Tim said, "This doesn't look good." Behind them, the sounds and flashing lights of emergency equipment rapidly gained on the two vehicles. Moving to the right to allow a fire truck and ambulance to pass, they followed them to a house engulfed in flames. Pulling to the side of the road, they exited to watch the firemen fight the blaze. A highway patrolman walked toward them.

Ryan pulled his badge. "What happened?"

"We got a 911 call from a resident down the road. They heard an explosion, and when they stepped outside to check, saw the flames."

"Was anyone inside?" Ryan asked.

"We don't think so. According to the neighbor who called, the house should be empty. Until the fire is out, we can't be sure someone didn't camp inside. What are you doing here?"

"Following up on an investigation that may have involved the use of this house." Handing him a business card, he said, "I would appreciate your contacting me if you find any evidence the house had been occupied."

As the trooper walked back to his vehicle, Adrian expressed the sentiments felt by the team. "There goes more evidence. These guys sure are into explosives."

On the way back to town, Ryan's phone rang. It was Blake. "We had another kidnapping, Senator Thompson's son." Then added their theory on Harmon's motives and the link between the governor and Thompson. "And, the boss is getting ready for a face-to-face meeting with the President."

"Jeez, I think you trumped my information," Ryan said as he relayed the night's events.

"Another link back to Harmon," Blake said.

"Any idea what the President wants?" Ryan asked.

"Yeah, the down and dirty on what we've found, and Scott knows the man won't be happy his best bud is our prime suspect. The other bad news is the auction may happen in a couple of days. I'm waiting to hear back from Dave Jenson in El Paso. He's trying to get more details from his contact in Mexico."

His voice bleak, Ryan said, "God damn! We're running out of time, and it's not looking good."

"Yep, and it's the same here," Blake said before he hung up.

While Ryan had talked, Kerry had turned in her seat to look at him, and Tim watched in the rearview mirror.

In response to the questioning look on their faces, Ryan said, "Another kidnapping and the auction may have been scheduled. As soon as we get back to BSI, I'll fill everyone in on the latest." His head turned to stare out the window as he pondered the horrible fate of the children if they couldn't get to them in time.

Once everyone had reassembled in the conference room, Ryan covered the details of the latest kidnapping and the link back to Harmon, along with the theory of his motives.

Kerry added, "I don't think there is anyone here who doesn't believe he is the mastermind behind this," and received a nod of agreement from everyone around the table.

His tone even more somber, Ryan said, "Blake picked up a rumor the auction will be held in a couple of days."

"Goddamn!" Mike interjected.

With a nod, Ryan continued, "I suggest we get a few hours' sleep. Then start back by examining each piece of property owned by Harmon. My instinct tells me those kids are somewhere in Texas."

Not wanting to leave her truck parked at BSI, Kerry followed Ryan and Adrian back to the hotel.

Walking into her room, the accumulation of stress and the aftermath of adrenaline dumps sent waves of exhaustion rolling through her. Dropping the backpack on the bed, she wanted to collapse alongside it and forget the shower. Laying her keys on the table, she reached for her phone. It wasn't in her pocket. Great, just great, it's still in the truck. She stared at the keys as she debated whether to leave it. *No, I'd better get the damn thing. Someone calls, and I don't answer, they'll call out the troops.*

Exiting the elevator in the underground garage, she quickly scanned each of the parked vehicles as she passed. The only sound was the click of her heels on the concrete. Tapping her remote control, she unlocked the door as she approached the truck.

Reaching for the handle, a faint scrape of a footstep turned her insides to ice. She spun, but there was no time to grab the gun hidden under her jacket. A man, his face covered by a black mask faced her, a pistol pointed at her chest. She caught a glimpse of movement behind a vehicle on the other side. *At least two of them and no one knows I'm down here.*

Motioning with the gun, the man growled, "Move!"

They need me alive so they can find where Tristan is located. It gave her an advantage.

"Move! Now! I can shoot your kneecap, then carry you out of here. One way or the other, you're going with us."

Hoping to keep him talking, while she figured out a way to escape, she said, "What do you want? My purse is upstairs."

"We want the kid. I'm telling you for the last time—move!"

Kerry sidestepped along the side as the second man, whose face was also hidden behind a mask, came into view, a gun held along his thigh.

"Please don't hurt me. I'll tell you where he is," she cried, infusing a note of fear in her voice.

With a snort of derision, he said, "I didn't figure you'd be very tough, even if you are an ex-cop." His eyes glittered in disdain through the holes of the mask, and the menacing laugh sent chills surging down her back, but the hand with the gun dropped—ever so slightly.

She twisted, raced around the end of the truck to the other side, fell to the floor and rolled under the adjacent car. Caught by surprise, the gunman's shot went wide, the sound reverberated in the confined space of the garage.

Kerry continued to roll and crawl under the vehicles until she reached a concrete column. Slipping behind it, she pulled the gun from the holster in her back.

The first man shouted, "Shoot, but don't kill her."

The second man, crouched behind a vehicle on the opposite side, fired. Chunks of rock flew when his shot hit the column, and blood trickled down her face from a piece that struck her forehead. She leaned out and fired, but the man had ducked back behind the car.

She caught a glimpse of the first man who was weaving around the row of vehicles in front of her. In a matter of seconds, she would lose the protection of the column. Any direction she moved, one of them would have her in his sights. They could remain behind cover and pick her off. With the wall of the garage behind her, she had nowhere to go.

Twenty-two

Ryan's phone chimed as he walked through the door. It was Scott. "Have you talked to either Nicki or Blake?" his boss asked.

"Blake called, filled me in on the latest developments," Ryan said, then brought Scott up to date.

When Scott learned a second house owned by Harmon had been destroyed, he said, "Another link. Our theory is Harmon has his sights set on the White House and is taking out his competition along with a financial pitfall in the process."

"Makes sense," Ryan said. "Harmon believes he is above the law."

Scott added, "It's why I think the children are still in Texas at one of his properties. He wants to be close and control every aspect of the operation."

"Blake said you've got an upcoming meeting with the President. Where do you think, it will leave us?"

"I'm not sure. I have to convince him that a trusted advisor and best friend is behind this operation, and then we go from there."

Ryan said, "We'll check every one of his properties, though it will take time since we can't get any other agencies involved. No telling who Harmon knows and if word gets back to him, well … I don't want to think about the consequences."

"I agree. We need to keep a tight lid on our investigation."

Ryan added, "Cooper plans to talk to the D.A. to find out about Lane's other clients. Maybe one will be another member of the gang. We still don't have any leads on Moore's whereabouts, though we do have his picture."

The thud of a door closing broke his focus on the conversation. That's strange, it sounded like Kerry's door whose room was next to his.

"Scott, I need to check on something. I'll call you in the morning."

Slipping his gun back in his holster, he walked into the hallway. The elevator door was closing. Stepping to her door, he knocked several times. A ripple of anger flowed over him when she didn't answer. Where'd she go? Striding to the elevator, he watched the light indicator stop at the garage level. What the hell is she doing down there and didn't like the strange sense of foreboding at the thought of her alone in the garage?

He raced down the stairs to the lobby. As he ran past the check-in desk, the attendant called out, "Is there something wrong, can I help you?"

Ryan ignored him and hit the bar to open the door to the stairs leading to the garage. The sound of a gunshot sucked the air from his lungs as a stab of fear clamped down his chest. Another shot rang out. He burst through the door and dove to the side of a car. Two masked men moved toward the back of the garage. A third shot echoed, and one ducked behind another vehicle.

Holy hell! Kerry's trapped behind a column. He fired at the man advancing toward her, then at the man on the opposite side who was behind the car.

Ducking, their heads turned in his direction before sprinting to a vehicle parked near the entrance. Ryan fired another shot, but both were out of view in seconds. Tires squealed as the car sped out of the garage.

Holstering his gun, Ryan ran toward the column. When Kerry stepped into view, a surge of relief flowed through him until he saw the blood running down the side of her face.

"God, am I glad to see you." She leaned against the column and slipped the gun into her holster. A siren wailed in the distance. "Guess someone called the cops."

Grabbing her shoulders, he looked for a bullet hole. "Dammit! What were you thinking, coming down here by yourself?" he shouted.

"I left my phone in the truck. I didn't plan on someone waiting in the garage, on the off chance, I might stroll down here," she snapped back.

A squad car skidded to a halt, followed by a second. The screech of sirens abruptly stopped. Two officers leaped from the car, guns drawn. One hollered, "Raise your hands."

Hands extended, Ryan turned to face them. "I'm an FBI agent. The assailants just left in a black SUV."

The other officer said, "Step away from the woman and let me see your identification."

Kerry surveyed the two officers with their pressed uniforms, polished shoes, and faces that didn't look old enough to vote. *Rookies, and it's why I don't know them.*

The officer that stepped out of a second car hollered, "Stand down! I know the woman. Damn, Branson! What are you up to now?" The two officers holstered their guns as he walked up to Kerry.

Grinning, she said, "Leon, you old dog, thought you'd be retired by now. I'd hug you, but I'd probably leave blood on your uniform, and that for sure would upset your wife."

Kerry turned to Ryan. "This is Leon Porter, my field training officer when I came out of the academy. Leon, meet FBI Tracker Ryan Barr." The rookies hovered behind the veteran officer.

Leon's face turned serious as he examined a gash that still trickled blood. "The last time I saw you, you were lying on the ground with a bullet hole in your head. So, what happened this time?"

With a quick glance of warning at Kerry, Ryan answered, "Kerry is helping with an ongoing investigation, and tonight's attack is related."

Leon's eyes flicked from Kerry to Ryan and back, "In other words, you can't tell me diddly squat."

"Yeah, that's the short and long of it," Kerry said.

Turning, Leon looked at the two rookies. "I'll handle this. You can clear and go back on patrol."

Kerry grinned in sympathy at the look of annoyance that crossed their faces. There's no one more nosey than a cop.

Once the two were in their car, Leon turned back to Kerry. "Now, tell me what really happened here."

Kerry hit the highlights of the investigation, culminating with the reason for the assault by the two men.

"What a hell of a mess," Leon said.

"Yeah, it is, and why I'm asking that you not file a report," Kerry said.

"That's not a problem, though you know the newbies will talk it up in the locker room."

She nodded. "I can't stop the talk, but I don't want an official report to back up their comments."

"Take care of that wound, and if you need anything call."

Kerry watched Leon's car pull out. "There goes one honest, hardworking cop."

The garage door opened, and the night clerk's head peeped around the edge before he stepped out.

"Uh, oh, we've got company," Kerry said.

"I'll handle it. Move to the car behind you and stay out of sight. Don't need him seeing the blood," Ryan said.

After a brief conversation, the clerk headed back inside. Kerry retrieved her phone and a first aid kit from her truck on the way to the elevator.

As Ryan punched the button, she asked, "What did you tell him?"

"A car backfired."

With a note of incredulity in her voice, she said, "He believed all those shots were nothing more than a car backfiring?"

Ryan shrugged. "It seemed to satisfy him. I don't think he really wanted to know."

As they stepped into the elevator, Kerry said, "I'm beginning to believe you also have a touch of Irish blarney."

Leaning against the wall, she added, "I'm certain the one I encountered by my vehicle was Moore, even though he had on a jacket and gloves. Cocky, arrogant, even disdainful, he was the one in charge. Oh, by the way, how did you know I was down here?"

Ryan explained hearing her door close and then following her downstairs. "I thought we agreed you wouldn't go anywhere alone." Anger slipped back into his voice as the sounds and images from the garage floated in his head.

"We did. I really didn't expect anyone would be watching the garage. If I hadn't left my phone in the truck, I would never have gone down there. It would seem to be a waste of time to stake out my vehicle." She abruptly straightened. "You don't think they planned on breaking into my room?"

Stunned, Ryan rolled the question in his head. "Damn! You might be right. It makes more sense than sitting in a garage all night on an off chance you might come back to your truck."

Exiting onto their floor, Ryan walked to Kerry's door. Expecting him to leave, she turned to say goodnight.

"We're changing rooms. Get your stuff."

"What! I don't need to swap rooms. All it will accomplish is to put you in danger, and I'm just as capable of defending myself as you are." Irritation bubbled inside her.

"This is not a question of your ability to defend yourself. I know you can. It's about common sense. If I hadn't by chance heard your door close, consider what might have happened tonight. Switching rooms puts me on one side and Adrian on the other. So, let's get this done."

A grin split his face. "Unless ... you would like me to bunk with you. That's your other option."

Pushing open her door, she said, "Humph, not in your wildest dreams. I'll get my gear."

Ryan chuckled to himself as he quickly packed his suitcase and grabbed his backpack and laptop. The sexy Kerry Branson did have a prickly side.

Back in her room, he dropped his gear on the bed, then followed her out the door.

Glancing over her shoulder, she said, "Now, what are you doing?"

"I'm going to clean that cut."

"Really! I am quite capable of cleaning it."

Grinning at her irritation, he said, "Probably so, but for my peace of mind, I plan to make sure."

Marching into her new room, she realized he was not going to go away as he grabbed the first aid kit from her hand and headed to the bathroom.

Kerry followed, her nerves sent alarms tingling over her body. She had laughed at Cindy's comments, but what she hadn't wanted to admit was the attraction she felt. In the small confines of the bathroom, she could feel the heat from his body. An aroma, a masculine and seductive scent filled her senses. God, he oozes sensuality. Okay, it had been a long time since she'd been this close to a man who stirred her emotions. It was only natural her senses were in overdrive.

She almost groaned as she watched his long and elegantly shaped fingers squeeze the cloth. Holding herself rigid, afraid any movement would betray the desire pulsating through her body, she stared at the sink. His breath tickled her cheek, and the cloth was warm on her skin as he gently washed away bits of concrete.

"It's not as deep as I thought. But then, a head wound always seems to be worse than they actually are. Hey, are you okay?" With a note of amusement in his tone, he added, "Your face is turning red."

Kerry took a deep breath. "Uh, yeah. A bit warm in here."

"Hmm … guess so. A little antibiotic cream and a band-aid, and that should take care of it until the morning. I'll check it again to make sure it's not getting infected."

"Uh … you, uh … don't worry about it. I'll be okay." *Great, now I'm stuttering.*

Fingers smoothed the cream over the cut. Ryan lightly pushed on the ends of the tape, then trailed his fingertips down her cheeks. The heat inside her rose. When he pushed up her chin, her eyes met his.

"I'll head to my room. We don't have many hours left to get some sleep, and we need to get what we can." The huskiness in his voice matched the desire that simmered in his eyes.

She realized her hands were on his chest. *God, what am I thinking? This is not the time or place.* She pushed back and walked into the bedroom. Avoiding any glance at the bed, she held the door open. As he stepped into the hallway, she said, "I haven't thanked you for your timely appearance tonight."

"Not necessary, but I'll keep it in mind. I might come up with a way for you to say thank you when all this is done." He flicked a finger over her nose. "Don't forget to lock the door behind me."

The man was undoubtedly sexy as hell, but he was also insufferable as she came close to slamming the door.

Two rings and Moore disconnected. A few minutes later, his phone chimed.

"Do you have the woman?"

"No. Interference at the last minute from her associate."

Moore didn't think it was possible for the voice to drop any lower. But as he listened to the ominous tone give him his next set of instructions, the hackles on his neck rose, and it wasn't caused by the cold night air. Over the years, he had been involved in dangerous and potential life-threatening incidents. He had dealt with the dregs of human society, dope dealers, and terrorists. None were more frightening than his boss.

He fought the urge to slam the phone against the wall as rage flowed through him. The damn bitch had eluded his grasp once again and all because of a bumbling FBI agent. Now, he had to adjust his plans since he didn't have the Murdock brat.

He took a deep breath to slow his racing heart and bring a body that had started to betray him under control. The doctor had warned him to take it easy, not get excited or upset. Slipping his hand into his pocket, he fingered the small vial of nitroglycerine tablets.

He had his contingency plans in place, and the auction would go off as scheduled. A grim smile crossed his face as he contemplated the consequences of the sale. Once he knew the buyer, he would launch the next step in his plan to destroy the parent's political career. As for Murdock, well there was another way to get rid him, along with that meddlesome woman and idiot agent. He didn't tolerate interference.

Twenty-three

Washington, D.C.

The sun was barely over the horizon when Scott walked into the office, his hair still damp from the shower located in the gym on the ground floor of their building. At the sound of the door, Blake looked up and motioned to him as he continued his phone conversation. Nicki had swiveled her chair to face Blake's desk as she listened to his side of the conversation.

Ending the call, he looked at Scott and Nicki. "That was the agent in El Paso. He's confirmed an auction to sell several children will be held the day after tomorrow. An agent has been embedded in one of the Bolivian drug cartels for the last six months. Somehow, Dave came up with a way to contact him. The agent discovered his boss has signed up to bid and has already received pictures of the kids."

Blake's words—the day after tomorrow—pushed the ever-present fear deeper into Scott's mind. He glanced at the clock on the wall. "Any opinion on how the auction would be set up?" he asked.

Blake said, "Nicki, and I have been playing the what-ifs on that. The most logical would be a website with a sign-in code for each buyer and an account in a country willing to look the other way. Then broadcast a live stream of the kids as each is sold. Buyers would enter a bid from their computer. Scroll the high bid across the screen along with a clock counting down the time to bid. Sit back and let the buyers 'duke it out.'

Once the winner wire transfers the money, then ship the child to the location designated by the buyer."

Scott said, "It's the way I would set it up. Those kids have got to be in Texas. I keep coming back to the control. He will want ... no, he'll need to stay on top of the auction. I bet he'll even be nearby when the sale goes down."

His phone chimed. It was the White House.

Texas

When Ryan walked into the breakfast bar, the only occupant was Adrian who lounged in a chair with a cup of coffee and an empty plate in front of him.

"I almost called you last night. A lot of noise, slamming doors and voices, in the hallway. Sounded like you and Kerry. I decided not to interrupt. Figured, if you needed me, you'd call." A smirk crossed his face.

"Not what you think, so get the shitty grin off your face. Kerry was attacked in the garage. Our old pal, Moore. I hope I get a chance to take that bastard down."

Adrian bolted upright as he listened to Ryan. "Is she okay?"

"Other than a cut on the forehead, she's fine." He explained what had occurred.

"Smart idea to change rooms."

"Since I rebuked her about a trip to the garage, she wasn't happy about the move."

"Shouted at me would be a more appropriate description," Kerry said as she joined them at the table.

Ryan's lips curled in a sheepish grin before he said, "Well, it was the heat of the moment, and ... you were dripping blood, so my actions were understandable."

"Humph!' She shot him a look of derision before taking a bite of eggs.

Adrian leaned back and grinned at the two of them.

Hoping to divert her attention, he leaned forward to examine the skin around the band-aid. "How's your head?"

"It's fine. I called Cindy. Luke brought home a puppy. Tristan has been having nightmares, and he thought it might help. They've become inseparable, and the pup is sleeping in Tristan's room. This morning the dog was snuggled under the covers."

She took a bite of egg before adding, "Since Tristan hasn't had any more nightmares, she said whatever the dog wants, the dog gets. I hope the Murdock's like dogs …." Her voice broke, and with a note of distress she said, "The other kids, how bad is it for them?"

Looks of anguish crossed Ryan and Adrian's faces. Ryan broke the silence; his voice was harsh. "Let's get to BSI."

"Luke wants to talk to us later this morning. He may have a lead on Moore and is waiting for a phone call from a military buddy," she said as they picked up their equipment and headed to the elevator.

Tim was pulling into the parking lot when they arrived. Seeing the bandage on Kerry's forehead, he sighed and asked, "What happened now?"

Hoping to avoid any lengthy explanations, she said, "I'll tell you later."

In the conference room, Dan was studying the map on the corkboard. Yellow push pins had been added to the red from the night before.

Coop was seated at the end of the table with a laptop in front of him, and John was on his computer at the other end. As they walked in, Kerry's injury immediately got their attention. While Ryan explained, she headed to the coffee pot.

Mike walked in behind them and heard Ryan's comments. He glared at Kerry. "I need to get you a helmet. It may be the only way to keep your hard head safe."

Kerry waved her hands in the air. "I know. No lectures, please. I promise to be more careful."

Mike growled. "There might not be a next time if you don't. These guys aren't playing around." He pulled out a chair and dropped a file folder in front of him. "Bartenders are a good source of information. Last night, I checked out a couple of bars near Harmon's estate before I headed home. I met a gardener who works for him. Interesting conversation."

Kerry recognized the hidden meaning behind Mike's comment. He was one of the best when it came to interrogation. He could extract information, and no one ever suspected they had been pumped dry by an expert.

Mike slid a paper to John. "Those are the coordinates for the estate. When you get a chance, print out an aerial map. We might need it. The gardener said a helicopter and single-engine aircraft are usually parked on the estate. The last few days there has been an unusual number of flights for both. What got his attention is that Harmon wasn't on any of the planes. Evidently, seldom does one leave unless he's on board."

He took a sip of his coffee. Everyone's attention was riveted on him as they leaned forward to listen.

"From the gardener's comments, the man is fanatical about security. It seems excessive even for someone with his money. Guards patrol the perimeter and monitor the activity of the servants working on the grounds. At night, they use dogs. Cameras are mounted everywhere, inside and out. Keypads are on all the doors. Servants are buzzed in from a control room inside the house where the guards watch video feed around the clock. His limo has bulletproofed windows, and he always has two guards with him when he leaves. It will be difficult to set up any type of surveillance on the place."

"Can we find out where those planes went. Any chance a flight plan would have been filed?" Kerry asked.

Coop said, "I doubt it, as they are only required under certain conditions. I'll check with a friend in the FAA."

"Customs and Border Protection might be able to help," Ryan said.

"Their flight tracking system monitors flights across the U.S. I'll hand this one to Scott. He's got the clout to gain access to their data."

Rising, Coop said. "Before I leave for my appointment with the district attorney, I have one other item." Anger crept into his tone. "I found out who recommended Moreland. A letter of recommendation from Harmon's attorney, Stuart Lane, was in her application file. That bastard planted her months ago, just waiting until he set his plan in motion."

Remembering his contact with the woman, Adrian interjected, "I'm not surprised. She was the perfect dupe."

Ryan walked to the map and studied the pin locations for several seconds, then glanced at Dan. "What are the yellow ones?"

"Has a house," Dan replied.

"Anyone know a good pilot," Ryan quipped. Nodding his head toward the map, "That's a lot of locations we need to look at and do it fast."

"As a matter of fact, I do," Mike replied. He headed to his office.

Kerry's phone chimed. Digging into her backpack, she pulled out the burner phone she still used to call the Shelton ranch. "Kerry," she answered.

"It's Luke. I've got information on Moore."

"Hold on, let me get a pad to write on." John slid one toward her. "Okay, what do you have?"

Luke said, "Calvin Moore was a Navy Seal, dishonorably discharged five years ago. He killed another Seal during an insertion training exercise. He claimed it was accidental, but the circumstances were suspicious. They couldn't prove the man's death was intentional, but that combined with his record was enough to get Moore kicked out. My contact knew him. He is cold-blooded and cruel, and everyone had to continually watch their back around him. If he didn't like you, accidents happened. Since then, there have been rumors he hired on as a mercenary. Now that I have a name, I'll dig deeper, see if I can find out who hired him."

Kerry had jotted down Luke's info and pushed the notepad toward Ryan. "Thanks, Luke, I hear you have a new addition to your household."

"The kid loves the puppy. He's named it Rex. Got to go, my other phone is ringing."

Mike walked in as Kerry disconnected. "We have additional information on Calvin Moore," she said and covered the details Luke had provided.

Mike said, "I'll put out a few feelers. I've got us a plane. It's at a small airport outside of town. Bruce Grayson's the pilot. Flew F-16s when he was in the military. A good man to have on your side and knows how to keep his mouth shut."

"Let's divide up the locations. The ones close by can be checked by car. Kerry and I will handle the others by plane," Ryan said.

"I need to stay here as I have a few more informants I want to locate. Maybe I can get a lead on Moore's location," Tim said.

It was agreed Mike would team with Dan and Adrian with John. Ryan left Kerry with the task to divide the sites as he stepped outside to call Scott.

When he answered, Ryan said, "There was another attempt to kidnap Kerry last night. We're certain it was Moore, and his first name is Calvin. He's a former Seal. Coop also found out Lane recommended Moreland."

"I take it Kerry is okay."

"Yeah, other than a cut on the head from a flying piece of concrete during an exchange of gunfire."

"Hmm ... sounds as if they are getting desperate. It's probably because the auction is scheduled for the day after tomorrow. Blake received confirmation from Dave Jenson."

Chills shot through Ryan. "Damn! We don't have much time left. Once those kids are sold, it will be nearly impossible to find them."

"I know, and I'm still convinced they are in Texas at one of Harmon's properties."

Ryan explained their plan to check the locations and added a request for flight data on the movement of Harmon's planes.

"I'll pass the information on Moore to Nicki. The meeting with the President is this evening."

I don't envy him, Ryan thought as he walked back into the conference room to pass on the bad news.

There was a moment of silence as everyone absorbed the implications of the auction deadline. Mike was the first to break it. His voice barked as if he still ordered a group of Marines. "Let's get the hell out of here. We have to find those kids."

❧

Nestled in a small valley surrounded by rocky hills, shrubs, and trees, the airport was a private field, with one runway. A couple of hangars and a small building with office printed over the door bordered one side. Inside, a man, gray-haired, his face seamed and wrinkled was seated at a desk. Rising to greet them, he barely topped Kerry.

After introducing themselves, Ryan explained they wanted to check several properties and spread a map on the desk marked with the locations. Bruce studied it for a few minutes, jotting details on a small pad he pulled from his pocket.

The plane was a single-engine Cessna that seated four people. Kerry opted for the back seat so she could spread out the map. Passing the first set of coordinates to Bruce, he programmed them into his flight navigator. As the plane rolled down the runway, her heart raced with a familiar sense of anticipation. She loved to fly and hoped one day to have the time to get a pilot's license.

As the plane lifted off, Ryan glanced over his shoulder, his eyes gleamed with pleasure as a broad grin crossed his face. A quick sense of a shared bond of joy briefly overshadowed the ominous reason for the flight.

Reaching the first location, Ryan asked Bruce to circle overhead before dropping for a closer view. An old farmhouse was flanked by empty fields. There were no cars or any sign the house was occupied. The pilot buzzed the top of the house. The front door and windows were boarded up.

Kerry crossed it off her list, gave Bruce the next set of coordinates and sent a text message to Mike and Adrian. It became the pattern for the trip. Every location was vacant, and more properties were eliminated as she received messages from the other teams.

The sun was sinking into the west when they turned to head back to the airport. Kerry's shoulders drooped from disappointment as she gazed out the window at the checkerboard pattern of fields, houses, and curving county roads. Nothing, where are they? What have we missed? All that remained were a couple outside El Paso. Wait, El Paso. Didn't Ryan say it was an agent in El Paso that found out about the auction?

Impatient, she had to wait until the pilot landed and taxied to the hangar. Exiting, they thanked Bruce and headed to Kerry's truck. Once they were far enough away so their conversation couldn't be heard, Kerry stopped and grabbed Ryan's arm. Excitement vibrated in her voice. "Who's in El Paso?"

Distracted by the warmth of her hand on his arm, his mind didn't connect to the question. "What?"

"You mentioned a contact in El Paso. Who is it?"

"An agent, Dave Jenson. He's the one who confirmed the auction. Why?"

"Don't you think it's odd an agent in El Paso came up with intel that no one else had found? Harmon owns properties in the El Paso area."

"Good Lord! You might be on to something. We need to learn more about those properties. Let's get back to your office."

As they reached the truck, Ryan caught a flicker of light from the low ridge of hills on the opposite side of the airport. Swiveling his head, it flicked again. "Sniper, get down!" Pushing Kerry to the ground, he dropped on top of her as a shot rang out.

Kerry crawled under the vehicle as Ryan shoved against her, pushing her backpack off her shoulder. A second round kicked up dirt and rocks a few feet from where his head had just been. Another shot, this one close to the tire.

Ryan wasn't sure what would happen if a round hit the gas tank, but getting trapped under the truck wasn't the way to find out.

Twenty-four

Washington, D.C.

Scott glanced at his watch. Time to leave. Picking up his file folders, he nodded to Nicki and Blake on his way out the door.

"I'm glad it's not me on the way to that meeting," Blake said.

Nicki sighed. "Amen."

A black limo waited in front of the building. A Secret Service agent stood at the rear door, ready to open it as Scott approached. Seated inside was FBI Director, Paul Daykin.

As Scott slid onto the seat, the Director greeted him, then said, "I thought it would be a good idea to talk before we met with President Larkin. Where do we stand on the investigation?"

Scott quickly recapped the known facts and his conclusions.

For a few seconds, Daykin was silent, a stunned look on his face. "Are you absolutely certain?"

"Yes, I am."

"Well, if you're wrong, your career just went into the dung heap. I hope you realize that."

A grim smile crossed Scott's face. "Only too well!"

"I'm getting a lot of pressure from the parents to know what is happening with the investigation. The desperation to do something is pushing them, especially since there has been no demand from the kidnappers. The media coverage has become rabid in their pursuit of information. I don't know how much longer I can keep them away from you."

Scott nodded. "I appreciate what you have done so far. I've been keeping an eye on the news, and it's getting vicious."

An agent escorted them into the White House. It was quiet, no hustle or bustle in the hallways. The lights were dimmed, and the silence was eerie. When he first joined the Bureau, he had taken a tour, but it didn't include the President's office. Now, striding down the hallway, knowing he was on the way to the Oval Office brought an unexpected level of anxiety.

When the agent reached a door, he tapped, then opened it motioning for them to enter. As Scott walked in, the historical significance overwhelmed his senses. Images of the presidents who had occupied the room filtered in his mind. The large desk prominently placed in front of the windows, the presidential seal on the rug, the elegant décor all combined to create a sense of elegance, power, and authority. Somehow, he had expected the room to be larger. Then he looked at the man seated behind the desk, and all thoughts of room size fled.

Though they had spoken on the phone, Scott had never met Arthur Larkin. Close to sixty years of age, he looked ten years younger and was the exception to the rule presidents aged quickly. At six-foot, one-eighty, with streaks of gray in the dark hair, he had a commanding presence. He stepped around the desk to shake hands with Scott.

A door opened, and the Secretary of Homeland Security, Vance Whitaker, walked in. After Whitaker greeted Scott and Daykin, the President motioned for Scott to take a seat in a chair. He and the other two men settled on the sofas. The fact he was seated in front of them didn't escape Scott's notice. *I'm the man in the hot seat.* Perched on the edge of his chair, unable to relax, the trepidation over the outcome of the meeting had his heart racing and nerves tingling.

Larkin said, "Scott, I've received several reports regarding your extraordinary ability in resolving difficult cases. I'm sure you are aware the carte blanche given to your new command is unprecedented in the history of the FBI. When Director Daykin first broached the concept for the Trackers unit, I must say I was skeptical, but his articulate arguments convinced me." The President stopped to look at Daykin, who smiled and nodded his head in agreement.

Turning back to Scott, Larkin said, "This current situation is unparalleled. Where do we stand on the investigation?"

Showtime—would he still have a job when he walked out the door? "Mr. President, I appreciate the confidence you have expressed in the Trackers. The team is extraordinary, and I believe has uncovered a remarkable amount of evidence that points to the mastermind behind this plot."

Scott had their attention as his gaze flicked from face to face. "I must insist the information is kept confidential. If any word of it leaks out, it will result in the death of the kidnapped children."

"Paul mentioned the same concern when I suggested the four Senators and Governor Simpson attend this meeting. Your concerns are noted. Go ahead with your briefing."

"I think it's best to recap the events that have occurred to ensure everyone's understanding." Starting with Kerry Branson, he detailed the events that had transpired.

Then, he moved to the findings of the team's research. "We didn't understand why there were no demands. Was there another reason for the abductions? Something that connected Murdock, Berkstrom, and Wademan? The only tie we found was their potential candidacy in the next presidential race. Then two more abductions and neither parent had any connection to the election. It could have been a major setback except for one reason. Agent Allison found a link between Senator Thompson and Governor Simpson."

He paused. Whitaker had leaned forward, his gaze unwavering as Scott continued, "It's a bill the Senator has sponsored to stop construction of the Danver pipeline through Utah. Having identified that, let me set it aside for a minute."

His voice incredulous, the President interrupted. "You actually believe the motive behind the kidnappings is a legislative bill and a remote possibility a senator might run for the presidency?"

Scott glanced at Daykin. The man slightly inclined his head—a nod of support.

"Yes, and if you bear with me, I'll connect the dots for you. The two houses that were destroyed were purchased by a company owned by, let me call him Mr. X for now. An attorney who had on multiple occasions defended the kidnapper murdered in Austin, was the attorney of record for the purchase of the properties. The county sheriff who searched the Shelton ranch and allowed one of the kidnappers to pose as a deputy received a hefty contribution to his campaign fund from this same attorney.

"The attorney also recommended the young woman we identified as the mole in the Austin FBI office. The woman kept her grandfather, who works for Mr. X, appraised of the details of the investigation. That information resulted in the attack and search of the Shelton ranch, the burglary of Kerry Branson's home and the attempts to kidnap her. The men involved are mercenaries, and Mr. X has vast overseas operations with an extensive, ex-military security force."

Scott paused again. The faces of the President and Secretary Whitaker held a look of astonishment. Daykin had settled back against the cushion with a stoic demeanor. He knew what was coming.

Continuing, Scott said, "We have identified an auction has been scheduled. There is considerable chatter on the wiretaps over the valuable commodities that will be sold. Today, we received confirmation from an undercover agent in one of the drug cartels. The auction is scheduled for the day after tomorrow, and several children will be sold. There is no doubt who the children are."

A soft whisper came from Whitaker. "Holy Hell!" The President darted a glance at him and nodded in agreement.

"As one of my agents so succinctly stated a couple of hours ago, once the children are sold, they will disappear and be impossible to find. The parent's personal lives will be devastated, and their professional actions discredited if people believe they can be controlled by whoever owns their child. The loss will effectively destroy their political careers."

Once again, he paused, looking each man in the eye. "I have come full circle to the reason Murdock, Berkstrom, and Wademan were targeted, and subsequently, Simpson and Thompson. A year ago, Mr. X was considered for his party's nomination for president. He needs the pipeline and will lose millions if it's not built.

"This is an intricate and complex plan, one that required money and resources. It took months to get all the pieces in place. There is only one person, at the hub of all the strands, who has the financial resources and connections to pull off such an elaborate plot. A plan that would eliminate his competition for a run for the presidency and stop a financial disaster."

Shifting to lean forward, the President looked at Scott in disbelief, and even a hint of trepidation as he asked, "Who ... is Mr. X?"

Scott's voice was flat and devoid of any emotion. "Mitchell Harmon."

Abruptly, Larkin stood and walked to a window. His hand rubbed the back of his neck as he stared at the garden landscape. Scott glanced at Daykin and Whitaker. Motionless, their gaze was fixed on the man who had just been dealt a devastating blow.

Turning, Larkin stared at Scott, his face stunned and confused. "How certain are you?"

"I am absolutely convinced Harmon is the mastermind. Every path leads back to him. We are continuing our search, and I expect to find additional evidence. Has he contacted you or asked any questions regarding the investigation?" Scott asked.

Larkin sighed, then said, "I've had a couple of calls since this began. The type we normally have. Two friends touching base with each other."

He paused, his eyes narrowed in concentration, then continued. "No, he didn't specifically ask about the kidnappings, but we did discuss the upcoming presidential race and any possible changes to the candidates for nomination. It didn't occur to me his questions were unusual as he is on the election committee. Now ... with what you have told me, yes ... he did seem to be fishing for information."

When the President paused again, Whitaker said, "I received a call from Mitch."

Larkin's attention swiftly shifted away from Scott as he asked, "What did he want?"

Whitaker looked at Scott and said, "Next month there is a conclave of governors in Austin." Turning his gaze to Larkin, he added, "Mitch knew I planned on attending the meeting and invited me to dinner."

Larkin asked the question that hovered on the tip of Scott's tongue. "Did you discuss anything else?"

"Yes. He mentioned the kidnappings, expressing sympathy for the parents and hoped the children would soon be found. At the time, it didn't seem strange, but under these circumstances, I must agree with your assessment, Mr. President—he was looking for information."

"What did you tell him?" Larkin asked.

"Thanked him for his concern, then declined the invitation, and we ended the call. Whatever he hoped to learn, he didn't get."

Scott asked, "How did he know you would be in Austin? Your travel schedule is never publicized."

"I assumed he heard about it from the President. None of the governors have been notified that I will be there."

"No, I didn't tell him," Larkin said. His gaze flicked between Daykin and Whitaker. "Opinions, gentlemen."

Daykin answered first. "I heard most of this in the car on our way here. I've had more time to evaluate Scott's information and conclusions. At first, I was skeptical, there had to be another explanation. After getting past my initial shock, and listening to the details again, I believe he is right. The pieces fit."

"I can't disagree," Whitaker said. "Your team has assembled an impressive amount of information in a short period, and I have to add his phone call to the list."

The President sank back onto the couch. Somehow, he seemed older as the man's fingers rubbed his forehead. "I've known Mitch since we were freshmen in college and have considered him one of my best friends. He's my daughter's godfather, for Christ's sake. This is beyond belief. I thought I knew the man, but apparently, somewhere he took a turn I didn't see."

"I am curious about something. Do you know why Harmon dropped off the radar for a run for the presidency?" Scott asked.

Larkin stared at him, his eyes widened. "Dear god, did I bring this about?" he muttered. His voice stronger, he said, "Yes. A year ago, I asked him to stand down. I believed and still do that he is the wrong candidate for the party nomination. I had several concerns. The major issue was his wealth from his oil and gas company and that it would work against him with the voters. I felt Murdock or Wademan would be the better choice."

"Sir, you didn't cause this. All the fault can be laid at the feet of an individual who believes he is above the law and is obsessed with obtaining the power of the Presidency." Scott never imagined he would be in the position of reassuring the President of the United States.

"Of course, you are right. It's hard to get past the years I've known him."

Standing, the brief bout of melancholy and disbelief had vanished. His gaze cold and hard. "What do you need?" the President asked.

"Access to the U.S. Custom and Border Protection flight tracking system. Harmon's planes have been flying at an unusual rate over the past week. If we can figure out where the planes went, we might find where the children were taken. As for the rest of the investigation, we are tracking every possible lead. I expect the next twenty-four to forty-eight hours will be critical. Let my team continue to do their job without interference," Scott said.

"All right. This is how we will handle it. Vance, considering the call you received, Harmon may have access to someone in your department. As of now, the investigation is classified as top secret."

Whitaker nodded in agreement as the President continued. "Get that flight data and assign a coordinator to interface with Scott's team. Make certain the person understands the details are top secret and not to be shared, even with their chain of command."

Turning to Scott, he said, "Contact Secretary Whitaker if you need access to any other agency's information. I know they don't like to divulge their secrets, but you'll have whatever you need. Notify me immediately of any new developments. Before you leave, you will receive a security code that will provide immediate access no matter where I am, even in the damn toilet. If you need any additional personnel or anything else, contact Director Daykin. Paul, he has top priority on any request."

Larkin gazed at Scott with anger and determination on his face. "Do whatever you believe is necessary to find those children. You have the full support of this office."

The meeting was over. Walking out the door, Scott thought, *one of my questions was answered. I still have my job.*

Alone in the limo on the way back to his office, he replayed the conversation. His heart still hadn't returned to normal, but for the first time since the notification of the Murdock kidnapping, he had a sense of optimism. Pulling his phone, he called Ryan. It rolled to his voicemail.

Twenty-five

Texas

Coughing from a nose full of dirt, Kerry said, "We have to get behind those boulders."

She scooted until she could crawl out the other side. Hunched over, arms wrapped around her backpack, she ran for cover, dropping to the ground behind a formation of large rocks on the edge of the property. Ryan fell beside her.

A shot rang out, seemingly from the office building, followed by another from the hillside. Then a deafening roar, and a ball of flames and black smoke erupted. Glass, metal, and engine parts rained down. Thick, pungent smoke filled the air and flames crackled that incinerated the remains of Kerry's truck.

Rage overwhelmed her. "You bastard!" she screamed.

Ryan's hand gripped her shoulder. Covered in dirt, his face bleak, he said, "We need to get to the back of the building."

They stepped over low bushes and weaved their way from tree to tree using the rocks to shield them. Sirens sounded as they rushed inside. Bruce was positioned by the front window with a rifle cradled in his arms. At the sound of the door, his head whipped around. His face sagged in relief. "I called 911, but thought you two were goners for sure. How'd you escape?"

Ryan started to explain when a deputy sheriff burst through the door, gun in hand. Not seeing a threat, he holstered his weapon and said, "Damn, Bruce, who'd you piss off?"

Motioning to Ryan and Kerry, he answered, "You need to talk to these two."

Ryan held up his badge case as he explained what happened.

The deputy pulled his radio, directing officers to search on the other side of the airfield.

Ryan turned to Bruce. "Did you see anyone?"

"Nah, without a scope, just shooting blind. Rocks blocked my view. All I could do was try to distract him."

"Well, we appreciate the cover fire," Kerry said.

"Been awhile since I got to shoot this old gun," he said, patting the side of the rifle. "It belonged to my dad. Damn good rifle." He hesitated, a look of uncertainty crossed his face. "There was one thing. Don't know if it means anything but that last shot sounded different."

Another deputy walked in. "Fire department's here. We found tracks behind a pile of rocks. Nothing else, not even a spent case. How many shots were fired?"

Kerry said, "Uh, I think four."

Ryan nodded in agreement.

"Whoever it was knew what he was doing since the cases are gone," the deputy said.

While Ryan finished up with the deputy, Kerry walked outside to watch the firemen. Water sizzled as dense sprays coated what was left. Thank god, they managed to hang onto their backpacks. At least they hadn't lost their laptops. The rest of her possessions could easily be replaced. The thought of how close they came, though, sent another surge of rage to burn inside her.

Ryan walked out, cell phone at his ear. Disconnecting, he said, "Adrian is on his way. By the time we get to BSI, Coop will have a vehicle waiting for you to use until we can get your truck replaced."

"How the hell do I explain this to my insurance company?"

"Look at it this way. Now you don't have to explain the bullet hole or the front-end damage." His feeble attempt at humor brought a weak smile to her face.

The remains of the gutted vehicle smoldered as the flames died away. One of the firemen walked up. "I was told this is your vehicle."

"Yeah, I guess what's left can be considered mine."

"It needs to cool overnight before you have it removed. Sounds like a close call for both of you."

A car pulled up, and Adrian exited. He stared at the burning vehicle and whistled. "I knew I didn't get the full story when you called me to pick you up."

"I'll fill you in on the details on the way back to town," Ryan said. Turning to the fireman, he asked, "Is there anything else you need from us?"

"No, Deputy Tate will be filing a report, so that should take care of it."

Kerry took a last, lingering look. The what-ifs sent shivers racing down her back. In the car, she leaned her head against the seat, shut her eyes and let her mind drift. Despite the dirt on her clothes and the stink of smoke that seemed permanently implanted in her nose, it felt good to relax. Adrenaline dumps, last night in the garage and again this afternoon, had started to take their toll. Arms and legs were beyond tired, her body felt heavy and lethargic. She needed a shot of caffeine to jump-start her system and debated whether to have Adrian stop so she could get a cup of coffee. *No, I'll wait until we get to BSI.*

Over her objections, Ryan was in the back. Leaning forward, he explained what happened.

"Any thoughts on how he found you?" Adrian asked.

"Kerry and I were watching for a tail on our way to the airport. If anyone had followed us, we'd have spotted him which leaves one other option. Someone put a tracking device on her truck. Would have been easy to do."

At the sound of her name, she tuned back into the conversation. *A tracking device, hell, I should have thought of that.*

"Ryan's right, it's the only explanation," she said.

"Which brings me to another concern. This time, it wasn't a kidnapping attempt, it was to kill you," Adrian said.

For a few seconds, the only sound was the hum of the engine. "Holy hell, and I thought my biggest problem was to keep them from grabbing me. What changed?"

"Good question," Adrian said.

Ryan leaned back. "Harmon's band of mercenaries wouldn't do anything without orders. He doesn't pay them to think. And if they don't follow orders, well, look what happened to Bullman."

He paused, a furrow crossed his forehead, as he pondered the complication. "I suspect he's written off any further attempts to get Tristan back."

"That's all well and good, but why kill me?"

"You interfered, screwed up his plan and that can't be tolerated. This is a psychopathic individual, without normal emotions, who is obsessed with becoming the next President. He will kill or destroy anyone who gets in his path. You got in the way."

A bleak look settled over Kerry's face. *How do I avoid the next attempt?* Her phone chimed. Tim's icon was on the screen.

He said, "I just talked to one of my drug informants. Word on the street is a contract has been put out on an ex-cop and an FBI agent. The man didn't have names, only that it was big bucks. It doesn't take a rocket scientist to figure out it's you and Ryan."

"Someone has already tried to collect. My truck is toast," she said, then explained what happened.

"Where are you now?"

"Adrian picked us up, and we're headed to BSI."

Saying he'd see her there, he rang off. Sticking the phone in her pocket, she turned her head to look at Ryan. A smirk on her face, she said, "That was Tim. There's a contract out to kill me ... and you. Guess Harmon doesn't like you either."

Walking through the front door of BSI, the tantalizing aroma of pepperoni drifted in the air.

"Praise be to the gods, someone ordered pizza," Adrian exclaimed.

Inside the conference room, pizza boxes covered the table. Dan, John, Tim, Coop, and Mike chomped on huge slices, heaped with cheese.

"Hope you saved some for us," Kerry quipped.

Motioning with a half-eaten slice with yellow strands hanging over the edge, "I think there's one small box at the end of the table." Mike joked back, though his eyes were filled with concern as he scanned her and then Ryan from head to toe.

Ryan and Adrian grabbed a paper plate and piled on several pieces before sitting at the end of the table.

"I'm going to wash my hands and face, so somebody had better make sure there are a few pieces left when I get back," she said as she glared at the circle of men around the table. With a pointed look at Ryan, whose clothes and face was covered in dirt, she added, "Unlike some people, I like to have clean hands to eat," and marched out of the room.

Mike looked at Ryan and Adrian and grinned. "Drinks are in the cooler against the wall. Tim filled us in on what happened and the contract on both of you. We need to come up with a plan."

"I haven't heard all the details," Cooper said. "Tell me what happened, then I've got new information for you."

Between bites, Ryan covered the details of the shooting, the loss of Kerry's truck, and his theory on Harmon's motives.

Kerry walked in as Ryan finished. Looking at her, he said, "I brought everyone up to date on what happened." His phone chimed. It was his boss. Stepping into the hallway, he quickly relayed the details of the attempt on their lives.

Kerry shoved a slice of pizza on a plate and sat next to Mike. She kept an eye on Ryan through the open door as she ate. While she couldn't hear his comments, when a stunned look crossed his face, she knew something had happened. *God, what is the bad news now?*

Pocketing the phone, he walked in and announced, "The President gave us the green light. Whatever action we need to take, he'll back us," as he explained the outcome of Scott's meeting with the President.

"I don't know which is more astonishing, a sniper after your hide or the President green-lighting our activity," Adrian said.

Ryan quipped back. "Personally, I opt for the sniper."

Adrian chuckled. "Yeah, I can see how you would think that."

"Dang, that's some heavyweight support your boss got," Mike exclaimed. "So, where do we go with it?"

Grabbing a can from the cooler, Ryan sat back down and pushed aside his empty plate. Popping the lid, he took a swig, then said, "Kerry came up with a theory I believe has merit. The only confirmation on the auction so far is from an agent in El Paso."

Ryan motioned toward the map, saying, "Harmon owns three properties there. The kids could be at one of them. Scott is contacting the Border Patrol to see if there is any record of flights in and out of Harmon's property in the tracking system."

Turning to Coop, he asked, "Do you have someone who can keep an eye on Harmon's estate. If another plane takes off, we need to make sure it's being tracked. Same with the jet at the other airport."

"I'll set up a rotation of agents starting tonight. Also, the FAA had nothing on any flight plans," Coop said.

Ryan said, "If one moves, notify Blake. He'll coordinate with the Border Patrol personnel. I wish we had someone inside Harmon's estate who could let us know who is on those planes, especially if it is Harmon. With this man's ego, he'll want to be near the site of the auction."

Mike said, "Hmm … let me contact the gardener. I got the impression he disliked Harmon. He might be willing to get us the information. I'll toss in a hefty bribe to help encourage him."

"If you think there is a possibility, he'll go to Harmon, back off. I don't want to jeopardize the kids. Harmon tried to take Kerry and me out because we got in his way. Imagine what would happen to the children if he even gets a hint we suspect him."

Turning to John, he said, "See what you and Dan can find on the El Paso properties, aerials, floor plans, security systems. I'll call Dave Jenson, he's the agent stationed there and bring him in on this. I'd like to get pictures of any of the structures that might be a possible location."

"What about the contract on you and Kerry? There's no telling who could come after you," Tim said.

Kerry tossed her paper plate in the trash. "There's nothing we can do, except watch our backside, and not get caught in a position where someone can take a shot at us."

"You need one of us following you wherever you go. I suggest Adrian, and I take on that job," Tim said.

"He's right. One of us needs to tag along behind you, and it would help if you stayed together," Adrian said with a hint of a smirk on his face that earned him a glare from Ryan.

Coop said, "The D.A. added two more names to our suspect list. T.J. Webb and Bart Matthews. Both have been represented by Stuart Lane on several criminal offenses, assaults and drug possession. According to the D.A., he's not a full-time defense attorney, only the three clients, these two and Boyd."

Cooper picked up his briefcase next to his chair. Flipping open the locks, he pulled out two photographs. "Mugshots and physical description from the last time they were arrested."

Mike picked up the pictures and studied them, then passed them on so the others could examine them. He said, "T.J. Webb, the name rings a bell, but I can't place it, and I don't recognize him. I'll make a few calls before I leave."

Tim said, "When you're ready, let me know, and I'll follow you. Adrian can keep an eye on Ryan and Kerry."

Mike nodded. "Appreciate the backup."

Snapping a picture of the two men with his cell phone, Ryan shot them off to Nicki and Luke, explaining his action to the others.

Kerry replied, "Good idea. Luke might recognize them. Now, I'm headed to the hotel for a shower and clean clothes. Then I'll come back and help with the research."

"Let's go," Ryan said.

A set of keys slid down the table. "A black SUV is parked behind the building. One of those keys unlocks a case with a rifle, tactical gear, and ammunition. Doesn't replace your truck, but will give you wheels until then," Coop said.

"Thanks. I'll try to get it back to you in one piece," she said and grinned.

Twenty-six

Washington, D.C.

The Secret Service agent opened the door, stepping back to allow Scott to exit the vehicle. He thanked him and headed to the front door.

"Good luck, sir."

Scott stopped, turned, and their eyes met. The young man nodded before sliding into the passenger seat of the limo. Scott watched the vehicle as the driver pulled away from the curb. *Protection agents are like servants, no secrets, they know everything.*

When he walked into the office, the sympathetic look on Blake's face made him wonder if he looked as drained as he felt.

"We got the full approval of the President and access to the flight tracking system. Where's Nicki?"

Blake's expression changed to a gleam of satisfaction as he said, "Catching a few zzz's on the couch in the breakroom. There's a pot of fresh coffee, and I ordered deli sandwiches. They're in the refrigerator."

As he headed along the hallway, Scott made a mental note of another need for their new office, a couple of good sofas and a small kitchen.

The internet, communication technology, and computers had changed the complexion of investigations. While fieldwork was still a fundamental and essential element, investigators skilled in manipulating and mining the internet and its proliferation of data, now played an even more prominent role. The days of a lone detective pounding the pavement in search of clues was gone. High tech was the name of the game, and it meant long hours for the individuals involved.

Nicki and Blake had worked this investigation almost 24/7, catching a few hours' sleep when they could. Gazing at the woman stretched out on the couch, her arm draped across her face, he knew he had one of the best in the business.

The clink of the glass coffee pot, sent her feet flying as she sat up. Dazed, she stared around the room. Seeing Scott, she yawned and rubbed her eyes. "Well, boss man, I see you survived your trip into the netherworld of politics. How'd it go with the big guy?"

"Green light all the way."

"Dang, glad to hear it. I gave you a fifty-fifty chance considering our prime suspect." Greedily eyeing the one in his hand, she asked, "Where'd you get a sandwich?"

Her light relief was what Scott needed. "In the frig, grab one, and then I want a meeting with you and Blake."

He glanced at his watch as he walked into his office. Ryan hadn't called him back. Setting the cup and foiled wrapped sandwich on the desk, Scott tapped his phone. When Ryan answered, he listened to what transpired at the airport. Alarm and apprehension rolled through his system, tying his insides into the knot which never seemed to completely go away as he processed the implications. Harmon had just ramped up the stakes.

While Ryan brought him up to date on the investigation and Kerry's theory on El Paso, Scott jotted notes on his notepad. Before ending the call, he relayed the results of the meeting with the President.

His coffee and sandwich forgotten, he walked into the bullpen area. "More bad news in Texas."

As he listened to the details, Blake was the first to make the connection. "Harmon's changed the game plan."

Scott said, "Yeah, he has. Nicki, find out every detail you can, no matter how small, on Harmon's properties in El Paso. I believe Kerry is onto something. Blake, contact Dave, I want him fully in the loop."

"I just got off the phone with him. His contact called, and the news isn't good."

"How can it get any worse?" Scott muttered to himself.

"The man's boss received a notification of the other bidders, which includes eight terrorist cells operating in the Middle East and South America, in addition to a list of the largest drug cartels. Harmon is letting everyone know who their competition is, and they had better be prepared for high bids."

"Is it still set for Saturday?"

"Yes, the notice included the time, twenty-two hundred hours, along with payment instructions. Dave's worried. The agent said Eduardo Munoz, head of the cartel, is getting suspicious of the agent's questions. The agent is pushing hard for information, maybe too hard, and it could cost him his life."

Nicki's phone chimed. "It's a text from Ryan." She scrolled down the screen. "We've got two more suspects. He sent pictures and names of two men Stuart Lane defended." She swiveled her chair to face the computer.

Scott sat in a chair at one of the empty desks. His mind hummed as thoughts raced. A pen pulled from his pocket tapped the desk.

Nicki said, "Both men were dishonorably discharged from the military and work for Harmon as security guards."

Another link dropped into place. Abruptly, he stood, "Blake, call Dave. Set up an emergency extraction of the agent. I'll handle the coordination on this end. I should be getting a call from the Border Patrol with a contact name. I want you to take the lead on tracking the flights, so Nicki can concentrate on El Paso. Any questions?"

When both agents shook their heads no, he glanced at the clock. The emotionless tone belied the grim look on his face, "We don't have many hours left."

His first call was to Will Cooper.

"Will, it's Scott Fleming." He explained the latest intel from the El Paso agent.

Coop replied, "We're running out of time, and we still don't have a location. My agents are watching the planes. If any move, we'll know it."

"If we find a location that looks promising, I want Ryan and the team he has assembled sent to El Paso. What do you need to get it done?" Scott asked.

"I can get us there. I've got a plane and will have the pilots on standby. I'm not sure what we'll need in the way of transportation, depends on where the property is located. Do you want me to coordinate it?"

"No, let Dave handle it. My biggest concern is to minimize the people in the know. The more that are involved, the greater the chance of a leak."

"Ryan expressed the same concern. I've taken extra precautions to ensure Moreland has no opportunity to learn any of the details. Harmon knows the BSI personnel are involved, but nothing we've done would trigger any concern on his part and make him believe we're onto him," Coop said.

"Well, let's hope we can keep it that way."

"We suspect a tracking device was on Kerry's truck. Both were certain they hadn't been followed. Oh, by the way, if you haven't talked to Ryan, there's a contract out on them."

"When I heard of the attack, I suspected Harmon had shifted gears. If you think of anything else you need, call me," Scott said.

His second call was to Ryan.

"I hear there's a contract on your head."

"Now, how did you find out?"

"Cooper told me."

"Ah, so he let that one out of the bag. I hadn't intended on telling you."

"I figured as much," Scott countered, then covered the gist of his conversation with Cooper.

As Scott hung up the phone, he realized events were moving beyond his grasp. In a few hours, it would be entirely in the hands of Ryan and his team, and two of them had a bounty on their head.

Texas

The shower and clothes that didn't smell of smoke had improved Kerry's frame of mind. As she parked behind BSI, Ryan pocketed his phone. "So ... he found out about the contract," she said.

"Yeah, from Coop. In the short time I've worked for Scott, I've learned not much gets by him."

A tap on the window and Ryan's door opened. "You might want to consider continuing your conversation inside, where it is a lot safer," Adrian said. He had followed them to the hotel and back.

Walking into the conference room, they saw the pizza boxes had disappeared and been replaced by a large map of West Texas. John was bent over, studying a section that included El Paso. Dan was attaching aerial maps to the corkboard.

Ryan dropped his backpack on a table by the door. "Webb and Matthews both work for Harmon as security guards."

"Now, isn't that interesting," Dan said.

Kerry asked, "Has anyone heard from Mike or Tim?"

"Not yet, and Coop's at his office setting up surveillance," John answered. Motioning toward the aerials, "These are the three locations from the list Nicki sent. They are large ranches, and each have a house."

Kerry stepped to the corkboard and examined the maps. Anyone of them would be an ideal location. "Do we know if anyone is living in them?" she asked.

"Not yet. I'm searching utility accounts for water, gas or electric. It will take time," John said.

Eyeing him, Kerry wasn't about to ask how he had gained access to the utility database. John could hack most any system though he seldom was called on to use those particular skills.

Ryan had stepped next to her, "Utilities, good idea. It would be the fastest way to eliminate a location. Anything I can do to help?"

Caught off guard, John stammered, "Uh … no … uh, don't think so. Being a fed, it's better if you weren't involved."

Ryan stared at him for a few seconds, then said, "Tell you what, let's agree what happens in this room stays in this room," and grinned.

A look of relief crossed John's face. "Deal!"

"So, what happens if we find a location," Kerry asked.

"We go get them," Coop said as he walked through the door.

Surprised, the BSI personnel stared at him.

"When you say we, do you mean all of us?" Kerry asked after a few seconds of silence.

"Yep. Fleming doesn't want to bring in any other personnel for fear word will get back to Harmon. So that leaves it up to us. I've already arranged to have a plane on standby. The official reason is to get Adrian back to Washington, and that's how the flight plan will be filed. Once we take off, the pilot will divert to El Paso."

"He's right. I got the same from Scott just a few minutes ago," Ryan said.

Coop added, "We're to coordinate with Dave on what we need for transportation."

Ryan's phone chimed. "It's Jenson," and stepped out of the room.

"Ryan, Blake called and filled me in on the details of your investigation. What do you need from me?" Dave asked.

"We know Harmon owns three properties outside of town. If we can identify a possible location, we'll be on a plane. Do you have the addresses?"

"Blake sent them."

"Any information you can provide would be helpful, especially floor plans and security systems. We'll also need transportation, vans, maybe even helicopters. I can't be more precise until we have the location pinpointed."

"I can get what we need from Ft. Bliss. I'm friends with the base commander."

Ryan said, "If you do encounter any opposition, let Scott know. He's got the backing of the President for anything we need."

"Blake didn't mention that interesting tidbit. I'll keep it in mind, but it shouldn't be a problem."

Back in the conference room, John had headed to his office, saying he would be searching databases if anyone needed him. Kerry, along with Coop, Dan and Adrian were studying the maps.

Kerry turned as Ryan pulled out a chair. "Anything new?" she asked.

"Dave's on board. Whatever we need he can get from Ft. Bliss."

"Good, then all we need is to come up with a game plan."

"Game plan? Now, what's happened?" Mike asked as he walked in followed by Tim.

Kerry explained, then asked what happened with the contact with Harmon's gardener.

"Well, I didn't need to bribe him. He already knew Harmon planned to leave though he didn't know when or where. Seems he is friends with the chef who was told to cancel the menu for the weekend. The only reason a menu is canceled is when Harmon is gone. Anyone want to take a bet he may be headed to El Paso?"

"No, I won't take any part of that action," Adrian said, and the others nodded in agreement.

Coop's phone rang. "When?" He listened, then asked, "Could you tell who was on board?" Disconnecting, he said, "A helicopter just lifted off. It turned west."

Ryan tapped the speed dial for Blake and passed on the flight info.

Mike said, "It can't be headed to El Paso, too far for the range of most helicopters without refueling. So, where is it going?"

John walked in. "We've got a problem, none of the locations in El Paso have the utilities turned on."

Kerry's heart dropped, a sinking feeling of disaster turned her face bleak as she looked at Ryan. His face mirrored her emotions.

"Did we get this wrong?" she asked.

The mood in the room turned solemn. Ryan looked at the clock. Less than thirty-six hours until the start of the auction.

Twenty-seven

Washington, D.C.

Scott choked down pieces of his sandwich with sips of cold coffee. The food sat like a lead ball in his stomach. Hearing Blake's voice on the phone, he tossed the remains in the trash and headed into the bullpen.

"What have we got?" he asked as soon as Blake hung up.

Hearing the explanation, he exclaimed, "A helicopter. Can they track it?"

"It's doubtful."

"Have they come up with any flights over the last week."

"Frank said they are still searching. He hopes to let us know one way or the other within the next couple of hours."

Nicki's phone rang. "It's Ryan." Listening, her shoulders drooped, and a look of distress crossed her face. When she hung up, she said, "The three properties in El Paso are a bust, none have the utilities connected. Ryan plans to have Dave run a visual as soon as it is daylight, but right now they appear to be vacant—another dead end."

Scott glanced at the clock.

Texas

"God, where do we go from here," Kerry asked.

219

"Maybe the Border Patrol will find a flight in their archived data. Other than that, I don't have a clue," Ryan said.

A phone rang. *Dang, it's the burner. Now, where'd I put it*, patting her pockets? When she answered, Luke said, "Kerry, around three years ago, Calvin Moore formed a mercenary team comprised of ex-military buddies, and they hired out to a drug cartel in Columbia. Webb and Matthews are part of his crew. Both were kicked out of the military for a variety of charges, along with four others, Stan Barton, Donald Grimes, Creel Jones, and Jack Davis. Word is, they would do anything for money and were vocal about their dislike of the government. A year ago, they dropped off the radar. My contact figured they had been killed."

Kerry had rapidly written the names. "Thanks, Luke, this helps more than you know. How is Tristan?"

"Oh, he and the damned dog are joined at the hip, inseparable, but he doesn't have any more nightmares. It's worth the wet spots that have popped up around the house. Hey, watch your backside. These guys are very bad news."

"I know." She wasn't about to tell him she was already a target. Cindy would call every hour to make sure Kerry was okay.

"Moore is the leader of a mercenary team, and here's a list of their names," she said and pushed the notepad to Ryan. "We know two of them, Webb and Matthews, are working for Harmon," as she added the rest of Luke's information.

"Let me have the list. I'll send the names to Nicki," Adrian said.

"I bet it was some of Moore's team on the helicopter. From what the prostitute said, we know at least three were in town," Coop added.

No one wanted to leave even though the investigation had hit a major roadblock. Ryan headed to the break room. His system needed caffeine. He stopped in the doorway of John's office. *Damn if it doesn't mirror Nicki's computer setup. I need to get them together. It would be a match made in heaven*, Ryan thought as he surveyed the multiple computers and printers on tables shoved together. John was back on his computer and focused on whatever was scrolling across the screen. Not wanting to break his concentration, Ryan continued down the hall.

Grabbing a cup, he filled it with the remains of a pot that was probably several hours old. At least it was still hot, he hated cold coffee.

Leaning against the counter, he contemplated the latest events. Had they missed a lead, was there another angle they could pursue. His gut was a quivering ball of fear at the possibility they had taken a wrong turn. The consequences were unthinkable. Maybe he needed to approach this from another direction. *I'm a profiler for god's sake. So, get into Harmon's head, figure out what and why.*

Closing his eyes, his mind drifted back to the meeting with the man. He had picked up on the arrogance, the sense of superiority. Power and money let him do whatever he damn well pleased, and he didn't believe he could be touched. He had built a billion-dollar business on cold, calculated plans. The elaborate kidnapping plot would have been constructed using the same methodical process. He would need locations, personnel, and a communications network.

He forms LPJ and buys properties. *Um ...I wonder when and how many properties were purchased by the company.* Pulling his phone, he tapped Nicki's number.

"Hey, tell me you've got something good because it's looking dismal on our end," Nicki said.

"Not yet, but I'm working on it. I need two pieces of information. When was LPJ set up, and how many properties were purchased?"

"I'll get back to you."

Picking up his coffee, he took a sip. Damn, it's cold. As he set the machine to brew another pot, he considered the other criteria Harmon needed. Personnel, someone, and more than one, with the skills and knowledge to pull off kidnappings and set up the auction. He hires a team of mercenaries who worked for the drug cartels. They would know the ins and outs of the underground drug network and how to contact prospective buyers. He puts Moore in charge of the operation.

Another call to Nicki. "Can you find out what Moore and his band of thugs did in the military?"

"Your brain must be working overtime."

With his power and influence, Harmon could easily keep track of the investigation. He plants a young woman in the local FBI office, who unwittingly passes on the details. He has access to the President and other high-ranking government officials that he can tap for information. Once everything is in place, Harmon sets his plan in motion.

Tristan is kidnapped and taken to the house in East Texas. The Wademan girl is next and ends up in the same house. Then Tristan escapes, and the whole plan goes awry. They had to move to another location when they found out Kerry picked up the boy. It was only a matter of time before someone put two and two together and came looking for the house. Which meant there was an alternate plan in place, maybe several. If I were Harmon, I'd have multiple locations ready, just in case. I'd want to keep all the children together as it would limit the number of guards. Since Moore and his band are still in Austin, it must mean the kids are close, so why not hold the auction here?

He rubbed a hand across his forehead. Were they totally wrong in their theory, was Austin the site for the auction and not El Paso? Why take a chance on moving them?

The machine beeped. Pouring a cup, he took a sip, savoring the heat that flowed down his throat.

His phone rang. Nicki said, "LPJ was set up a month before the house in East Texas was purchased. Since then, the company has acquired seven more properties. Four around Austin and the three near El Paso. Nothing yet on the military background request. It will take longer."

"Was one the property at Lytton Springs?"

"Yeah, it was."

"Send me the address of the other three properties near Austin."

Ryan's mind kept revolving back to the El Paso connection. Why there? No, they weren't wrong. Ryan knew it deep in his gut. Suddenly, the pattern he was looking for emerged in his mind. El Paso was a perfect choice. Harmon had to consider how to move the product. Shipping was a huge component of his oil and gas business.

El Paso connected to Ciudad Juarez, Mexico. The two cities formed the largest metropolitan area on the border between the U.S. and Mexico. It was the gateway for narcotics flowing into the U.S. and known as the El Paso/Juarez Corridor. With the daily movement of people and vehicles crossing the international bridges, drug traffickers had unlimited opportunities to move their products. What better place to hold an auction and then immediately smuggle the children into Mexico.

If that's the plan, was there another property. One they hadn't found. And if there was another property, was there another company? He tapped a quick text to Nicki—'other companies at same time as LPJ?'

Excitement flushed the despair from his system. Moore's next step would be to get the children to El Paso. The best time to transport them would be during the night, and most likely they would use a van, enclosed so no one could see what was inside. It would be too difficult by plane. If they had a problem, it was a lot easier to pull to the side of the road, than to find a place to land. No, the men wouldn't want to be cooped up with four kids in a small plane. If the helicopter had Moore's men on board, did it mean they were getting ready to move? So, how do we find where?

Washington, D.C.

Feet propped on his desk, Scott glanced at his watch. A sense of helplessness pushed his emotions into a state of despair. It was a strange sensation, and one he had never experienced in an investigation. His two agents pounded their keyboards and made phone calls. There was nothing he could do except stay out of their way and let them do their job. When he heard Nicki talking to Ryan, he couldn't stand the isolation of his office any longer. He had to know.

When footsteps sounded behind her, she turned in her seat. "Ryan's gone into overdrive, he's got something working. He's made two calls wanting to know about LPJ's acquisitions and what Moore's men did in the military."

"Hmm … interesting," he said, stepping to a chair at a nearby desk. Tilted back, Scott propped his feet on the surface and pondered Ryan's questions. When Nicki relayed what she had found, it started a new train of thought, examining the logistics of a complicated operation. Unknowingly, his mind moved along the same track as Ryan's.

"Nicki, were any other companies formed at the same time as LPJ?" Scott asked.

"I don't know. I just got a text message from Ryan asking the same question. I'm cross-checking my data results, but it will take a few minutes to find out." She opened another screen on her computer and accessed a file folder. Scanning the entries, she stopped at one toward the bottom of the list. Clicking on the title, she opened the company's profile.

"I'll be damned. SynDike, Inc., was set up in the same month as LPJ."

"Any assets?"

"I'm looking."

Blake's phone rang. Nicki stopped to listen to his conversation.

"Are you sure," Blake asked. "Okay, thanks for the info."

"That was Frank from the Border Patrol. The helicopter wasn't up long enough to get a lock and track it. He found two flights this week that originated from the vicinity of Harmon's estate. One dropped off at a small airfield near Edmund, Oklahoma. The date coincides with the abduction of Wademan's daughter. The other was to Utah, same scenario. Both were small aircraft. The flights didn't trigger an alarm for possible drug or terrorist activity, so there was no follow-up."

Blake paused, tilted his chair back as he mused, "A small airplane could get the team to each location, grab the kid, and be out of the area quickly. Buy an abandoned rural farm with a house like the one in East Texas, land at any nearby small airport, many of which don't even have a control tower, transfer the kid to a waiting car, and be back in the air. Easy and relatively undetectable."

"Call Ryan and let him know," Scott said.

Nicki turned back to her computer. "SynDike owns a Cessna aircraft, purchased shortly after the corporation was formed. I don't have any other assets listed, but I bet the company owns property in El Paso." Her fingers flew over the keyboard.

He knew his agents were onto something. A sense of optimism slowly crept into his mind. They weren't dead in the water yet.

Texas

Armed with three addresses, Ryan strode into the conference room.

Dan stared at the aerials. Tim and Mike had slid down in their chairs, eyes closed, and Adrian and Coop were in a conversation on drug trafficking.

"We may have a lead," Ryan said. His words immediately energized everyone around the table.

Examining the aerial map with the push pins, he asked, "Dan, where are these three addresses." As he relayed each, Dan located it on the map.

"Were all three locations checked?" Ryan asked.

"Yeah, Mike and I checked two and John and Adrian the third. They were all vacant. Why?"

"It's what I expected," but before he could explain his phone beeped. A sharp tingle of anticipation surged through him. "Blake, what did you find?"

Blake put him on the speakerphone. Once he had relayed the flight information he had uncovered, Nicki's voice echoed in the background as she told him about SynDike.

I'm on the right track! Ryan thought. "I think the kids are still in the Austin area, and they'll be moved tomorrow night. There must be other properties we haven't located. One in the Austin area, and one in El Paso."

Scott's voice said, "We've come to the same conclusion. So far, Nicki hasn't found them."

Nicki said, "If it is a recent acquisition, it may be why they're not listed as an asset. I'm searching the county tax records, but it will take time."

"I have another option. I'll get back to you." Ryan was about to make the biggest gamble of his career, which location to go after. They had only a few hours to find the Austin location. By the time, they got to the property, the kids could be gone. No, it made sense to go for the El Paso location. But if he was wrong, they wouldn't get a second chance.

Heading down the hall, he walked into John's office. "Can you search the El Paso databases by name?"

"Yeah, but it takes longer as the address is the primary key used to identify a property."

"Look for SynDike, Inc., or Calvin Moore."

"SynDike?"

"Another company formed at the same time as LPJ."

"I'm on it."

Behind him, Kerry asked, "Did you come up with something new?" She had been asleep on the couch in the reception area, and the voices woke her.

"Yes, let's go back to the conference room, and I'll let everyone know."

Over the next several minutes, Ryan covered the profile he had mentally developed, adding the information from Nicki and Blake.

Coop said, "It makes perfect sense to use El Paso."

"I suggest we all get some sleep. This may be our last chance," Ryan said.

"Is everything set?" the toneless voice asked.

"Yes, my men are in place," Moore answered.

"The arrangements on the other end, are they finalized?"

"The shipment will arrive at the new location early Saturday morning. Each parcel will be ready to ship upon conclusion of the sale on Saturday night.

"Have the buyers been notified."

"The final notification was sent a few hours ago."

"Call when you arrive at your destination. Put out the word the price has doubled on the contract."

Moore pocketed the phone. The thought of what happened at the airport reignited his rage. They should be dead and would be if he'd used the RPG first instead of his rifle. But he wanted to watch, to relish the sight of the bitch's head in his scope as he pulled the trigger. He didn't understand how the agent knew he was on the ridge, or even how they got out from under the truck when he fired off the rocket grenade.

Still, two million bucks. Their escape wasn't such a bad deal after all. No, he'd keep this to himself. Since everything was set for the transfer, he had time. He'd take Creel with him. The two of them could easily eliminate Branson and Barr.

Twenty-eight

Ryan had stretched out on a couch in the waiting room. A hand shook his shoulder, and John's voice vibrated with excitement. "I found the property. The utilities were turned on a month ago under C. Moore."

"Where!" he exclaimed. Jumping up, he winced from the soreness in his body.

"Fifty miles west of El Paso. I have an aerial map in the conference room."

"Damn good work," Kerry said. As she slid off another couch, she groaned. At the questioning looks from Ryan and John, she explained, "Sore from yesterday. I hate to think about how many bruises I've got. I'll get the others."

The map with the push pins had been replaced with the aerial map of a section of West Texas. Surveying it, Ryan called Scott who answered on the first ring.

When he heard the news, Scott asked, "How'd he find it?"

"Uh, sure you want to know?" Ryan said.

"Okay, no more questions on that one. What's your next step?"

"Set up a tactical plan to extract the children, but we need floor plans. I'll contact Dave and ask if he can get a set."

Disconnecting, his next call was to Dave.

"Jenson." His voice was groggy from sleep.

"We've got a location."

His tone instantly alert, he asked where. Ryan relayed the address along with a request for floor plans.

"Whatever I can get, I'll send to you. It may take a few hours."

"Contact your friend at the base and ask for three helicopters and pilots. Tell him you need them for a training exercise and will get back to him later today on a location. Find a remote place where we can stage. We need at least two or three vehicles. We'll bring the tactical equipment with us. Will Cooper has a plane on standby to get us there. I'll let you know as soon as we have a timeline."

"If you need any extra help, I have several agents I trust."

"Since I don't know what we'll need in personnel, I'll get back to you on that one."

As the team members shuffled into the conference room, faces were tired, but their eyes held a gleam of hope.

"What have we got?" Mike asked.

Pointing to the map, John said, "It's a ten-thousand-acre ranch located west of El Paso with a large farmhouse and several outbuildings. Utilities are under Moore's name."

Certain they had found the location for the auction, a surge of exhilaration rushed through Kerry. As she looked around the room, the fatigue had vanished, replaced by an intent look of excitement.

They crowded around the corkboard to study the aerial view of the ranch.

"It will be damn difficult to breach, but at least it's not on a busy highway. I suspect there's not much traffic in that section of the desert," Mike said.

"I don't know about anyone else, but I need coffee to jump-start my brain," Dan said and headed the breakroom.

Kerry's phone rang. She followed Dan out the door as she answered. It was Luke.

"Seth and I are in town. Where are you?"

Puzzled, she said, "At BSI. What are you doing here?"

"Cindy's worried and insisted I check on you. Since I had a trip scheduled for next week to handle some business in Austin, I moved it up. We'll be there in a few minutes."

Stepping back into the room, she said, "Luke Shelton and his brother are on their way here."

Mike nodded, then said, "I wish we could get a sniper on this ridge to give us eyes on the place," and pointed to a section of rocks that jutted above the landscape. "I don't see any way we can get someone up there in time."

"Is there a place on the other side of the highway where someone could set-up?" Ryan asked.

"I'll print the map for that section," John said and headed out the door.

Adrian asked, "What about floor plans?"

Ryan said, "I asked Dave to get us a set."

Dan walked in with a pot of coffee and set it on the hot plate Kerry had dug up in the storeroom. Pouring a cup, he asked, "So, where are we?"

"Trying to decide if we can get someone in place for surveillance," Coop answered.

Kerry's phone rang. It was Luke, his voice tight with urgency. "I'm headed to your front door. Open it, someone's watching the building."

Racing to the door, she flipped open the lock. Two men, their hats pulled low over their faces, rushed inside.

Luke said, "Let's move out of this area. There's a man across the street."

Everyone had stepped into the hallway. Moving back to the conference room, Tim asked, "What happened?"

Luke said, "We came around the block, and our lights picked up a guy behind the shrubbery in front of the building across the street. He ducked back as we passed. I left the truck parked on a side street, and we walked here. Didn't want to leave it in the parking lot where someone could run a check on it and find out who we are. We kept our heads down, so it's doubtful he would have gotten any pictures."

"Good thinking," Mike said.

Tim said, "I'll notify dispatch and get a squad car out here."

In the conference room, Kerry introduced Luke and his brother Seth, then asked, "Is Tristan all right?"

"He's okay. Cindy's worried, that's all. I left Butler guarding the homestead. He drew the short straw." He grinned at his brother, then scanned the room. His eyes locked on the aerial map. "Need any help?" he asked with a hopeful note in his voice.

"Yes, we do," Ryan said. Seeing the doubt on Coop's face, he added, "Luke and Seth are former Seals."

Pointing to the map, Coop said, "This is the location outside of El Paso where we believe the auction will be held." His comment signified his acceptance of the two men.

"Auction?" Seth said.

Ryan realized they were unaware of the details of the plot and launched into a description of the events that had transpired. As he talked, their faces turned grim, then morphed to rage.

Luke said, "Holy hell! We'll do whatever you need to help get the bastards." He looked at Ryan. "What are you doing to protect Kerry and yourself?"

"If we leave, either Adrian or Tim follows us."

"Let us know if you need another body for the protection detail," Seth said.

"Did you bring any weapons?"

"Oh, yeah," Luke growled, his lips peeled back in a parody of a smile.

Tim stepped back into the room. "I talked to the patrol sergeant. Whoever was outside is gone. He'll try to keep a car in the area."

John walked in with another map. "I could hear what happened from my office," he said, and introduced himself to the two men. He tacked the map on the board next to the first. "This is the area directly across the road from the house. The mailbox on the edge of the road is in both maps for a point of reference."

Mike explained the difficulty of the insertion of a surveillance team.

"I can see the problem. It could be done, but it will take time to set up," Luke said.

Mike sighed. "We don't have the time."

"That's flat terrain with no cover. They can see anyone approaching the house from the highway," Seth added.

Luke turned to Ryan who stood at one end of the table listening to the discussion. It made sense to let Mike and the new additions to the team handle the logistics. They had probably forgotten more about tactical maneuvers in a desert environment than he would ever know.

"Did I understand you to say Moore's team is in charge of the auction?" Luke asked.

"Yeah, it's the current theory," Ryan said.

Luke's face was thoughtful as he turned back to survey the map. "I know a couple of his men and have heard rumors about the rest. You are going up against an experienced force of guerilla-style mercenaries, ruthless, battle-hardened soldiers. It would be better if you sent in a military team trained for this type of operation."

Ryan said, "I would agree, but it's not an option. The problem is Harmon. We don't know how deep his tentacles reach into the government. We're getting helicopters from Ft. Bliss and have to conceal the reason. For all we know, he could be best friends with the base commander. If Harmon gets the least bit suspicious we're onto him, those kids will end up in a grave somewhere in the desert. We can't take a chance."

Luke nodded, before saying, "Makes sense, foolhardy, but logical."

Ryan looked around the room at his small team of recruits. Six civilians, and four law enforcement. God, how bad are the odds against us? Out of the ten, only three had any experience in this type of operation, and … he hadn't given them a choice.

"I haven't asked, only assumed which is a mistake on my part. If anyone has doubts about being involved in this operation, now is the time to speak up."

"Dang, Ryan, don't go getting all melodramatic on us," Kerry retorted, waving her hand at the others in the room. "There isn't anyone of us who intends to back down from this fight."

"You ready to get back to work?" Mike asked and glared at Ryan.

He grinned as he felt the heat of a blush on his face, more from relief than embarrassment. "This is how I want to handle it. Mike, Luke, and Seth, you're in charge of the tactical operation. You have far more experience in this style of combat than any of us." He looked at each of the other team members who, one by one, nodded their head in agreement.

"I need a timeline, equipment list, and an operational plan," Ryan said. He explained the list of items he had requested from Jenson.

Mike said, "Dan, get the blackboard from the storage room. John, we need aerial maps of the surrounding terrain and the roads leading to the ranch. At least a ten-mile radius around the property."

"Seth and I will start on the equipment list while you are getting set up," Luke said. Then added, "Kerry, set up a list of items for the kids. We have no idea what condition they will be in. Anyone have medical training?"

John lifted his hand. "I do. I worked part-time as an EMT in college."

"Then you're our designated medic. Work up a list of medical supplies we can carry with us. Ryan, we will need to have ambulances on standby somewhere close to the ranch. I'm not sure how you can accomplish it, but I'll leave the task in your hands."

Ryan jotted down a few notes as Mike and Luke issued their directions.

"Give me the lists when you are done. I'll get the items," Coop said.

Tim added, "I'll help."

Kerry looked at Tim. "Are you certain you won't have any problems with the department?"

"Nope," he grinned, then said, "As of today, I'm on vacation. I can do whatever I damn well please, and a vacation in El Paso sounds like a pretty good idea." His comment brought a chuckle from everyone and helped ease the somber mood.

"Adrian and I will work on the coordination with Jenson in El Paso and keep our boss in the loop. Sometime today, everyone needs to get whatever personal items you need. What have we forgot?" Ryan asked.

Twenty-nine

Washington, D.C.

Scott paced. A nervous habit, and one he had never been able to break. Almost as bad as his pen-tapping. He glanced at the clock. As he turned, Nicki and Blake also glanced up at the wall. It seemed all three of them had become obsessed with time. Hard not to when the hours slipped away.

A computer beep broke the silence in the room. Nicki opened the incoming email. "It's the background information on Moore's men." She scanned the attached document from the commander of the unit where they had been assigned.

"Scott, this is worse than what I expected. Communications, Weapons, Demolition, Mountain Warfare, and those are only a few of the skills these guys have. Moore and Jones are also pilots. I'll forward this to Ryan."

He had stood near her shoulder and read the document. Scott didn't think it was possible for the knot in his gut to grow larger, but it swelled until he felt the pressure against his heart and lungs. He was all too aware of the limitations of training and experience of the team flying to El Paso, and there wasn't a damned thing he could do about it.

His phone chimed. It was Ryan. Tapping the speakerphone, they listened as he brought them up to date. When he mentioned the addition of Luke and Seth, Scott felt a slight easing of the tension. The men's background would be an invaluable asset to the operation.

"What do you need from us?" he asked.

"Nothing, right now. Once we lift off, I'll call."

As Scott disconnected, he looked at his two agents. "We've done all we can. Go home, get a decent shower and some rest. It will be another long night."

He headed to his office to call the President and his boss.

Nicki said, "I'm not leaving. There is one more item we haven't tried to find, and it's the website for the auction."

"You're right. With both of us searching, we might locate it. I wonder if Dave's contact can tell us," Blake said and tapped his phone.

"Dave, it's Blake. Are you still in touch with your agent?"

"I talked to him an hour ago. He said his situation is getting tense. An extraction team flew into Bolivia last night and is near his location, waiting for his call."

"We were hoping he could get the information on the website for the auction and the passcode."

"I'll call him, but I'm not hopeful," Dave said.

Texas

Kerry handed her list to Coop. As soon as he had the rest of the lists, he and Tim headed out the door. Acquiring everything would take a couple of hours, plus Coop had decided the equipment and supplies should be loaded in a van for transport to the airport.

Dan had posted the additional aerials of the ranch. An old farmhouse was across the road. A major discussion had ensued over the use of the place for an observer. If any of the three ex-military men were in El Paso, it would have been an easy solution. Instead, there was the issue of recruiting another person who could get into place without blowing the whole operation.

Finally, Ryan stepped into the fray and asked, "Do you know anyone stationed at Ft. Bliss?"

Mike said, "I don't."

"I've lost touch with a lot of the men I worked with, so I wouldn't know," Luke said.

Seth leaned back in his chair, a thoughtful look on his face. "Luke, do you remember an old-head sergeant we both had when we went through boot camp? Sergeant Duggan."

"That old bird, I sure do. Why?"

"I think when he retired he moved to El Paso. His daughter and grandkids live there."

Turning to Mike, Luke said, "There's our man if we can find him. As mean as a rattlesnake and as ornery as they come, but you can trust him."

"I'll make a few calls and see if I can locate him," Seth said and walked out.

Ryan's phone chimed. It was Dave.

"I've sending you a floor plan of the house. The helicopters are on standby, and I have your vehicles. What's the latest?"

Ryan filled him in on the details along with the information on Sgt. Duggan. "Seth is trying to find him. See what you can do. We need to get eyes on the ranch as soon as possible. If you locate him, get a number, and I'll have Luke or Seth call. They know him."

Dave said, "Nicki is trying to find the website for the auction. I talked to my agent in Bolivia. He said he might be able to get access to the site address and password and would get back to me." He added the information on the extraction team.

"Sounds like he is cutting it close."

"Yeah, he is, but he has two kids. Call me when you lift off."

Ryan turned to look at the timeline on the blackboard. They had agreed the optimum time to make entry was the hours before dawn. A raid in the daylight would significantly increase the risk factor, not only to themselves but also to the children. *My god, I hope I haven't read this wrong.* What if they don't move the kids tonight? What if the time of the auction changed? Ryan rubbed his head in frustration, so many ways this could go all wrong, and it would be the children who would pay the price.

Mike said, "We've done as much as we can until we get more intel. This might be a good time to get any housekeeping items you need."

Luke said, "We're set. We have our tactical gear in the truck."

Ryan looked at Kerry who had been silent during the discussion though he had noticed the intent look on her face as she sipped her coffee and listened. "Are you ready to head to the hotel?" he asked.

Adrian had also taken a backseat to the discussions, but when Ryan mentioned the hotel, said, "I'll follow you."

Kerry grabbed her backpack, then dropped it on the table. Shoving her gun in the waistband of her jeans, she followed the two men out the door to the SUV parked behind the building. She slid behind the wheel and waited for Ryan who stood outside talking to Adrian.

Once he was seated, she asked, "Everything all right?"

"Yeah, just a little coordination." Pulling his phone from his pocket, he tapped the screen.

Adrian's voice answered, "Okay, you two. Keep it clean. Big brother … will be listening," and chuckled.

Ryan said, "We decided to keep the phone line open in case he spots something."

"Don't worry, I've got you covered," Adrian said.

Kerry said, "Great idea, though, what can happen in the few blocks it takes to get to the hotel?"

When she pulled out of the lot, Kerry surveyed the shrubs across the street and the parked cars as she passed. Adrian pulled behind her, then backed off until there were a couple of car lengths between them. Her eyes flicked between the roadway and the rearview mirror.

"Anything?" Ryan asked.

"Hmm … just a motorcycle, and Adrian," she said as she turned onto the side street leading to the hotel.

"Yeah, I'm still with you. Biker went straight. Now, if we can just get you back in one piece … Jump! Jump! Get out!" Adrian screamed.

Instinctively, Kerry hit the brakes, popped the seat belt, pushed the door open, and jumped, rolling as she hit the pavement. For an instant everything slowed, the car moving down the street, and then—a ball of fire erupted. This time she didn't have the protection of large rocks, and the force of the blast shoved her against the tires of a parked car. A roar pulsated in her head. Flames and smoke shot into the air.

Pieces of debris rained from the sky. A twisted chunk of metal that looked like a part of the door landed a foot from her legs.

She screamed, but couldn't hear the sound. *Ryan, oh my god, where are you? Did you get out?* Terror clawed its way into her mind.

A face leaned over her. A hand shook her shoulder, and his mouth moved, but the roar still filled her ears. Dazed, she shook her head, then recognition flashed through her mind. Adrian, it's Adrian. The deafening buzz lessened, and she could hear him calling her name.

"Ryan, where's Ryan, do we need to get to cover?" she cried out. Moving her legs, she pushed herself up against the tire. Everything worked, nothing seemed to be broken.

"Kerry, can you hear me?"

She nodded her head yes.

"The shooter's gone, and Ryan got out. He's on the other side of the street."

Shifting her eyes from Adrian's face, she searched until she found him. He was on his back on the sidewalk. Panic shot through her.

"What's wrong with him? How bad is he hurt?"

"He's just dazed and has a cut on his head."

She sighed with relief. "Anyone else hurt?"

"No, your car was the only one on the street."

"What happened?"

"I'll explain later. I need to get you checked out. The ambulance is on the way."

"I need to get to Ryan."

"You're not going anywhere except to the hospital."

"No, I'm not. Help me get up." Clutching his arm, she pulled herself up, then leaned against the car as a wave of dizziness swept over her.

Adrian shook his head, a look of frustration on his face, but he slipped his arm around her shoulder to steady her.

Taking small steps, she weaved her way through the debris littering the pavement. The intense heat and smoke from the burning car made it difficult to breathe. She fought back the bile that rose in her throat.

Ryan was arguing with a paramedic who didn't want him to sit up. When he spotted her, he brushed aside the man's hands, pushed up and swung his legs to sit on the edge of the curb. "Are you okay?" His hands reached for her as she sank down beside him.

"Yes." Her eyes skimmed over him. The only injury she could see was the cut on the side of his head. His arm slid around her, and he pulled her close.

Laying her head on his shoulder, she stared at the flames and black smoke. "We really need to stop meeting like this."

Adrian squatted in front of them. "You both need to go to the hospital."

"No!" they uttered at the same time.

He grimaced, then said, "Okay, but it's against my better judgment. I feel I should force you into the ambulance."

"You know why we can't do that," Ryan said.

Adrian sighed. "Yeah, I do. Both of you stay here and don't move. I need to make a few calls and ... try to explain this to the cops."

Mike answered the phone at BSI. Loud curses rang out when he heard what happened. The next call was to Scott with much the same effect.

When he disconnected, Adrian said, "Scott wants you to call as soon as you are up to it. I'll talk to the police, then we need to get out of here."

Walking to Adrian's vehicle, Kerry steps were still unsteady, and

Ryan wasn't much better. She crawled into the back and collapsed. Her mind had just begun to process how close they had come to being killed—again—and a thrust of anger shot through her. Eyeing the back of Ryan's head and the bits of trash that clung to his hair, she asked, "Do you have any idea what just happened?"

"No. Adrian screamed—jump—and I did."

Rage flowed through him. The goddamn plan should have worked. He'd hired local talent to tail them. If they turned toward the hotel, he'd be waiting. If not, the biker would call with their location. One way or the other, he'd get a chance to take the shot and be a million bucks richer.

Instead, the damn bitch and cop had escaped again. Just as he pulled the trigger, they jumped. How the hell did they know? Moore wanted to kill them with his bare hands, see their life trickle away as he squeezed their necks, especially Branson.

His voice harsh with anger, Creel said, "I told you this was a bad idea. You let this woman get under your skin. You should have put out the word on the contract and let someone else take care of it. This could jeopardize the entire operation." He drove onto the freeway entrance ramp.

"We got away, no one saw us." He glanced at his watch. He still had a few hours, could he set up another ambush?

Then, another possibility occurred to him. He'd met an old army buddy in a bar a few weeks back who was looking for work. If his boss had been willing, Moore would have hired him, but the Man didn't want to add any men. I'll hire him, pay him a hundred thousand to get rid of Branson and Barr and keep the rest.

Moore's eyes slid to the man behind the wheel. He wouldn't have to split the two mill with Creel since he wouldn't be involved. Settling back in the seat, his mood flipped. He was feeling damn good. They'd be dead, and he'd have the money.

Thirty

As Adrian pulled away from the curb, Ryan asked, "What happened? It was that bastard Moore, wasn't it?"

"Yeah, it was. He stepped into the street with an RPG, fired, then ducked into an alley and disappeared. Thank god, we had decided to keep an open link with the phones. Even with that, it was too damn close."

"How the hell did he know we were on our way to the hotel?" Kerry exclaimed.

"My guess is the guy on the motorcycle. He had on a helmet and could have been talking to Moore on the phone," Adrian said.

"But … Moore was already in place, waiting. We might not have turned. That's pretty iffy," Kerry said.

Ryan said, "Not really. It's a safe bet we'd be headed to the hotel. If not, the biker probably had orders to stay with us until Moore could catch up. He could even have set up a tag team, hand us off from one tail to another. It was only a matter of time before Moore took that shot."

"Adrian, what did you tell the cops?" Not that she cared. She ached from head to toe.

"Someone would be in contact to file a report, but for now any information was classified. They weren't happy. I gave them my card and said if there was a problem, call Washington. That shut them up."

Kerry chuckled. Hell, here she was again, a co-conspirator to the FBI 'national security edict.'

Adrian dropped them off at the front door. Kerry hobbled inside followed by Ryan. The desk clerk eyed them with suspicion as they crossed the lobby. *I can't blame him, we're a mess*, clothes dirty and torn, and Ryan with a bandage on his head. As they passed, Ryan flipped open his badge case, held it up for the desk clerk to see and kept walking toward the elevator.

Adrian caught up with them as they waited for the door to open. "I'll get my gear packed and be ready to leave whenever the two of you are ready."

"You might be in for a wait if the shower feels as good as I think it will," Kerry said. Even walking was a painful experience.

Inside her room, she stripped off her clothes and stuffed them in a plastic bag along with the smoke-laden ones from the truck explosion. Adrian would have to swing by her home. She needed more clothes, plus what few she had weren't suitable for what was ahead.

The sight of her body in the bathroom mirror brought a squeal of dismay. She was a kaleidoscope of colors, and new, long red marks were on her hip and leg where she had skidded along the pavement. *Dang, is there a color I don't have?* At least most of the bruises would be hidden by her clothes. Leaning against the shower wall, the hot water beat on her skin, and she groaned with pleasure from the warmth and relief to her aching muscles.

Dressed, she began to feel half-way decent, though she knew she would be stiff and sore for several more days. She packed her gear and called Adrian to let him know she was ready.

Ryan and Adrian were waiting in the lobby. "We're going out the back. We've agreed that it's a good idea if we stay out of sight until we leave for the airport," Ryan said.

Adrian made a quick pass by her house, then headed to BSI.

When they walked into the conference room, Coop quipped, "Didn't I hear her say she'd get the vehicle back to me in one piece or ... did I just imagine it?"

It brought a chuckle from everyone, but they still had to run the gamut of questions. Adrian did most of the talking as he detailed the ambush.

The only comment Ryan had was about the rocket launcher. "I bet the RPG is what he used to blow up Kerry's truck."

Once everyone was reassured they were okay, Ryan managed to get the conversation off them and back on the operation.

The big news was Seth had talked to Sgt. Duggan. After numerous calls between Seth, Dave, and Duggan, they had come up with a plan to get him inside the abandoned house.

"How soon will he be on site?" Ryan asked.

"Within the hour," Coop said.

"We've worked out an approach, and need to go over it before we leave," Mike said, motioning to the blackboard covered with diagrams.

Luke picked up the briefing. "We have to deploy after dark. If the kids get there tonight, we can make entry before daylight. Otherwise, we'll have to wait until tomorrow night. We examined every possible approach, and it's impossible during the day. Moore's men would see us coming from more than a mile away. With firepower like an RPG, it's a risk we can't take."

Mike added, "We'll use vans instead of the helicopters. In the desert, sound carries, and helicopters have a distinctive sound. It would be a dead giveaway."

Luke stepped to the blackboard, and said, "We'll park the vehicles at this point, two miles from the house. We go in on foot in teams of two. Team assignments and radio designations are on the corkboard. I've checked the weather forecast, clear but cold, with a full moon."

Kerry looked at the list. She was teamed with Ryan.

Mike said, "Dave sent a floor plan. A copy is in the briefing packet," motioning to a stack of files on the table. "Between now and when we get there, everyone needs to study it. Your life could depend on knowing where you are and what is ahead of you."

Luke waited until everyone had grabbed their packet, then said, "I hope Duggan will be able to provide intel on the security force before we get there, but I'm not counting on it." Indicating another diagram on the board, he added, "This is the route each team will take to approach the house. Duggan will meet up with us and team with Dave.

"The house is approximately four thousand square feet. There is a large family room at the back that overlooks the patio. It's likely this is where they'll set up a video camera for the feed to the website. Dave learned a large satellite dish was installed last week. One of Moore's men is probably already there getting the communication system set up."

Ryan said, "I haven't had a chance to tell everyone, but Nicki sent me the military records on Moore's men. Webb is a communications expert."

Luke nodded. "Once we breach the front door, Kerry and Ryan will head upstairs to the bedrooms. The rest of us will secure the outside and first floor."

He paused and glanced at the group assembled at the table. "There is a difference in a police action and a military one. This is a military operation. No warnings, no hollering police as we break through the door. You shoot first and to kill, no warning shots. The men you are up against won't hesitate to kill you. Don't give them a chance."

Adrian said, "Since someone is keeping tabs on our activity, we could be followed to the airport."

"That's a good point, considering Ryan, and I almost got blown out of existence—again!" Kerry interjected.

Luke said, "After Adrian called, we knew we had a problem. Coop came up with a plan. Adrian, did you park in back?"

"Yeah," he replied.

"Good. Move Kerry and Ryan's gear and anything you want Coop to take to his car. Just don't put anything on the backseat floor."

He glanced at his watch. "In a few minutes, a furniture van and cab will arrive. Adrian, you take the cab to the airport. We want you seen leaving. The furniture van belongs to one of Mike's clients and will back up to the front. With the back doors open it will block the view of the front door. Everyone, expect Mike and Coop, will get into the back. The van will return to the furniture store, and two cabs will be at the back door. Seth and I will take one back to our truck. We didn't want to take a chance on someone following if we left here on foot. The other cab will take the rest of you to the airport."

Luke looked at Mike, a twinkle in his eye. "Mike will leave the lights on, so it appears all of us are still here. Mike and Coop will go out the back. Mike will have to squeeze down on the backseat floor, so he's out of view when Coop drives away."

Mike's deep voice growled.

"Did you say something?" Luke asked, a broad grin on his face. A glare from Mike was his only response, as Luke continued, "Coop will drive to the FBI office and park in the parking garage. He'll be seen entering his office. The van is already there loaded with the items from your lists. Mike will move the gear from the car into the van. Coop will go down the rear stairs to the garage, and they'll leave for the airport."

Coop slid a piece of paper to everyone. "I had the plane moved inside a hangar to prevent anyone from seeing us board. This is the hangar number. Once everyone, except Adrian, is on board the pilot will taxi to the executive terminal where Adrian will be waiting.

"The pilot has already filed a flight plan for D.C. Once we're in the air and out of view of the airport, he'll turn west to El Paso. Dave made reservations at a hotel on the west side. As a precaution, I suggested he not use our real names, so he blocked the rooms under the guise of a training conference. He also made arrangements for us to land at the Army airfield instead of the commercial airport."

Coop's phone chimed. He listened, then asked, "Could you see who boarded the plane?"

When he disconnected, he said, "A plane took off from Harmon's estate a few minutes ago," as he tapped in a number on his phone.

"Blake, a plane just left the estate." After a few seconds, Coop said, "No, my agent couldn't see who got on."

Pocketing the phone, he said, "I bet Moore and his partner are on the plane. Blake will call if the tracking center locates the flight."

A knock sounded at the front door.

"Showtime, let's move," Luke said.

Washington, D.C.

Blake passed on the flight information to the flight center. Back on his computer, he continued his search for the auction's website. While he located several suspicious sites, none were the right one. Running his hand over his face, he couldn't recall the last time he was this exhausted. He and Nicki had been on their computers, nonstop for hours, and he needed to stretch his legs. "Do you want anything from the breakroom?"

"A can of soda and not a diet one. I need a full shot of energy," she replied.

As he walked down the hall, a phone rang. When a loud "Yes!" rang out, he raced back.

A look of elation on her face, she rapidly wrote down the information. Then her expression turned solemn. "No ... oh, no. Let us know as soon as you hear."

"What?" Blake asked.

Nicki stared at her computer screen for several seconds, then slowly swung her chair to face him. Tears glittered in her eyes. "That was Dave. His contact was able to get the web address and the passcode."

"That's good news, so what's wrong?"

"The agent may be dead. Dave heard gunfire and shouting in the background. His contact was obviously under duress as he hurriedly relayed the information, then the phone went dead. Dave hasn't been

247

able to reach the extraction team."

Scott had walked out when he heard Nicki's shout of elation. Rage and despair raced through him as he listened. "If the agent has been killed, we can't let his death be for nothing. Work the problem and let's take down the bastards and get those kids back."

Nicki swiveled back to her computer, her fingers stabbed the keyboard as she typed the address she had been given. A couple of tears dropped onto the keys.

As they watched, a page appeared. In the center was a coiled rattlesnake. Its tail of rattles was upraised, the head extended and jaws open, the protruding fangs ready to strike. Under the hideous image was the space for the password. Typing it, the site opened, and pictures of the four kidnapped children filled the screen.

"Holy Hell!" Scott whispered as he watched her flip through pages that contained more pictures, information on the parents, bidding, and payment instructions. The hatred that had slowly taken root deep in his soul for Mitchell Harmon intensified as he viewed the vile and revolting advertisements to sell four innocent children. *Work the problem, just like you told Nicki.* "Can you trace where the feed originated?"

"I'll try," she said, her tone reflecting the forbidding look on her face. "It may take several hours. Blake, pull the site up on your computer," and passed him the codes. "Monitor it for any changes."

Watching her and Blake, Scott had never seen such grim determination or focus. Once again, he felt an immeasurable sense of gratitude they were members of his team.

Pulling his phone, he called Ryan, it rolled to his voice mail. His message was terse and to the point. "We're into the site."

Texas

Kerry gently leaned back in her seat, trying to ease her aching muscles. Coop's plan had gone off without a hitch. The pilot had turned west and notified them they could use their electronic devices. Seated next to her, Ryan tapped the button to power up his phone.

A beep sounded and as he listened to his voice mail, he exclaimed, "They're in."

Across the aisle, Mike asked, "In what?"

"The website," he said as he called Scott.

"Where are you?"

"In the air headed to El Paso. Just got your message."

Scott explained Dave's phone call and what Nicki had found. "She's attempting to trace the origin," then told Ryan the bad news.

As he disconnected, Ryan felt sick at the thought the agent may have died trying to save the lives of four children. With a deep sigh, he stood and moved into the middle of the aisle, so everyone could hear him as he relayed Scott's information. When he sat, the only sound came from the plane's engines.

A phone chimed, it was Seth's. When he disconnected, he said, "Duggan says there is a single vehicle parked in front of the house. He's only seen one man working on the satellite dish in the backyard. He also spotted a modification that wasn't on the aerials. A long section of ground has been plowed and packed down. It's a runway."

"Is it possible the children will arrive by air?" Kerry asked.

"Maybe. We know both Moore and Jones are pilots. It could also be they plan to fly the children to Mexico rather than take a chance on transporting them across the border by car," Ryan said.

Mike told everyone to take advantage of the opportunity to get some rest. Most everyone kicked back in their seats and were soon asleep.

Restless, Kerry tried to doze. She couldn't seem to shut down her brain. Had they made a mistake? What if the kids weren't at the property? What if the communications setup in El Paso was to relay the auction from another location? If they were wrong, they wouldn't get another chance. The what-ifs circled and drove her deeper into a sea of doubt and worry. She knew sleep would continue to elude her.

A snore broke her concentration. It was Ryan. Glancing at him, at first, she was exasperated, *how can he go to sleep at a time like this?* Then another small snort brought a smile to her face. He had removed the bandage, but the edges of the gash were still raw and red.

The memory she had shoved back, refusing to accept its meaning, rose in her mind. The terror that had clawed at her as she screamed his name, believing he had been trapped in the car, and the unbidden thought that had emerged. She couldn't lose him, not when he had become the center of emotions she had never experienced. Just his presence sent a surge of longing through her, to press against him and feel his arms wrapped around her. Kerry had never fallen in love, not the kind of love that sinks into your soul and locks around your heart.

His head shifted sending a blond lock of hair across his forehead. She gripped her hands together to resist the urge to reach up and brush it back. *Oh, my god. I am in so much trouble here.*

A beep sounded, it was the 'fasten your seat belt' sign. The pilot's voice said they were starting their descent.

Ryan jerked awake, glancing around him. The mischievous grin on Kerry's face raised the hackles on his neck. What was she up to this time? "What!"

"Oh, nothing," she muttered and fastened her seat belt.

His phone chimed. Steering with one hand, he grabbed the phone from the console with the other and hit the answer button.

"Status, Mr. Moore."

"Approximately three hours from the location."

"Will there be a problem with the delivery?" the toneless voice asked.

The image of the four unconscious children in the back of the van flicked in Moore's mind.

"No, the packages will arrive in good shape?"

"Excellent. Then the operation is on schedule?"

"Yes."

"Where is your competition?"

"Other than a representative who left by plane for Washington, they are still in Austin."

"Evidently, no one has fulfilled the contract."

"Not yet." He didn't want his boss to know he had tried twice and failed. Since the news reports had only referenced a truck and car fire, he was safe. The Man didn't tolerate mistakes.

"I don't understand why there haven't been any takers."

Moore could detect the anger in his boss's voice. "I'm not certain," he replied.

"Find out why," his boss demanded.

What Harmon didn't know was that he had deliberately made the information on the contract vague. He wanted the money and still intended to get it. He hadn't been able to contact his army buddy, and he didn't put out the word on the increase in the bounty. Once he finished in El Paso, he'd head back to Austin. This time he'd finish the job, even if it meant a trip to Washington, D.C.

Thirty-one

When the plane taxied to a stop, Kerry saw two vans parked along the runway. A man, dressed in jeans, boots, and a jacket emblazoned with FBI on the front, leaned against the front of one, his arms crossed over his chest. As the door opened, he straightened and strode toward the plane.

Grabbing her backpack and ball cap, she followed Ryan down the metal staircase. The agent waited at the bottom of the steps. Around thirty-five, he was tall and lanky. His hair was the standard Bureau haircut, short and neat. Wire-rim glasses on a round face made him look more like a professor than a federal agent.

"Dave, good to see you again. Wish it was under better circumstances," Ryan said as he stepped onto the concrete. Turning, he introduced the agent to the others assembled on the tarmac.

When Kerry shook his hand, Dave held it for a few seconds and smiled at her before saying, "So you're the person who threw a monkey wrench into Harmon's plans."

Kerry grinned back. "I guess it's one way of looking at it."

Dave said, "I suggest we head to the hotel and get settled. I talked to Sgt. Duggan. There hasn't been any new activity."

With everyone pitching in to help, it didn't take long to transfer the equipment from the storage compartment of the plane. Boxes of weapons and ammunition, medical supplies, tactical vests, bags that held helmets, radios and headsets and other pieces of equipment disappeared into the back of a van, along with their suitcases. Dave handed each a hotel key.

Climbing into the back of the other van, they sat on the facing bench seats which could easily accommodate five people on each side. Ryan and Coop sat in the front with Coop behind the wheel as they followed Dave.

Seth's phone rang. "It's Duggan." After a brief conversation, he disconnected and said, "A small plane landed, but only two people got off."

"Well, that answers the question of plane versus car to transport the kids," Adrian said.

The next call was from Blake to tell them the plane that left the estate had landed in the desert west of El Paso and did Ryan need the coordinates. Ryan said no, they already knew where the plane was located.

At the hotel, Dave said, "I have a meeting room on the third floor. Once you're settled, let's meet there."

Inside the room, a long table held an assortment of metal buffet servers, trays of cold cuts, bowls of salad and chips along with a variety of drinks.

"Good idea. I was wondering how we would get something to eat," Ryan said.

"I expected you would want to discuss your plans, and this seemed the easiest solution to ensure privacy. There are all the fixings for chicken or beef fajitas or sandwiches and salad if you want something on the lighter side."

Once everyone had filled a plate, Ryan said, "Mike, Luke, and Seth have developed the tactical plan for the raid."

A comment which caused Dave's eyebrows to raise.

Ryan knew exactly what Dave thought. It was unusual for civilians to be in charge. He said, "With their military background, they have the experience and knowledge for this type of operation. I'll let them explain."

Luke had laid a file folder on the table in front of him. Shoving his plate aside, he opened it, slid a set of documents to Dave and explained the details of the entry to the ranch along with the anticipated level of resistance they would encounter from Moore's team.

Dave said, "Any idea when the kids will arrive?" as he studied the documents.

Ryan said, "I believe it will be tonight since the auction is scheduled for tomorrow night. I don't think they will wait and move them tomorrow. That would cut it close if there was a problem."

Dave glanced at Seth. "Your Sgt. Duggan is, uh … an unusual individual."

Seth choked as he tried to laugh and swallow at the same time. Clearing his throat, he said, "For Duggan, that would be a compliment. He was the drill sergeant in boot camp and the meanest, most cantankerous man I've ever known. He made our lives miserable, but he knew how to turn a raw recruit into a soldier."

"What's the word on your undercover agent?" Adrian asked.

Dave's face turned grim. "I don't know. The extraction team hasn't located him. When they arrived at the hacienda, it was deserted. They found a pool of blood in one of the rooms. The team is searching, but now they're looking for a body. They want to bring him home."

"Damn," Kerry said, a sentiment which echoed in everyone's mind.

Dave called the front desk to request a waiter remove the remaining food and dirty dishes. Once the large table had been cleared, Kerry opened her laptop and checked her emails. She sent a quick message to her parents. There wasn't much she could say, other than hi, and she loved them.

Mike broke out a deck of cards and started a game of Texas Hold 'Em, a variation of poker. Occasionally, a glance would be directed to the large clock on the wall. The hours were slipping by. Already, less than twenty-four remained.

Another chime. "It's Duggan," Seth said as he answered. When he asked how many, cards dropped as everyone shifted their focus. Listening intently, he interjected an occasional question, then said he would call once they were on their way.

When he hung up, he glanced around the table. "They just arrived."

Kerry's gut tightened. The same tension was visible in the body language of everyone in the room.

"A car and delivery truck passed the old house where Duggan is hidden. When they pulled into the yard, someone lit up the place with floodlights. He got a head count, at least seven. With the truck backed up to the front door, he couldn't see what was inside. When they moved the van, they switched off the floodlights."

Sliding a copy of the floor plan to the center of the table where everyone could see, Seth pointed to a bedroom. "Lights came on in this room. Hopefully, they are keeping the kids together."

Luke looked at his watch. "Everyone get your gear and be ready to pull out in thirty minutes. Seth, call Duggan and give him our ETA. Dave, can we get out of the hotel without having to go through the lobby?"

"Take the stairs. They lead to a door that exits onto the parking lot," he replied.

Washington, D.C.

Nicki had dimmed the office lights, but her computer screen beamed like a neon sign. Eyes, gritty with fatigue, stared at the obscene website as she monitored it for any change. So far, she hadn't found the source of the transmission. Blake had made another pot of coffee. She glanced at the time in the corner of her screen, only ten minutes had passed from the last time she looked.

When Scott's phone rang, tingles of fear stabbed at her as she shot to her feet and headed to his office. Blake was close on her heels. They hovered in his doorway.

Scott was grim-faced as he listened. "Do whatever must be done to finish this," he said, his voice resolute. Disconnecting, he looked at his agents and said, "The children are at the El Paso ranch. The team is on the way and should be in position within the next hour."

They nodded and stepped back to their desks. There wasn't anything that could be said and nothing they could do except wait.

Tapping the number he had been given, Larkin answered on the first ring. "Mr. President, Scott Fleming. The children are at the ranch in El Paso and the team is going in." He listened and said, "Yes, I will."

His boss and Whitaker were with the President. He'd been invited to join them but had declined. His place was here with his team.

The call made, he walked out of his office. Blake handed him a cup of coffee. He took a sip, but if someone asked, he couldn't have said what he was drinking. "Have we heard anything about the status of the agent in Bolivia?"

"No, nothing."

This will be one long and hellish night.

Texas

Dave had located an abandoned plant several miles out of town that could be used as a staging area. Luke passed out the vests, helmets, and headsets, while Seth walked around with a black grease pen marking faces.

Once everyone had suited up, Luke went over the details of the raid one more time, then added, "Double check that you have nothing on you that makes noise. Make sure your cell phones are turned off, not even on mute. There is one change to the plan. Dave, in addition to disabling the vehicles, take down that damn plane. I don't want to take a chance on someone escaping in it. Questions?"

He looked at each person, then satisfied with what he saw, said,

"Let's get it done."

They piled back into the van. Luke drove, and Mike was in the front passenger seat. Dave and Adrian followed in the other van. Kerry was scrunched between Ryan and Tim and had to sit upright. If she leaned back the vest and a holder on her gun belt for extra magazines dug into the bruises.

Her insides were tied in a knot, her heartbeat was a hammer strike against her chest. She could feel the blood throb in her head. She had been on several raids when she was with the PD, but nothing like what was ahead of her. Surreptitiously, she wiped a wet palm, then the other on her pants and took several slow deep breaths to ease the tension rolling through her. It didn't help.

Luke slowed, cut his lights, saying "Three miles out," as he searched for the narrow dirt road that ran along the east side of the property. There had been considerable debate whether to approach the house by the road or across the desert. While staying on the road was easier and faster, there was a remote possibility a passing car could screw up the entire operation.

She suddenly realized how quiet it had become. John, Dan, Seth, and Coop were on the opposite bench. She glanced at their faces. They stared at the floor, their expression stoic. No emotion, though she saw John take a couple of deep breaths. They probably felt the same tension and apprehension.

Luke turned onto the dirt road, killed the engine, and the van rolled to a stop. Mike had disabled the overhead light before they left. He eased the passenger door open leaving it ajar. Luke's actions mirrored Mike's. Coop opened the back door, and they stepped into the harsh desert environment.

The sweat on Kerry's face turned cold as she looked upward to a night sky filled with twinkling lights. Light from the rising moon filtered across a flat landscape covered with bushes and cacti. A faint sound of yips and howls from a pack of coyotes echoed in the far distance.

They formed up in the order Luke had set. They would follow a formation of rocks, using it for cover until they were closer to the house.

Despite the moonlight, shadows from large clumps of cactus and mounds of rocks made the trek difficult. A couple of times Kerry felt the sting of thorns through her pants when she got too close to a large cluster. Though the air was cold, beads of sweat trickled down her back.

Two clicks sounded in her ear, followed by three more. It was the prearranged signal with Duggan. He had left the old farmhouse to intercept them. At a hand signal from Luke the team halted. A man rose from behind a large boulder and trotted toward them, a rifle cradled in his arms. Seth handed him a vest and helmet he had been carrying. Duggan's voice whispered in her ear, "no guards," as he quickly donned the gear.

In the briefing, Luke said he was counting on the fact Moore's men would be complacent. They wouldn't be expecting trouble. Still, he had put in place a contingency plan had there been a guard.

As they rounded the end of the rocks, Kerry had her first view of the house. It was a large structure, two-story with a full porch that extended across the front and down one side. In the rear was a detached garage that could house four cars. A covered walkway connected the garage to a side door. A large delivery van, along with two vehicles were parked in front of the garage. The plane sat on the end of the runaway. Lights shone through the large windows at the back and front of the house.

The team moved to the rear of the garage where they split into three units. Seth, Coop, Tim, and Adrian would enter through the kitchen door. Luke, Mike, Kerry, and Ryan through the front door. Dave and Duggan would disable the vehicles and plane while Dan and John secured the outbuildings and perimeter.

Kerry followed Luke and Mike as they crossed the driveway to the front of the house. Looking up, she saw a sliver of light that shone around the drapes in an upstairs bedroom. Luke slipped along the porch to the side of the front window. He held up one finger and pointed to his eyes to tell them he saw one man. He clicked his radio once to signal to the other groups. Two clicks answered. Three men accounted for, four were left if Duggan was right.

Luke slid to the side of the front door, nodded to Mike and whispered, "Go."

Mike's size twelve foot struck the door with the power of a two hundred and fifty-pound man. The door frame shattered. Shoving the broken door aside, he rushed inside. A shot rang out.

As Kerry cleared the doorway, her gaze quickly scanned the entryway and living room. She ignored the man on the floor as she turned and headed to the stairs with Ryan close on her heels. The man was probably dead, or Luke and Mike wouldn't have been running down the hallway that led to the family room.

More gunfire erupted. Blocking out what was happening downstairs, her focus was on the landing as she sprinted up the steps, hugging the wall. Behind her, Ryan was offset to provide cover fire. Stopping on the last step, she peered around the corner before moving into the hallway. Ahead were seven doors, five bedrooms, and two baths. The light she had seen came from a bedroom on the right side. When a door opened on the left, Kerry dropped and felt the thud of Ryan's body land alongside her. A man leaned out, fired two quick shots, then ducked back into the room. Gunfire continued to echo from downstairs.

"He's trapped unless he decides to take a dive out the window," Ryan whispered. "Can you get into the bedroom?"

The door was several feet ahead of her. "Yeah, if you can keep this guy out of the hallway."

Luke's voice came over the radio. "Ground floor secured, five down."

Damn, that left two men. One was ahead of them. Where the hell was the other?

Thirty-two

In a belly-crawl, she pushed forward, and her eyes scanned the doors ahead of her. Ryan fired several shots at the doorframe of the open door as she inched closer to the target bedroom. His voice echoed in her ear as he told her to hold up and cover him. He needed to change magazines. She popped off a couple of rounds to keep the man out of the hallway.

When Ryan gave her the all clear, she rose, squatted on her heels, her back to the wall, and reached for the doorknob.

A voice inside shouted, "Pull back, or these kids are dead."

Kerry whispered, "Keep him talking."

Ryan popped off another round at the open door. Wood shrapnel flew into the hallway.

"What do you want?" Ryan shouted.

Kerry flashed three fingers.

The voice hollered, "Safe passage out of here, or I start shooting kids."

Kerry's fingers had gone to two then one. Grabbing the doorknob, she shoved the door open and dived through the doorway, rolling as she entered the room. It was all that saved her as a shot passed over her head. Calvin Moore stood in the middle of the room. Even as he swung the gun towards her, her mind registered what was behind him, twin beds, each with two small mounds.

On her back, the gun gripped in her hands, she double-tapped his chest. Blood bloomed on his shirt. His gun fell to the floor as he weaved on his feet, a look of shock and recognition on his face as he stared down at her.

He dropped to his knees and cried out, "You bitch! I should have killed you in the garage," then fell forward onto the carpet.

"Target bedroom secure, one down," she said as she rose, kicked his gun across the room, then knelt to feel for a pulse. Moore wouldn't be blowing up anyone or anything else ever again.

In the hallway, more shots rang out. Feet pounded, and doors crashed open. Then Ryan's voice echoed in the headset, "Upstairs secure, one down."

She stood, turned to the beds and checked the pulse of each child. They were alive but unconscious. Relief overwhelmed her, and she fought back the tears as she perched on the edge of a bed.

At the sound of Ryan's voice, she turned her head. Adrian leaned against the wall, blood dripped from his fingers. "Hold this tight," Ryan said as he pressed a folded towel against the side of Adrian's arm.

"Ryan, how bad?" she asked.

"A round caught him in the arm."

"It's not bad, just hurts like hell," Adrian said.

"Anyone else hurt?"

"I don't know," Ryan said.

Luke entered the room. He stopped in front of Adrian to check the wound. He said, "We were damn lucky, this is the only injury."

The room soon filled as the other team members trickled in, stepping over and around Moore. As the men looked at each child, seemingly wanting to be reassured they were alive, Kerry saw the raw emotion on their faces, even the normally stoic two brothers, and her boss.

"I called for the medivac helicopter," Dave said when he walked in. Instead of an ambulance, he had the helicopter on standby, in case of an injury in their alleged training session.

Ryan stood with Coop and Dave conversing in the corner of the room and kept an eye on John as he treated Adrian's injury.

Control had shifted to the federal officers. It was their responsibility now to handle the containment of the crime scene and set up damage control. She took one last look at the filth on the floor. *You, slimy bastard, I hope you and your team rot in hell.*

Shifting her focus, she gazed at the four children. Faces, dirty and tear-stained, wrenched at her heart. One stirred, Senator Wademan's daughter. Her eyes slightly opened, and she murmured, "Mama?"

Kerry pushed the hair from the girl's forehead, then picked up her small hand, and lightly stroked the back with her fingertips. "No, sweetie, not yet. But soon your mama will be here."

Ryan glanced at her as he listened to Coop. Her helmet was on the floor, and long strands of hair had come loose and hung around her face. She leaned over one of the little girls who was awake, holding the child's hand. She must have sensed his stare. When her eyes met his, a smile lit up her grease-smeared face, and he felt he had just been sucker-punched. How had he not known? He was the hotshot profiler and hadn't even seen it. He'd never met a woman who moved him the way she did. She was everything a man could ever want. How did I miss it, she's my future?

Coop stopped talking when he realized Ryan had acquired a dazed look and tuned him out. He turned his head to see what had prompted the deer caught in the headlight stare. Seeing the focus of Ryan's gaze, Coop grinned. Hell, anyone could have seen this one coming from a country mile away.

Washington, D.C.

Scott had paced until his legs were weak, his system saturated with endless cups of coffee. As minutes turned into hours, nerves tingled as the fear intensified and settled deep into his gut. Glancing at Nicki and Blake, their faces lined with fatigue, he could see the same emotion in their eyes.

Nicki's shout, "Oh, my god! The website's gone. Does it mean they found them?" sent him spinning toward her desk and Blake bolting out of his chair.

Scott stared at the blank screen where a few minutes before the obscene snake had filled the screen. Fear mixed with hope raced through him. He wasn't sure what it meant, but that it was gone could only be good news.

His phone rang, it was Ryan. Tapping the speakerphone, Ryan's first words would become indelibly imprinted in his mind.

"We have them, they are alive." Cheers rang out from Nicki and Blake as they clapped and high-fived each other.

"The kids have been drugged. We can't detect any physical injuries, though, we won't know for sure until a doctor examines them. A medivac helicopter just landed, and as soon as they are loaded, they will be on their way to the hospital."

"Was anyone on the team injured?" Scott refused to give voice to the word killed.

"Adrian caught one in the arm, other than that no. We've got seven dead men, including Moore. We got lucky, they didn't expect us and weren't prepared when we stormed the house."

"What's the status of the website?"

"John and Dan pulled the link down. It's gone."

"Nicki was monitoring it and saw it disappear. Were you able to find any evidence that connects to Harmon."

"No, there's not much here. Dave's crime scene unit is on the way, but I'm not hopeful we'll find anything. I expect we'll be here for the rest of the night. I'll provide an update in the morning."

"Ryan," he hesitated, searching for the right words, but realized nothing he could say would remotely be adequate for what an improbable group of people had accomplished.

"Yes, something else?" Ryan asked.

"No. I'll talk to you in the morning."

He looked at Nicki and Blake. "Go home and get some sleep."

He walked into his office. He had one more call to make. Tapping in the code he had been given, the call was answered on the first ring.

"Yes."

"Mr. President, it's Scott Fleming. The operation was a success, the children are alive and on their way to a hospital in El Paso."

"Damn good work, Scott. What is the status of your team?"

"One injured, but it's not severe? Harmon's men were killed."

"Have you notified the parents?"

"No, sir. I thought you might like to have the honors on that one."

"Yes, I would, thank you. We still have unfinished business. I want a full briefing in the morning, ten a.m. in the Oval Office. Please have a list of all the individuals involved."

White House

Larkin hung up the phone and leaned back in his chair. Paul Daykin and Vance Whitaker sat across from him. "They pulled it off! The children are alive and on the way to the hospital. Paul, when you told me who was on your team, I thought we would have dead civilians as well as your agents littering the West Texas countryside." He shook his head in amazement, then said, "Arrange for immediate transportation to get the parents to El Paso. I want both of you here tomorrow for Scott's briefing. It should be enlightening."

The two men rose to leave. Larkin's voice stopped them. "Paul, any word on the missing agent?"

"No, sir. The extraction team is still searching, but the outlook is bleak."

Larkin nodded, an intense look of sadness crossed his face.

Picking up the phone, he said, "Get me Senator Wademan."

Texas

Kerry stood in the front yard and watched the helicopter lift off. She was incredibly tired from the after-effects of adrenaline that had pumped through her body for the last several hours. Dizziness, fatigue, nausea, it had all hit as her system spiraled down. *God, I'd give next year's pay for a cup of coffee.* Instead, she settled for the bottle of water a medic gave her.

Twisting the cap, she took a sip and stared at the beehive of activity. Cars lined the highway and drive. Crime scene techs, medical examiner personnel, agents from Dave's office and others that she had no idea who or what they did had swarmed the house and vehicles.

She had overseen the transfer of the children and then decided to get out of the way. Seth and Luke had made the trek to their vehicles, and they were now parked in front of the M.E.'s van. The team had stashed their gear in one of the vehicles. Getting rid of the weight had helped ease the fatigue that consumed her.

A footstep sounded behind her. It was Mike.

"Ryan said there was no reason for us to stay, though he, Coop, and Dave can't leave yet," he said.

Adrian was in the helicopter. John had field dressed his wound while they waited for the medics, but it would probably require a few stitches and a couple of shots.

"I'm ready to get out of here. Did he say when we would fly back?" she asked.

"It'll likely be late afternoon. Dave requested we take both vehicles back to the hotel. They'll catch a ride with one of the other agents. Sgt. Duggan also plans to stay. He said this is the most fun he has had since his last boot camp." Mike chuckled, then said, "He's wandering around, examining everything and making a nuisance of himself."

Sitting on the bench seat, the contrast between the two trips was surreal. For one thing, nothing poked her in the back. The most noticeable change was the demeanor, still not much conversation, instead there was an occasional snore from either John or Dan. The tension and apprehension had vanished, replaced by a sense of a job well done. The good guys had won, and even though seven men had died, she felt no remorse for their death. Four children would soon be home with their parents instead of a life of sexual abuse, slavery or even death. No, she felt not one iota of remorse as her head drooped, and she drifted off to sleep.

⚜

Gently, Mitchell Harmon swirled the golden liquid in the thick, hand-cut crystal glass and breathed in the smoky aroma of the Irish scotch whiskey. The doctor had warned him to lay off alcohol, but this was a special occasion. Sometimes, he believed the man deliberately overreacted, a ploy to get him back to his office for another hefty fee. The liquid slid down his throat as he savored the taste.

Moore had called to inform him the children were at the El Paso location. Less than twenty-four hours before his plan came to fruition. His private jet was fueled and ready to fly him to El Paso. The thought of being nearby appealed to him, and he had arranged to have dinner with the Mayor and several high-ranking law enforcement officials and their wives. The paradox in the gathering had been deliberate. He chuckled at the thought.

In his hotel room, he'd wait for Moore's call to inform him of the identity of the buyers and the amount of their winning bid. Then, the next phase of the plan would begin. The parents would receive an anonymous letter advising them of the fate of their child. The devastation of the knowledge and the ensuing media campaign to discredit the three Senators and the Utah Governor should destroy their political careers.

Since he didn't have the Murdock child, he'd already come up with a plan to remove the Senator. He would conveniently die in a car accident.

Relaxed in the leather-padded executive chair, his eyes skimmed the room over the rim of the glass. The décor of his library office exuded power and elegance. A collection of rare, first edition books filled the built-in bookcases. He'd never read them, but they impressed his visitors. His cherry wood desk and chair were positioned, so his back was against the tall, narrow windows that overlooked his rose garden. He smiled. He always thought the garden was such a nice touch.

On the wall opposite his desk was a fireplace with a hand-tooled mantle. In between were two chairs, the backs to the fireplace and two matching couches that faced each other. His many guests had never grasped the irony of the design since it wasn't oval.

Occasionally, his eyes flicked to the screen of the small computer on his desk. It had been purchased for one specific reason, to monitor the website. Each time he looked at the logo, it triggered a deep sense of satisfaction. When Moore had suggested the design, it struck a chord. Like the snake, Mitchell was coiled to strike. His competition would be eliminated though they didn't know it yet. And, he would soon be rid of Moore and his team. Their deaths had already been arranged.

Picking up the matching glass decanter, he refilled his glass. The set had been a gift from the Prime Minister of Ireland. Over the extra sips he allowed himself, he envisioned his hand on the bible as he took the oath of office. If his money could get Larkin and other politicians elected, he knew he could buy his way into the White House.

His eyes flicked again to the computer. The screen was blank. Stunned, he stared at it. What the hell! His fingers quickly typed in the address. A message flashed—*server not found*. He must have made a mistake and re-entered the address. The same response appeared on the screen. It's gone, no it can't be, it must be there. His fingers trembled as he tried again, and then again.

The thud of his heart pounded in his chest as he tapped the speed dial. The voice that answered wasn't Moore or Jones, his alternate contact. Jabbing the button to end the call, he stared at the phone. Shock, then fear streamed through him as it slid from his hand and hit the floor.

He slumped in his chair as the awareness swept over him. He didn't know how but was certain it was over. The plan he had set in motion when Larkin had the gall to tell him he wasn't the right person to be President of the United States had been destroyed. A hot rage erupted, its heat coursed through his body.

Branson, that bitch, this was all her fault. He'd up the ante on her and Barr, make it two million each and advertise it through his drug contacts. There'd be a taker, dozens of them, they'd come out of the woodwork.

To slow his racing heart, he sucked in several deep breaths. Revenge would have to wait. His immediate concern was to discover what happened. He'd been very careful not to leave a paper or money trail. There was nothing to connect him to the kidnappings, except his property and Moore and Jones. The property was not a concern. He'd plead ignorance, and there wasn't anyone who could dispute it other than the two men. His only hope was both were dead.

Thirty-three

The ring of a phone sent Ryan scrambling from the bed. Dazed, he looked for his cell phone, then realized it was his wake-up call. Three hours' sleep, but it would have to do.

Processing the crime scene had taken hours. As he had predicted, the house yielded little in the way of evidence that could convict Harmon. Agents would trace the video equipment installed in the house, but it was all probably purchased by Moore or one of his team. The cell phones they found were burners. Call logs would be investigated, but Ryan didn't believe they would find any calls that would incriminate Harmon.

The only interesting incident happened with Moore's phone. It rang as the tech was bagging it. Ryan had answered, and the caller immediately disconnected. He was sure the person on the other end was Harmon.

Showered and dressed, he called Kerry. "Where are you?"

"We were wondering when you would surface. Everyone is downstairs at the buffet."

"I need to make a call, then I'll be down."

The conversation with Scott took longer than he expected as he provided the details of the assault and its outcome. Scott informed him of his upcoming meeting and the President's request for a list of people involved in the investigation.

"Any idea why he wants a list?" Ryan asked.

"Don't have a clue, but I expect I'll know shortly. When will you be back in Austin?"

"This afternoon. Once I get everyone rounded up, we'll leave for the airport. Coop has the plane on standby, ready to lift off."

Ryan typed up the list on his laptop, and along with his report emailed it to Scott, then headed downstairs. The aroma of bacon and coffee filled his nose as he walked through the door. The team had pushed several tables together. With a plate piled high with bacon, sausage, scrambled eggs and hash browns, he grabbed a cup of coffee. Kerry pulled out a chair for him as his hands were full.

Eyeing his plate, she said, "Are you planning on feeding an army?"

He grinned. "Yeah, this one-man army. I'm starved."

Adrian sat across from him, his arm in a sling.

"How's the arm?" he asked.

Adrian shrugged. "It's fine. The bullet didn't hit the bone. A few stitches that's all."

Kerry chuckled, then said, "I told him that unshaven look and his arm in a sling makes him look mysterious and dangerous. The women will love it."

"Ignore her. She's been rambling on about it since she sat down," Adrian quipped back.

Laughter erupted from the others as Tim and Mike added a few comments of their own.

Mike's question brought the light-hearted mood back down. "Do you know the status of the children?"

Ryan said with an edge of anger in his voice. "I talked to Dave a few minutes ago. He's at the hospital. The doctor said they are dehydrated and suffering from the residual effect of the drugs used to dope them, but otherwise, they're fine. Their mental condition may be another story. It will take time to recover from the trauma they've experienced."

He took a sip of coffee, then said, "The parents are starting to arrive. Where's Coop?"

"He left to check on the plane. When are we leaving?" Adrian asked.

"As soon as everyone is ready." In between bites, he covered what had transpired after they had left the scene.

"Any chance you'll be able to charge Harmon?" Tim asked.

"I doubt it, so far we don't have any hard evidence that will stand up in court."

"It sure sticks in my craw he might walk on this," Luke said. Murmurs of agreement echoed around the table.

"I know. It does in mine too," as Ryan pushed back his plate and stood. "Let's get the hell out of here."

Washington, D.C.

A couple hours of sleep, a hot shower, and clean clothes worked wonders for Scott's mood as he prepared for another meeting with the President. He didn't have the same sense of trepidation he experienced with the first. A file folder was filled with notes on the investigation and several copies of the list Larkin had requested. Reading Ryan's lengthy report, his amazement had risen over what had been accomplished within such a short time.

At the sound of footsteps, he walked to his office door. Nicki and Blake had walked in. "What are you doing here? Why aren't you at home?"

"We decided you might want some help, and someone has to man the office while you're playing at the White House," Blake joked.

Wondering how they knew, he said, "Well, since you're here, there is some follow-up information I need," and listed his requests. The first was to find out the latest on the condition of the children.

Armed with answers on every possible detail the President might question, Scott waited for the limo to arrive. This time his boss, Paul Daykin wasn't in the car. Within minutes the driver had turned into the gate at the White House. Walking down the hallway to the Oval Office, people and conversations flowed around him. A far cry from the silence of his first visit. Waiting for the guard to open the door, his sense of trepidation re-emerged.

Inside, the President was seated on a couch next to Vance Whitaker, and Paul was on the opposite couch.

"Scott, right on time. Have a seat," Larkin said as he stood to shake his hand, then motioned to a chair positioned at the end of the two couches.

Ah, the hot seat again as Scott shook hands with the other two men.

The President started by asking for the latest on the children's condition. Thankful that Nicki had talked to the doctor, he said, "They are doing fine. All the parents have arrived. The results of the blood test identified significant traces of multiple drugs. The doctor believes they were heavily sedated. They are dehydrated and have lost weight. It will be at least two days before the doctor will even consider releasing them."

"From what Paul has shared with me, it was a close call," Larkin said.

"Yes, sir, it was. The effort of the individuals involved in this investigation is impressive," Scott said.

"How is Agent Dillard?"

"A flesh wound that only required a few stitches."

"Tell me what happened," the President asked.

Over the next hour, Scott outlined the steps the team had taken, the attempts on Ryan and Kerry's life and the contract to kill them, and finally, the assault on the house and its outcome. The President stopped him numerous times to question a detail or person's action.

"Where is the team now," Larkin asked.

"Headed back to Austin."

"Were you able to acquire the list I requested?"

Scott reached into his folder and removed a stapled set of papers. Passing a copy to each of the men, he said, "Agent Barr sent this to me this morning. It not only lists the people involved but also a description of their activity."

There was silence as the three men absorbed the contents of the lengthy document. Scott watched the President as he read. A couple of times, he flipped back to a previous page and reread the entries. When he finished, he said, "Absolutely amazing," then glanced at Daykin and Whitaker. Each man nodded as if in agreement with a preconceived plan.

"Scott, what is your assessment of filing criminal charges on Mitchell Harmon?"

"I think it would be a waste of time. So far, we've not found one piece of solid evidence, paper or a money trail that ties him to the plot. His attorneys will argue he was an innocent dupe. He had no idea a few security guards hired for protection had gone rogue and used his property for criminal activity. Public opinion might convict him but in a court of law, no."

"Your supposition is Paul and Vance's belief as well. I plan to ask Mitchell to fly in for a meeting tomorrow afternoon under the guise of discussing the presidential nomination. I want your team, agents Cooper and Jenson, and Ms. Branson, as well as yourself, to be here. If we can't cut off the head of the snake, I can pull its fangs, and that's precisely what I plan to do."

Scott found Larkin's reference to a snake, strangely omniscient since no one other than himself and his two agents had seen the logo on the website.

Texas

Luke added a bit of excitement once the plane was in the air. He had called his wife to let her know he and Seth were coming home. Cindy had described in explicit detail the landing of a helicopter in their front yard and Tristan's reunion with his parents. The puppy had made quite a hit, but during the excitement had peed on the suit of the Secret Service agent who was holding the dog.

Listening to Luke describe the call, Kerry laughed and knew she had to hear the story firsthand. She'd call Cindy once she was home. Tristan had stolen a piece of her heart and hoped one day she might get a chance to see him again.

After that, most everyone fell asleep. Kerry dozed off, her head braced against a window. The sound of Ryan's phone woke her. Listening to his end of the call it was his boss. He glanced at her, then said, "I'll set it up."

Rising, he walked toward the back of the plane where Coop was seated. Kerry twisted her head, curious what he was up too. He shook Coop's shoulder to wake him, talked to him for a few minutes, then returned to his seat. Coop had followed him, then continued to the cockpit.

Unable to contain her curiosity, she asked, "What's happened?"

"Adrian, Coop, and I are headed to D.C. Scott is notifying Dave to catch the next flight out of El Paso."

Kerry's heart sunk, she knew this was inevitable, he would have to leave.

Ryan saw the look of disappointment that crossed her face and hoped it meant she didn't want to see him go. He added, "You are going too."

"What! I can't go to Washington. You're joking, right?"

"Nope ... and, darlin', I don't believe you have a choice. This is a Presidential order."

Stunned, she stared at him. He had to be joking. "All right, what's the punch line?"

"It's not a joke. Scott had a meeting with President Larkin and was told to have—you—at the White House tomorrow afternoon."

She squealed, panic in her voice. "Oh, my god! I have nothing to wear." Her hands fluttered in the air. "What do you wear to meet the President?"

Her voice woke the others who wanted to know what was wrong. When Ryan explained, a roar of laughter erupted from Mike. "She doesn't blink an eye when she shoots the badass leader of a mercenary gang trying to murder her, but is sent into a tailspin over what to wear to the White House."

When everyone joined in the laughter, she snapped back. "I'm glad you all think it is so damn funny, but you're not the one meeting the President. If you were, I bet you'd change your tune."

"Don't worry," Ryan reassured her. "Coop is setting up the flight with the pilot. There will be time for you to go home and pack before we leave. Adrian and I need to retrieve our gear from the hotel. I expect you might even have time to stop at the mall, or we can go shopping tomorrow morning."

Suddenly, a warm feeling gushed through her. *I like the sound of that. We ... can go shopping.*

Unusually tired, Harmon chalked it up to a lack of sleep. He'd spent most of the night pacing and watching the news channels. While confident that with one call he could find out what happened to Moore and his men, he couldn't take a chance. There was still the issue of his property, and he didn't want someone to remember the call. He had to wait.

His flight and dinner engagement in El Paso had been canceled, and he'd spent the morning in his library. His secretary had handed him several contracts to review before he left his office. He forced his mind to concentrate on the details of each, though his eyes continually flicked to the news channel on the wall-mounted, flat-screen TV. The uneasiness and fear that clutched at his chest were an unfamiliar sensation.

When the red banner scrolled across the screen signaling breaking news from El Paso, waves of panic surged through him as he increased the volume.

A reporter stood on the side of the road in the desert, her voice vibrated with excitement as she said the abducted children of several politicians had been found. The camera zoomed to a house behind her with several vehicles in front. She described the shootout that had occurred when law enforcement officers raided the house and killed the gang of kidnappers.

He hit the off button on his remote. Any hope that lingered disappeared. At first, a sense of relief overwhelmed him. He was safe, then anger and hatred built. He'd find out who raided the house and add them to his list along with Barr and Branson. In the meantime, he'd regroup and come up with another plan. He would not let an opportunity to be the next President pass him by.

His private line rang. He almost ignored it but didn't want anyone to wonder what was wrong. Answering, he heard the President's voice.

"Mitch, how are you?" Larkin asked.

"Art, good to hear from you. I'm doing fine. Looking forward to our meeting next week with the presidential election committee."

"Well, that's why I am calling."

Paranoia sent spikes of fear shooting through him. Was it possible he knew? No, how could he? "What do you need?" Harmon asked.

"I'd like to have a meeting with you to discuss strategy before we meet with the committee. Some of the potential candidates may decide not to run. The kidnapping of their children has changed their perspective on the campaign."

Hope surged through him, maybe the kidnappings weren't a lost cause. "When do you want to meet?" Harmon asked.

"My schedule is booked this next week, except for tomorrow afternoon. Can you fly in for a four-p.m. meeting?"

Since being elected, Art Larkin had become a pompous windbag and always made a point of his hectic schedule, as if no one else was busy as well. "Shouldn't be a problem. All I have planned for tomorrow is dinner with the governor. A president trumps a governor any day," then chuckled at his joke and waited for Larkin's answering laugh.

Odd, there was a moment of silence before Larkin replied, "I'll see you tomorrow."

His voice had an edge Harmon hadn't heard before. As he disconnected, he wondered at the strange tone, then decided it was his imagination.

Thirty-four

The plane seemed empty with only four people on board, three of whom had waited on Kerry to arrive.

Coop had told her to take one of the vehicles waiting at the airport when they landed. Her first stop was to drop Ryan and Adrian off at the hotel and pick up what she had left in her room, then she headed home. She showered, changed into black slacks and an oversized shirt for the flight.

Considerable time was spent in front of the closet flipping through the hanging clothes. Kerry hadn't been kidding when she wondered what someone wore for a meeting with the President. She finally decided on a red suit, trimmed in black and a white silk blouse. She also added a pair of black and orange silk pants and a matching camisole style top. The perfect attire if they went to dinner. A few other outfits, the just in case kind, were added to the growing pile.

As she contemplated the possibilities on this trip, she decided to stop at the mall on her way to the airport. Since Coop had said he would pick up Ryan and Adrian at the hotel, she had extra time and intended to put it to good use.

When she arrived at the executive terminal, the three men were seated at a bar, sipping a beer and watching a ballgame on the TV. They didn't seem perturbed at the delay though all three grinned when they saw the size of her suitcase.

Once the plane was in the air, Kerry kicked back the seat and relaxed.

She glanced at Ryan seated next to her.

"Any idea why I've been called to the White House?"

"Nope. Scott will be waiting for us when we land. I expect we'll find out then."

"Any speculation? Come on, you must have some clue."

"All I know is Scott was told to bring his team, Coop, Dave and you to the meeting."

"Think it has something to do with Harmon?"

"It might, but I can't imagine what the President would do." He cleared his throat and added, "I ... uh ... wondered if you might like to go sightseeing after the meeting tomorrow. The lights at night in downtown D.C. are truly remarkable, though they might be a bit of a letdown after being in the Oval Office."

Yes! as she high-fived herself in her mind. "Since I've never been in D.C. at night, that would be fun."

"Okay, that's good." His fingers lightly caressed the back of her hand where it lay on the armrest.

A wave of heat burst through her as she gazed at those long, elegant fingers and envisioned them sliding and caressing her bare skin.

"Scott told us to take a couple of days off. If you don't have to rush back to Austin, we could, um ... take a tour of the Smithsonian, maybe stop by Arlington Cemetery, have dinner somewhere."

She folded her other hand over the top of his. "Mike told me the same, take a few days, and enjoy myself. I'm sure we can find lots to do," she said as her eyes met his.

Behind them, Adrian and Coop grinned like a couple of goofy kids at each other.

Washington, D.C.

Dave's plane had arrived earlier, and Scott had dropped him off at the hotel where Nicki had made reservations. Now, he waited at the executive terminal for Ryan's plane to land. Since he needed a meeting with them, he didn't mind playing chauffeur.

Adrian was first off the plane, his arm still in a sling, a grim reminder of the danger they had faced in El Paso. Coop followed, then Kerry and Ryan. Ryan's hand at the small of her back as they walked down the steps didn't escape his notice. *Ah, so that's the way the wind blows.*

Scott greeted Adrian, then Coop who he hadn't seen for a couple of years. Ryan introduced Kerry, a note of pride in his voice. Scott liked what he saw. Tall, and slim, she carried herself with authority. Intelligence and even a hint of determination sparked in her eyes. Her face and figure could have graced the cover of any fashion magazine, but she had chosen one of the most challenging professions for a woman.

Scott held her hand for a minute as he gazed at her face. "I am so pleased to meet you and thank you for coming."

Kerry had expected an older man, instead of one in his late-thirties. He only topped her by a couple of inches, but his build was solid. His face was rough-hewn, with a small scar that split one eyebrow and another curved over his cheek. His eyes were dark, his gaze knowing and watchful.

"Who can resist an invitation from the President?" she responded and smiled.

Scott thought, *My, god, her smile could destroy a man's soul. No wonder Ryan looks besotted.*

Asking Ryan to drive so he could talk, they pulled out of the airport. "I wanted a chance to discuss tomorrow's meeting, then let you have an opportunity to relax and enjoy your stay."

Turning in the seat so he could see their faces he said, "The general opinion is we won't be able to charge Mitchell Harmon with a crime. There is no hard evidence to tie him to the abductions. But it doesn't mean the man will escape justice. As the President so succinctly stated, 'we may not be able to cut off the head of the snake, but I can pull his fangs.' Harmon has been invited to a meeting tomorrow at the White House. I'm not sure what the President has up his sleeve."

"Will we be at the meeting?" Kerry asked.

"No, I don't believe so. The President requested you arrive an hour early, so he can talk with each of you. I wish I could tell you more, but this is in the President's hands now."

At the hotel, Scott shook their hands again and said he would see them the next day. Ryan handed the suitcases to the hotel bellman, then walked over to Kerry. "I have to pick up my car at the office. Would you like to go for a drive later this evening?"

She nodded, and said, "I'll be waiting."

As Ryan weaved through the heavy D.C. traffic, he asked, "Do you really not know what is going on, or was it for Kerry's benefit?"

"I have too much respect for that young woman to play games with her. I really don't know. The President has not confided his plans to me though I suspect Daykin and Whitaker are in on the plot. They will both be there tomorrow. Would you get Kerry, Dave, and Coop to the office by two p.m.? I'd like for Nicki and Blake to meet them, and we'll go together to the meeting."

Ryan glanced at Adrian in the back seat, "Are you sure you're okay to drive? I'd be glad to take you home and pick you up in the morning."

"No. I can use my arm if I have to, but it's more comfortable to have the support of the sling."

Ryan parked in the covered garage and unloaded the suitcases from the trunk. Adrian grabbed his case and headed to his vehicle with a wave and, "I'll see you tomorrow."

Handing the keys to Scott, Ryan said "Tomorrow, then." He grabbed his cases and turned to walk to his car.

Scott's voice echoed behind him. "Tell her I said goodnight."

He grinned and picked up his pace.

Thirty-five

When Kerry woke, all that remained of Ryan's presence was an indentation in the pillow, and the earthy masculine scent she had come to associate with him. She vaguely remembered a light kiss on her forehead when he left. He wanted to stay, but with the upcoming meeting, he had to go home, change clothes, and then head to his office. He'd be back later in the day to pick her up along with Coop and Dave.

She stretched, languidly content. Her mind drifted back to the memories of their night together. When Ryan returned, they'd walked to a nearby restaurant. Over dinner and a bottle of wine, they talked about everything except the events of the last week. She felt she was in a game of catch up with the man she already loved. There was so much she didn't know but wanted to learn. Last night was their beginning.

When he walked her to the door of her room, the raw desire in his eyes as he bent to kiss her had sent waves of heat crashing over her. The sexy red lingerie she had picked up at the mall on her way to the airport was still packed in her suitcase. She smiled. *There's always tonight.*

Rolling, she looked at the clock. *Oh, my god! It's almost noon.* Tossing aside the covers, she scrambled out of bed. She couldn't believe she had slept so late. Ryan would pick her up in little over an hour, and she had to get dressed for the meeting of all meetings—with the President of the United States.

Her nerves were in overdrive. Nothing worked. Her makeup had to be applied three times before she was satisfied. Her fingers kept slipping on the small buttons of the silk blouse. When Ryan knocked on the door, she had just slid her feet into the three-inch high heels. When she opened it, his reaction eased some of the tension.

Thunderstruck, he gazed at her. It was the first time he had seen her dressed in anything other than pants and a shirt. Her slim red skirt ended at the top of the knees. He couldn't take his eyes off her legs. The memory of them locked around his body drove the blood from his brain. His eyes finally moved upward, to the long curls that brushed her shoulders. God, the woman, was gorgeous.

She laughed, then twirled, as his dazed look consumed her. "I take it you approve of my outfit."

When he reached to pull her into his arms, she backed away. "No ... oh, no, not until after the meeting. I just spent thirty minutes getting my makeup right."

"Woman, you drive a hard bargain, but only until we get back. Then all bets are off," he said as his eyes hungrily caressed her.

Coop and Dave waited in the lobby. When she stepped off the elevator, Coop let loose with a long whistle, causing everyone in the room to turn and look.

"Dang, woman. You clean up pretty good. Too bad, I'm a married man, or I'd give ole' Ryan here a run for his money," he quipped.

Dave grinned and nodded his head in agreement.

The teasing continued until they arrived at Ryan's office. Scott introduced Blake and Nicki. Even though Nicki had on high heels, Kerry towered over the petite woman. They hugged and did the air-kiss thing. Ryan figured Nicki didn't want her makeup messed up either. Blake started to wrap his arms around Kerry for a hug but stopped when he saw the glare Ryan gave him.

Adrian caught the byplay, and a smirk crossed his face as he looked at Ryan, earning another glare.

They followed Scott to the conference room. At his first words, the mood turned serious. "I'm not sure what the President has in mind today. I just spoke with Director Daykin who confirmed Harmon flew in early this morning. Does anyone have any questions?"

"Do you have a current report on the children?" Kerry asked.

"Yes, Nicki called this morning. The doctor said they are making a steady improvement and expects to release them tomorrow."

"What's the word on the undercover agent? I don't believe I've ever heard his name," Coop said.

"Peter Cassidy. The extraction team hasn't found him and believes he is dead. What they have pieced together is the drug lord found out he was an undercover agent. The gang abandoned the hacienda for fear the police would raid it," Scott answered.

Nicki was the first to break the silence. "Peter was the agent who first alerted us to the plot to sell the children in an auction. He managed to get the date and time of the auction to us, along with the website information."

A surge of anger flowed through Kerry, and when she looked at the others at the table, the same emotion was on their faces.

"Have the parents been informed of Harmon's involvement?" Dave asked.

"I don't know. I haven't spoken to them. I expect the President will decide on what and how much they will be told. So far, the motive behind the abductions is known to only a few people," Scott said.

"Who would believe it? It would seem to be utterly implausible, but he almost succeeded," Adrian said.

"Yes, he would have, if it hadn't been for a young woman driving down a remote Texas road and the bravery of a small boy," Scott said.

His words brought back the memories of that night, getting lost in the fog, seeing Tristan running toward her. The realization suddenly hit her, *My God, it was only one week ago.* She had lived a lifetime in that one week.

Scott glanced at his watch. "It's time to leave."

As they turned into the drive, Kerry's nose was glued to the window as her eyes swept over the White House. A Secret Service agent opened her door and helped her step out of the car. As she walked up the steps, her legs trembled. Whatever possessed her to wear three-inch heels? *That's all I need — to fall on my ass in the White House.* The humor at the thought steadied her.

They followed the agent down a hallway. He knocked, opened the door and stepped back. She followed Scott expecting they would be in a conference room. It took a moment to register she was standing in the Oval Office, and the President was walking toward her.

"Scott, would you make the introductions, please?" Larkin asked.

When Scott introduced her, the President held her hand for what seemed forever to her but was only a few seconds. "You are a remarkable young woman. May I call you Kerry?"

His words brought a blush to her face. "Uh … yes, sir."

He patted her hand, then stepped back. His voice turned hard and cold. "There will be another day for this group, along with the rest of the Texas team, to receive the acclamations you so deserve for the tragedy you averted. Today is for retribution. In a few minutes, Mitchell Harmon will arrive for a meeting. I will inform him of our knowledge of his horrific crimes and my intentions to destroy his financial empire. As the individuals responsible for stopping him, you have the right to be involved in the denouement."

Motioning to the two men who had stood behind him, "Director Daykin and Secretary Whitaker will wait with you in the Cabinet Room. At the appropriate time, you will step into the hallway outside this office, where Harmon will see you as he leaves."

"If you will follow me," Director Daykin said and led them to the nearby room. "Please make yourself comfortable. There are coffee and a variety of soft drinks on the table by the door."

Too nervous to sit, Kerry wandered, looking out the windows at the famous Rose Garden, then examined every piece of furniture, object and painting in the room, and wondered what was happening in the Oval Office.

The President stood at the window and gazed at the lush garden as he anticipated the painful confrontation. Despite the deep-rooted anger that throbbed inside him, there was also a sense of loss. Mitchell Harmon had been his closest friend and confidant for most of his adult life. The man's betrayal and the horror of his cold-blooded plan had struck at the very fiber of his integrity and moral conscience. It was difficult to reconcile the man he believed he knew, with the person about to enter his office.

When the knock sounded on the door, Larkin turned. As Mitchell Harmon entered, his hand flicked toward the couch. "Right on time, Mitch. Have a seat."

The President picked up a folder from the desk and strode to the opposite couch. Laying the file by his side, he gazed at Harmon's face. Where was the cruelty, the utter callousness that drove a man to commit such an abhorrent act? Why didn't he see it? Then Harmon's eyes met his. A soulless stare devoid of emotion and warmth. *Had it been there all along, and I just never realized it?*

Harmon eyed the folder, then looked at Larkin. The somber demeanor of the President sent a sense of uneasiness to trickle through him. This wasn't Art's usual greeting. He hadn't even offered to shake his hand.

"It's good to see you. How are you doing?" Harmon said as he crossed his legs and eased back against the cushion.

Larkin's tone was terse. "I've had better days. This has been a horrific week. The kidnapping of Senator Murdock's son, then the children of the other Senators and the Utah Governor was appalling."

"I was shocked when I heard the news of the Murdock child and the other children. What happened to the boy? The media broke a story the children had been found in West Texas, but there was no mention of Murdock's son."

"A young woman, a private investigator with a company in Austin, found the boy on the side of the road."

"How odd. Why wasn't it ever mentioned in the news reports?"

"The kidnappers made numerous attempts to get Tristan back, so she hid him at a ranch in East Texas."

A hint of anger flicked in Harmon's eyes, then disappeared. If Larkin hadn't been watching Harmon's face, he would have missed it. The telltale spark removed the surrealistic mood that had swirled in Larkin's mind and destroyed the lingering grief he felt. The man in front of him was a chameleon who used his money to cloak his psychopathic personality and deserved everything Larkin was about to instigate and more.

"Well, I'm glad he and the other children were found. What did you want to discuss about the presidential elections?" Harmon asked.

"Interesting you should ask because the elections are linked to the abductions."

Stunned, Harmon looked at him, then recovered and said, "That seems to be rather improbable."

"I thought so at first, but as events developed, the theory became less and less implausible."

A sheen of sweat broke out on Harmon's forehead.

"The kidnappers made no demands which led the investigators to search for other motives. What linked the senators? They found it, a run at the presidency," Larkin said.

"That can't be right. Governor Simpson's son was kidnapped, and she's never been considered as a candidate. As a matter of fact, neither has Senator Thompson."

"Their connection was the alliance to stop the construction of the Danver pipeline."

"Art, this doesn't make sense. I don't know why you're telling me this. I thought this meeting was to discuss the election."

"We are talking about the election. Details emerged that led to the individual behind the kidnappings and a hideous plot to sell the children in a high dollar auction. The undercover agent who discovered the plan was killed."

A sheen of sweat covered Harmon's face. "I'm not feeling well. I may have eaten something that disagreed with me. Since I'm not interested in these details, why don't we discuss the upcoming meeting at another time," he said as he stood?

"Sit ... down! I'm not finished," Larkin said.

"I don't know what's going on here, but I sure as hell don't like your attitude." Anger vibrated in Harmon's voice as he sat.

Larkin leaned forward, his body rigid, hands fisted on his knees, his voice harsh and contemptuous as he said, "What is going on is your sick and twisted obsession to become President. It was your plan to kidnap the children and sell them to the scum of the earth. The properties you purchased to hide the children, hiring Calvin Moore and his team of mercenaries to carry out the abductions, the spy you inserted into the Austin FBI office, a county sheriff you bribed, your plane to transport the kids, bounties to kill the investigators, the auction you set up—all the connections lead back to you.

"You thought you'd get the nomination by destroying the lives and careers of more qualified individuals, plus pick up a nice bonus by stopping a bill that would have cost you millions. Well, I've got news for you—you would never have become the next President!"

"You bastard. Who do you think put you in that chair? It was me, my money." Harmon angrily thumped his chest. "I made it happen. Then, you had the audacity to tell me I wasn't good enough for the voters."

"It was the voters who put me in this chair, not you," Larkin snapped back, his anger pushed him to the edge of the couch.

Harmon shrugged his shoulders and eased back as twinges of pain shot through his chest. "Well, it's immaterial now, since I plan on running with or without your help. As for the rest, I don't know anything about these ridiculous allegations. If you have any facts to support your absurd theory, I'll have my attorney investigate them.

Otherwise, it's all conjecture."

Larkin said, "Would that attorney be Stuart Lane?"

A look of shock crossed Harmon's face as the President continued. "Oh, yes, we have a revealing dossier on him and his involvement in your insidious plot. You might escape conviction, but the publicity will ruin your aspirations. But it will never get that far. I guarantee you won't get funding from the party coffers, and ... I plan to use every legal option I have to wipe out your assets."

Picking up the folder, Larkin opened it and pulled out a set of stapled documents. "This is a list of all your contracts with the federal government. By this time tomorrow, these will be null and void, millions in annual revenue gone. Your oil tankers must pass inspection. I can stop your shipments for months as they sit in port while every bolt and nut are examined. Your refineries will be shut down as they undergo the same intense inspection. I've ordered an IRS audit of all your companies and holdings. That's the short list of what I can do."

Sweat trickled down Harmon's face, his breathing had become ragged. His chest felt as if an enormous weight pressed against it.

Larkin's eyes flashed with scorn. "By the time, I'm finished, you won't have enough money left to get elected as the county dogcatcher. You are ruined, and this is the last time you will ever set foot in the White House."

Larkin stood and walked around his desk. His fingers triggered a button on the underside. "I hope I never lay eyes on you again. Now, you goddamn bastard, get the hell out of my office. Oh, on your way out, take a good look at the people standing by the door. They stopped your hideous plan and saved five children from a fate worse than death."

Harmon staggered off the couch. He had to get back to Austin and come up with a plan to stop Larkin's actions. Surely, he couldn't carry through with these threats, but the pain was intense, and he couldn't concentrate. The door opened as he reached it.

Outside, a group of people stood in front of him. His vision blurred, and it took a second to focus. A woman stood in the center. Damn, it's that bitch Branson and beside her was that bumbling fool of an FBI agent, Barr. They should be dead, not standing here looking at him with loathing and contempt. The rage that surged through him increased the stabbing throbs of pain in his head and chest.

He had to get to his car. Turning, he stumbled along the corridor. The heavy weight in his chest pressed against his lungs, he couldn't get air. Pulling his tie apart, he unbuttoned his collar. Sweat ran down his back as his lungs heaved. His legs gave way, and he fell.

Hands rolled him over, and a man peered down at him. It was one of the men in the hallway. He gasped, "pills, left pocket." Harmon felt a hand reach into the pocket, pull back, and search the other side. He tried to correct him, tell him no, go back.

When Harmon collapsed, Scott was the first to reach his side and rolled him over. Hearing the mumbled words, his hand slid into the pants pocket, and fingertips brushed the small bottle. Removing his hand, he searched the other pocket.

Harmon muttered, then a loud gasp echoed in the hallway and his chest stopped moving. Lifeless eyes stared at the ceiling.

Scott checked for a pulse, then stood. Unemotional, his face failed to reveal the retribution he felt at the sight of the dead man on the floor as he announced, "He's dead."

A large group of people had clustered in the hallway. A Secret Service agent said, "A doctor is on the way. Couldn't you find his tablets?"

Scott shook his head. "No, I didn't. You need to inform the President."

Larkin was seated at his desk when the knock sounded on the door. When it opened, the agent rushed inside.

"Mr. President, Mr. Harmon collapsed and is dead. Agent Fleming was there and tried to help, but he couldn't find Mr. Harmon's pills in time."

"Thank you, Agent Riley. I'm sure everyone did the best they could to assist Mr. Harmon. Let me know when the doctor arrives."

"Yes, sir."

During his earlier discussions with Whitaker, Larkin had remembered a comment Harmon had once made about his heart condition and the need to carry nitroglycerine tablets. Knowing Mitch, he believed he could use the man's ego and arrogance to push him into an emotional and stressful state. His plan worked. He felt no remorse for his actions, and even if he did all he had to do was think about five children. The President spun his chair to look out the windows that overlooked the Rose Garden and smiled.

Epilogue

Washington, D.C.
Two weeks later

Children's laughter echoed as they played a game of kickball on the White House lawn. Two Secret Service agents stood nearby, a smile on their face as they oversaw the vigorous activity.

A large crowd milled around the Rose Garden. The President had arranged for the parents of the abducted children to meet the individuals who had saved their child's life. Scott and his team, all the members of the Texas team and their families, along with Dave Jenson, and even Sgt. Duggan had been invited to the White House for a buffet luncheon.

Kerry stood next to Ryan, his arm around her shoulder. She watched Cindy and Luke as they talked to Senator Murdock and his wife. When Cindy had received the invitation, she had called Kerry, panicked at what to wear. Remembering her same reaction brought a grin to Kerry's face.

It had been an emotional day. Earlier, when Tristan saw Kerry, he raced toward her. She grabbed him, swung him around, then held him in a tight hug.

The Murdocks caught up with him, and he said, to everyone's delight, "This is my pretend momma." His parents had already heard the story and only grinned at their son's exuberant greeting.

Lightly tapping his nose, Kerry said, "That reminds me, young man. I owe you candy." Pulling a bag of candy bars from her purse, she handed them to his mother.

Tristan looked longingly at the bag, but his mother said, "Not now. You can have one when we get home. Don't forget to thank Kerry."

"Oh, yeah, thank you," he said and gave her that mischievous grin that had stolen her heart. "Kerry, I have a new puppy. His name is Rex."

His dad had muttered, "The damn dog pees on everything." His wife laughed and punched him in the arm.

Footsteps sounded behind her and brought her thoughts back to the present. Coop stopped beside them, and said, "I think we've wrapped up most of the lingering details," as he stared at the scene on the lawn.

Kerry asked, "What happened to the clerk and sheriff?"

"I transferred her to another agency. I couldn't fire her without revealing what Harmon had done. There was nothing I could do about her grandfather or the attorney. As for the sheriff, he was convinced it was in his best interest to resign. I tried to talk Luke into running for the position, but he said he couldn't deal with the politics that came with the job. Can't say I blame him."

At the sound of the President's voice, they turned. He had walked onto the steps leading to the garden. Director Daykin, Secretary Whitaker, and Scott stood behind him. Next to him was a young man. Cuts and fading bruises covered his gaunt face, his body thin and emaciated. One arm was in a sling, and he leaned heavily on a cane. Beside him was a young woman with a child on each side of her, their hand clasped in hers.

The President's voice rang out with a jubilant note. "If I may have everyone's attention. I have one more … very …very special guest I would like to introduce. An agent who for the last several months has been undercover in a Bolivian drug cartel, and played a critical role in the rescue of the children—Peter Cassidy."

A rumble of gasps rolled through the crowd, then people began to cheer and clap. Everyone had believed the agent had been killed.

Tears trickled down Kerry's face. *There goes my makeup,* but this time she didn't give a damn. She looked up at Ryan, a joyful look on her face that slowly turned to suspicion.

"You knew!"

He held up his hands. "Hey, I was sworn to secrecy."

"You and I are going to have a serious discussion about communications when we leave here," she said and punched him in the arm.

CPSIA information can be obtained
at www.ICGtesting.com
Printed in the USA
FFHW01n1944091018